CH00675889

THE FIRE IN OUR HEARTH

AVELINE BOOK 3

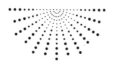

RAE WALSH

SMALL SEED PRESS

Books By Rachel Devenish Ford:

The Eve Tree: A Novel

A Traveler's Guide to Belonging

Trees Tall as Mountains: The Journey Mama Writings- Book One

Oceans Bright With Stars: The Journey Mama Writings- Book Two

A Home as Wide as the Earth: The Journey Mama Writings- Book Three

World Whisperer: World Whisperer Book 1

Guardian of Dawn: World Whisperer Book 2

Shaper's Daughter: World Whisperer Book 3

Demon's Arrow: World Whisperer Book 4

Azariyah: A World Whisperer Novella

Books by Rae Walsh

The Lost Art of Reverie: Aveline Book 1

A Jar Full of Light: Aveline Book 2

The Fire in our Hearth: Aveline Book 3

First published in 2021

Copyright © 2021 Rae Walsh

Small Seed Press LLC

racheldevenishford.com

God sets the lonely in families,
He leads out the prisoners with singing.
Psalm 68:6

CHAPTER ONE

Ani was in the bulk section, right in the middle of pouring chickpeas into her bag, when she stumbled. The dried beans scattered across the floor, clacking and rolling, the sound echoing in the quiet grocery store as though Ani had spilled a bucketful of dried beans rather than a few handfuls.

She sighed and closed her eyes, letting her shoulders slump a little before she bent down to start picking them up. She had only managed to grab five or six before two of the store employees arrived. Ani straightened to find Sheldon, the store owner, and Lucy, a part-time worker, staring at her. Sheldon was much taller than Ani, with black curly hair, an embroidered satin vest, and a purple fedora. Lucy only worked at Green's when she was called in. Usually, she worked at the Aveline Cafe, so Ani had had more than a few conversations with her while looking over the menu. Lucy was a short, middle-aged Thai-American woman whom Ani had liked right from the first.

The tiny grocery store was well-staffed. Ani should have known that the commotion wouldn't go unnoticed.

"Sorry," she said, making a face. "My leg gave way a bit when I was filling my bag."

"Don't worry about cleaning them up," Sheldon said. "We'll get a broom."

"You should see what happens when toddlers play with the spouts," Lucy said. She made a sweeping motion with one hand. "Candy everywhere."

"I want to keep the chickpeas," Ani said.

They both stared. "The ones in your bag?" Sheldon asked.

"The ones on the floor," Ani said firmly.

Lucy was frowning at her now. "It's okay," she said. "We don't make people pay for spills. Even though sometimes I think we should, especially if Trinity cannot keep her eyes on her toddler, and it happens every single time she comes in..." At a look from Sheldon, Lucy stopped talking abruptly.

Ani stood a little taller. "No, I want them. I try to never let food go to waste. If you had seen the things I have seen... well, those beans are in better condition than many I've eaten in my life. I'll just wash them well when I get home."

Sheldon nodded slowly, swallowing once.

"You've got it."

After they had finished gathering the scattered chickpeas and putting them in a bag for Ani, Lucy rang up Ani's groceries without commenting any further on the spill. Ani was lost in thought about how she always managed to make an impression on people in the weirdest ways. She almost didn't hear the older woman's question.

"I'm sorry?" Ani said. "I missed that."

"I said that I haven't seen you in the café lately. Don't be a stranger."

"Oh," Ani said. "I guess I've been really busy with work."

"Well, if it's my shift, I'll give you a free scone."

"Thanks," Ani said, smiling as she lifted her bag to her shoulder. The bell rang out as she left, grinning as she remembered the looks on Sheldon and Lucy's faces as she tied up the bag of dusty beans to bring home. They had been rendered speechless. Knowing Ani did that to people sometimes. They always thought they could get a read on her, and then she went and did something that surprised them. Or depressed them.

She tipped her face up to the early spring sun as she began to walk home with her grocery bags. The weather hadn't turned hot yet, and the sun was pleasant after the chilly store.

People in this town would get used to her sooner or later. And as soon as they did, Ani would be gone, on to the next place that was sponsoring refugees. Her smile wavered and dimmed. It was the life she had chosen, but it hurt to always be the one leaving.

Ani knew that the loss of place was just one way that she identified with the refugees she served. It seemed as though the world was constructed of two sets, two different realities, and Ani danced between the two of them. The world was dim with loss. The world was full of good things. The movement between the two was dizzying, and her own intensity because of her knowledge made it hard for her to find friends. Not to mention a boyfriend.

She was limping slightly. It was time to get home and get her leg elevated, but she had one more stop under the black oaks of Main Street before she could go home. The post-master had texted to let Ani know she had mail and needed to come in and sign for it. It was the packet she had been waiting for all week—the complete dossier of information about the refugees who would arrive in Aveline in two months. Ani was looking forward to reading about the Syrian families who would be moving to Aveline.

The sponsorship program was still relatively new. Ani had worked with three other sets of refugee families after training in Canada with a non-profit that specialized in this type of sponsorship. Those assignments had only been two families at a time in big cities, and this time with four families coming to the small university town of Aveline, the work felt different. It was both more and less intimidating. These families would have a significant impact on the structure of idyllic Aveline, and Ani knew it could be a beautiful, compassionate change. She only hoped others felt the same way.

Ani's last families had been from Syria also. She could still see the photographs they had shown her of their decimated homes after bombings. She should show them to Sheldon and explain how they had spent a year at a refugee camp, washing bugs out of rice. Maybe then he would understand why she had to bring the chickpeas home. Her heart fluttered as she got closer to the little building that was Aveline's post office. She couldn't wait to open the packet and see the first photos of the families staying in refugee camps, ready to come to their new homes.

She took a breath as she walked into the post office. Every wall was plastered with posters of the cosmos: constellations, planets, and colorful nebulas. She knew it was the postmaster himself who had put all the pictures up on the walls. The effect was like walking into a moving, shimmering galaxy. If she squinted.

At the front counter, the man gave her the large manila packet. Ani grabbed it and hugged it to herself, smiling at him. She knew she should remember his name, but it had disappeared into the mass of new things she had been learning since arriving in Aveline.

He was looking back at her. She liked the way he looked, with hazel eyes, brown hair streaked with blond, and a beard, not too long and not too short.

"This is all the information about our new refugee families," Ani told him. She glimpsed his name tag. Daniel. Right, that was familiar. "Where they come from, their names and ages."

"They don't send it by email?" he asked. His voice was surprisingly soft yet deep. He looked down when he talked, then glanced back up at Ani.

"No," she said. "We have emailed back and forth about the general details—how many families, what region they're coming from. But today is the day we learn the specific families. I love this part." She cut herself off suddenly. She was rambling to someone she only knew from seeing around town.

But he didn't seem put off.

"When will you open it?"

"Right away. I'm going to go home, make a cup of tea, put my feet up, and then spend hours reading the whole thing."

He had an interesting way of meeting her eyes for a moment and then looking off behind her or at his hands.

"What kind of tea?" he asked. "Do your feet hurt?"

Ani was taken aback. He seemed genuinely interested and very direct with his questions, but his directness didn't make her feel strange or imposed upon. It was refreshing. It was like the way her family talked.

"Right now, I'm going to make mint tea like my mom would make. If it was earlier in the day, I might make Persian tea. Have you ever had it? Do you like tea?"

"I like many things," Daniel told her, " especially when it means learning and trying things from other places."

"Well, I'll have to make you Persian tea sometime." She glanced down, feeling the steady ache from her right calf, knee, and hip that told her it was well past time to get home and off her feet. "One foot hurts," she said. "You've heard of polio?"

"Yes, of course," Daniel said.

"I had it as a kid in Iran. I know. It's eradicated now but still lingered back when we were kids. I was one of the last, I think." She smiled a pained smile. "Lucky me. My mom told me it's because I was meant to be special." She stopped herself again. Unbelievable! How had she gotten to the topic of her mother?

He was nodding and looking at her intently, as though he might ask questions about polio.

"I should go," she said.

"Yes," he said.

"See you around," she said.

"I'll be at the meeting next week," he told her.

"Oh good, I'll see you then."

Ani was blushing slightly as she left, but she also found that she was smiling, and that the smile lasted all the way home.

CHAPTER TWO

The apartment was dark even though it was the middle of the afternoon when Ani got home. This was an unfortunate side effect of the small windows and heavy drapes of her temporary residence. Ani walked through the rooms, turning the lights on as she went. This place had not been her first choice in apartments, but she had tried for three others before she was finally approved for a rental. She was thankful to have a place to stay at all.

"I won't be here long," she said out loud as she threw her purse and jacket onto the sofa. Ani felt the need to remind herself of this from time to time, when the beige walls seemed sure to make her crazy. She went to the kitchen to unload her groceries, laying the bulky manila envelope on the table. She was tempted to rip it open standing there.

"Tea," she said aloud. "A good cup of tea will make the moment perfect."

While the water boiled, Ani changed into soft pants and an oversized T-shirt, then swirled hot water in her glass teapot, plunging the mint tea sachets in to steep.

She put away her groceries, humming, then opened the bag of chickpeas and dumped them into a large bowl, rinsing them by filling the bowl and then pouring off any dust or debris that floated up. She did this ten times, until the water was perfectly clear, then left them to soak.

Ani didn't love to cook, but she didn't love to eat out by herself either, so she made large batches of Persian lentil stew or hummus and ate them with salad and bread all week long. It horrified Ani's mother, but it worked for Ani. She half thought her mother disapproved because she ate hummus and pita almost daily. "It's not even Irani food," Ani's mother told her. But pita was easy to find, and Ani had gotten into the habit of making large batches of hummus when she lived with a Lebanese roommate in college.

"We survive on this," Ani's roommate told her. "It's better than noodle packets."

It certainly was. And Ani was still eating like she was in college.

Ani took the little glass teapot and cup to the table by the sofa, set them down, and put on some soft music. As she sank back into the sofa, she untied her hair, letting it spill down, sighing with relief. Perfection. Her legs up on the ottoman, comfortable clothing, a cup of hot tea, and a happy scalp. She pulled the dossier into her lap and used a pair of scissors to open the top flap.

"This is it, Ani. Time to meet the families."

For as long as she could remember, Ani had felt as though she lived a hairsbreadth from an abyss of sorrow that could consume her. She kept herself from the edge by focusing on little things—small comforts, her loved ones, and the few families that she could help.

She murmured a prayer before she pulled out the sheaf of papers.

"Let me be helpful, sensitive to loss, and affirming of these beloved people you are guiding to us. Help me to be strong against accusation." She paused as she pulled the papers out. "And bless Daniel, the man at the post office. He seemed nice."

Then she took a sip of tea and read the cover letter from Amanda at the organization.

Ani, here are the docs on the cases that are headed your way in a few weeks' time.

Listen, I know this is a surprise, and I would have emailed you all of this before, but I thought that maybe it would be better if you got it all at once. The team decided just two days ago that these changes were best for all involved, considering the makeup of Aveline and the fact that it is a small town.

Ani frowned, pulling the sheet of paper closer and taking another sip of tea.

. . .

HERE IT IS: *We have decided to send you four Venezuelan families rather than the Syrian or Afghani families we had initially spoken about.*

ANI CHOKED ON HER TEA, spraying it over the sheet of paper and hastily wiping it off with the blanket on the back of the sofa.

I FEEL *like I can already hear your protests. There are several reasons for our decision.*

1. The Reverend Francisco Rodriguez, the man behind this record number of sponsorships in a small town, is from El Salvador and is fluent in Spanish.

2. Aveline, as a small Californian town, has natural connections with Latin American citizens.

3. Most importantly, Ani, there is a major hiccup with the case of one of the families, and you have the most success of any of our workers in dealing with legal trouble and smoothing bumps along the way. (Shameless flattery, but true.)

We are being careful not to talk too openly about any of this at the moment, but all will become clear in the following pages and our phone calls over the next few weeks.

To tell you the truth, I wanted you to "meet" the families through their photographs at the same time that you get this news.

I know you will fall in love with them as I have.
Yours,
Amanda Tate

CHAPTER THREE

Ani sat back, letting herself be drawn into the cushions of the couch. Her head was fuzzy. *Venezuela. Venezuela!*

She didn't know what to do or think. So she did what she always did when something big came her way. She called her mother.

She wrapped herself more firmly in her blanket and smiled as she heard her mother's voice.

"Ani?"

"Hi, Mama," she said.

"Just wait," Ani's mother, Maryam, replied in Farsi, their shared language. Ani's parents were Armenian-Iranian and spoke Armenian together at home, but Ani had grown up speaking Farsi, the language of Iran, and had never been fluent in Armenian.

Ani could hear her mother walking through the house, opening and closing doors. She closed her eyes, imagining home, trying to conjure up the feeling of it. The colors of the kitchen, her father in his armchair with his sweater and socks on, leaning back with the newspaper—he stubbornly clung to reading the physical copy—in his familiar gentle hands. As the evening went on, Ani's father would move from the news to music—jazz, classical, or middle eastern—and literature or poetry. Later still, after dinner, Ani's parents would read a Psalm together and maybe sing an old Armenian hymn.

Her father might wander out to smoke his pipe in the tiny backyard in San Francisco. Or he might be in one of his stages of trying to quit. Ani checked the time. She may have interrupted her mother in the middle of cooking dinner. The smells of garlic and onion sauteed in a pan would fill the kitchen, and her mother would be humming as she reached for ingredients with the grace of a dancer.

Sure enough, Ani's mother came back to the phone and said breathlessly, "Are you still there, sweetheart?"

"Yes, I'm here, Mama."

"Okay, good, I just had to turn dinner off. It can wait a moment. Did you get your package today?"

"I did. Mama, you'll never guess what they've done."

"What is it?"

Ani took a deep breath. "I got a letter from Amanda Tate that says all four families are from Venezuela, not from Syria or Afghanistan like we thought."

There was a short silence as Ani's mother took this in. Ani pulled her blanket tighter around her. It was cold in her apartment, but she didn't like the burning carpet smell of the heater, so she wore layers and blankets instead of turning it on.

"Well," her mother said finally. "That is big, isn't it?"

"Yes! I've spent all of my time in Middle Eastern refugee communities. I know nothing about South America."

"But it will be very similar, no? Not the people, of course, but the work? Help them settle in, get the community on board with all that is required?"

"Yes," Ani blew out a short breath. "That is the same. But I speak Pashto, Farsi, and Arabic. I don't speak Spanish."

"Ah." Ani's mother was silent, and Ani could picture her in the house, looking out the front windows, perhaps, or folding laundry, or removing dead leaves from one of her house plants. "Did Amanda say why they chose to make a change?"

Ani huffed a sigh. "She said it was because the main pastor--the community leader here--is from El Salvador, and he speaks Spanish. And many people in the community are Spanish speakers or have roots in Central and South America.

"Ah," Maryam said.

Ani knew her mother's voice, both the in-person voice and the on-the-phone voice. She knew her morning voice and her late afternoon voice. She knew her night voice. She knew this voice.

"What are you not saying?" Ani asked.

"Oh, honey, I am just beginning to understand why this would be hard for you."

Ani smoothed her hand across the arm of the sofa. "What do you mean?"

"Well, if other people speak the language and you don't, you will have to rely on others. And you know you like to, how can I say this—be the most knowledgeable. You don't like to need others."

"Ouch," Ani said, laughing but actually a little stung. Her mother was right, but she had touched on something that Ani didn't really like about herself. At the same time, she didn't exactly know how to change this part of herself. She took things so seriously. She was the one in a group project who came up with all the ideas and then somehow ended up doing all the work. It wasn't Ani's fault that others didn't care about things as much as she did. But it was a lonely place to be.

"This might be exactly what you need. You will have to cooperate with others." Maryam laughed. "I wish I had thought of something like this when you were little!"

Actually, Ani reflected, it was past time she stopped calling her mother so often.

"Well, you've been a comfort," she said, her voice dry. Her mother laughed again, and despite herself, Ani closed her eyes to soak in the sound. Her mother's laugh was like sunlit rooms and flaky pastry dessert, singing the Psalms, or Ani watching TV with her legs on her mother's lap while Maryam massaged her calf and foot.

"I think you'll get through this and be changed for the better," Ani's mother said. "And maybe you will decide to settle down and give me grandchildren, also. What is this pastor like—the one who speaks Spanish?"

Ani rolled her eyes, though her mother couldn't see her. "So suddenly, you are okay with me marrying a man who is neither Armenian nor Persian?"

"I have given up on that."

"Good to hear it. Well, give up on Reverend Francisco also, okay? You know I can't settle down with my kind of work. No more matchmaking."

"Reverend Francisco. That's a nice name."

Ani didn't know why she bothered.

"Talk to your father for a moment, okay?" Maryam said. "And be nice to him."

Ani made a sound of protest. She was always nice to her father. But her mother was gone, and her father was already on the phone.

"Hi, Darling," he said.

Ani smiled, feeling tears prick at the back of her eyes.

"Hi Papa," she whispered.

They chatted for a while, and then Ani said goodbye. She let the phone drop into her lap and picked up the sheaf of papers again. Was her mother right about why this bothered her so much?

Maybe. Ani couldn't actually pick out any emotions right now, other than a feeling of not knowing what would come next or what she was supposed to do. It was a terrible feeling, anxiety that fizzed and bubbled inside her. She poured another glass of peppermint tea, holding her face over the steam, inhaling the calming fragrance. She drank the tea down quickly, then, feeling restored, she breathed another prayer, this one just for help.

As she looked through the pages, Ani could mark the very moment, the very beat of her heart when everything started to change, when the Venezuelan families turned from ideas to people. They were not a language she didn't speak, they were not a change of plans. These were families in need of a place to rest.

There were four families. That had not changed. A single father and child, a couple with three young children, and a couple with one child. Finally, scanning the pages, Ani came to a family with a single red star printed on the top of their dossier. Was this the problematic case?

Ani looked closer, unable to see an issue. They appeared to be a regular family with two children. But then she brought the papers closer and examined the photographs. The dates of the parents' birth and their pictures didn't match. These people were too old. Ani would be willing to bet that these were grandparents, and yet, they had filled out the forms as parents and lied about their birthdates.

She breathed in. Yes, this would be tricky. And that was putting it mildly.

CHAPTER FOUR

O n his way to the church, Daniel stopped walking for a moment to turn his face up to the sun. The weather had been rainy and cold all last week, and they needed the rain at this time of year; they needed all they could get. But today, the sunshine felt so good. Daniel held out his hands, admiring the shadows of the leaves, the way they moved and danced on the sidewalk and his skin. For a moment, he forgot everything and was nothing but himself.

The inside of his head had been so strange lately. Daniel wasn't sure he liked it.

After years of holding himself inside, close and rigid, Daniel was free from accusation and could feel tendrils of hope inside, like plants newly exposed to light. He was changing, and he didn't like change.

He began to walk again, watching the play of the shadows on the sidewalk or looking up to see the glow of light through leaves. For his whole adult life, he had kept his interests small and controlled. He had reduced his life to his job, his interest in cosmology, and music. The three things were a comprehensible block, a study with boundaries. But now, change came so quickly that Daniel couldn't quite catch his breath. He wanted more, and he didn't know what to do with the desire.

The boulder of accusation had been heavy on him for years. Daniel hated it, but at least it was familiar. People had been suspicious of him for most of his life. He grew up as a foster kid who had always been a little odd. Daniel knew he wasn't bad, but it wasn't easy to maintain that belief when everyone thought he had done things he hadn't. Sometimes he looked at his hands and feet, wondering whether they got up to stuff when he was asleep.

Ten years ago, nearly eleven now, Daniel had been wrongly accused of a cluster of robberies in the town. Two people had known it wasn't him— Daniel's friend Theresa and the person who had committed the crime. Reesey had left town for understandable reasons, and the criminal had not come forward, also for understandable reasons.

The rumors died down when there was no evidence to convict Daniel, but then last fall, it all erupted again when someone sprayed hateful graffiti all around town, and Daniel had once again been a person of interest. Daniel started to resign himself to this life, a life of shouldering unjust accusations.

But then Theresa had come forward and bravely told the truth. The vandal was not Daniel--it was Cam. Cam had committed all those robberies. Cam had assaulted and raped her ten years ago. Cam had spraypainted racist words on George and Mercy's office walls.

Overnight, the boulder of accusation against Daniel was gone. But Daniel found that some people found it hard to shake off its residue. They had become familiar with avoiding him and treating him with suspicion. Daniel couldn't blame them. He also found it hard to get rid of the leftover debris of shame. Every day, Daniel had to remind himself that he was free, that no one could hold another man's actions against him anymore. For a while, he had wondered whether it would be easier to move away and start over, but Theresa had convinced him to give life in Aveline another shot.

"You can't leave right after I moved here," she said. "Besides, I want everyone else to know what I know. That you're the best and sweetest person in this town."

Daniel smiled at her. "What about Sheldon?" he asked.

Reesey shrugged. "He's the best looking and funniest. But not the best and sweetest. Even he knows that."

Daniel laughed. No, he wouldn't call Sheldon sweet. But he wouldn't call himself sweet either. He didn't know what he would call himself.

He had chosen to stay, reminding himself that he did have more friends now. People like Sam and Francisco.

Daniel quickened his steps, hoping to arrive early for the town meeting, so he could help Francisco set up. It was a good example of the changes that moved swiftly into his life, like clouds in a strong wind. Daniel had never helped set up the church for a town meeting before. He had never attended a town meeting before. Meetings made him uncomfortable.

A lot had happened in the ten years since the robberies. One of these things was that Daniel had been diagnosed with autism. The diagnosis meant a lot to him. It explained why people sometimes had a hard time connecting with him, why people didn't understand him or found him suspicious. It explained why he felt like he was from another planet.

The best thing about knowing he was autistic, though, was that it explained his obsessions and even gave them permission to exist. The specialist who had helped Daniel with his initial diagnosis had explained that his heightened ability to focus was like a superpower.

"Not everyone can work with the depth and range of detail that you can."

In the past, Daniel had cycled through obsessions. Some of the most recent were working with efficiency at the post office, knowing every star or constellation, and memorizing and learning eras and genres of music.

But now. This change. Daniel would never stop looking at the stars or playing and learning music. But he had become interested in something that felt dangerous to him, like swimming with sharks or playing with tigers. His new interest was with people. Specifically, he had become fascinated with the refugee crisis. He couldn't stop reading or thinking about all the people in the world who were displaced. This was dangerous. This was not organizing mail systems or memorizing the names and movements of planets. This was about people.

Daniel had never been very good with people.

The smell of the church was familiar and welcoming.

Frankie was in the sanctuary, putting plates of churros on a table. He looked up as Daniel entered.

"Just in time," Frankie said. "I need help. Ani's using slides and setting up the screen is a two-person job."

"Did your mother make those?" Daniel asked, gesturing at the churros.

Frankie looked at him for a moment. "She did. Grab one while it's hot."

"I'm the lucky one," Daniel said. He picked up a churro, still warm and soft, and bit into it. "This is delicious."

"Help me with the screen?"

They rolled the portable screen into the room and set it on its stand, just as Ani walked in.

"Ani!" Frankie said, walking to meet her. "Good to see you! I'm excited about your presentation today."

Daniel watched from where he stood as Ani smiled at Frankie. Daniel was terrible at knowing instinctively what people were thinking by their facial expressions but really good at learning and remembering over time. Because Daniel had known Theresa for so many years, he almost always could pick up on her moods. He had learned her patterns. Theresa was more straightforward than most, though, because she was so direct and always said what she thought.

Working to understand people was hard work. Daniel tried to think of it as a game, though it mattered more than he let on. He had learned from a young age that knowing what people were thinking was a matter of personal safety. It helped you know when to disappear or just get out of the way. Most people took the ability to read moods for granted.

Daniel didn't know Ani well enough to identify any of her emotional tells yet. He wondered what she was thinking. Her face looked different than it had in the post office yesterday when she told him she was excited to open the documents. Her black hair was partially pulled up, with some falling around her shoulders, and she wore flowy pants and sandals. Now that Daniel knew about her disability, he could see that one foot turned out ever so slightly, though he doubted he would have noticed if she hadn't told him. Her T-shirt was a soothing salmon color. After a moment, Daniel realized he had been staring at the contrast between the black of her hair and the bright color of her shirt for too long. Staring had gotten him in trouble in the past. He shook himself and walked forward to say hello.

CHAPTER FIVE

Neither Frankie nor Ani seemed to have noticed his staring.

Daniel said hello to Ani, jamming his hands in his pockets. "Are you okay?"

She looked at him for a moment. "The letter I got yesterday contained a bit of a shock. I'll be okay, but I feel flustered."

"What kind of a shock?" Francisco asked.

"I'll explain it all when we start the meeting," Ani replied, tucking some stray hair behind her ears. "I'll feel better when we're set up and ready to begin, I'm sure."

Daniel nodded. That made sense to him. He finished with the screen and went to find an extension cord for Ani's computer. Francisco seemed to want more information, hovering near Ani as though she would change her mind and talk to him before the meeting, but Daniel had learned from experience that people didn't like it if you pressed them when they had made up their mind. It seemed to him that those with intuitive abilities into people's emotions relied too much on them. Frankie seemed to think Ani would confide in him if he hovered. Maybe that's what he would have do in her position. But Ani continued to look through her notes, ignoring the tall pastor.

Daniel's shoulders were tense. He moved them in circles to try to relax. Everything was ready and Ani was looking through her notes. People would soon begin to arrive, bringing their voices and movement into the sanctuary of the church, filling the space. Daniel poured himself a cup of coffee from the carafe and walked outside to stand on the church steps in the shadow of the old stone building, one of the oldest in Aveline.

The inside of the church smelled like the orange oil they used on the pews, and the outside smelled like the needles from the single redwood tree that grew in the yard. The buds on the cherry trees were close to blossoming, and when they did, the grass would slowly become littered with pink petals. Then, when Daniel looked up as he walked along the street, the branches would close overhead, lacing together in a pale pink canopy. He thought about the pink canopy, how it appeared every spring, how it looked with the light shining through it, and he began to relax, breathing slowly.

There had been too many meetings that were about problems, with him as the subject focus of attention. Was Daniel the one stealing? Had he defaced the buildings?

Now, waiting at the church for people to arrive, he reminded himself that this was a different type of meeting.

His body disagreed, holding tension, preparing for a getaway, in case the people turned on him.

They didn't know him at all, he reminded himself. They were only acquainted with their own picture, a mirror of their suspicion.

A voice from beside him. "And you? Are you doing okay?"

Daniel hadn't even heard Ani arrive beside him. She wasn't very big, only reaching his shoulder, and she held herself with a certain stillness. She was looking up at him now. He looked back out at the cherry blossom buds.

"I don't really like meetings," he said. "So many people, so many thoughts whizzing by." He shifted on his feet, pointing to the tree branches over the church year. "These trees are going to be beautiful soon, with thousands of pink flowers. They're all around town, and they only last for a little while."

He glanced back at her and saw her smiling faintly. She had very long eyelashes.

"Thank you," she said, putting a hand on his arm.

She turned and went back inside, and after a moment, he did, too. People began drifting into the church sanctuary. Daniel stood at the back, leaning against the wall. He saw Theresa and Sheldon arrive. Reesey went to give Ani a hug, and Sheldon spotted Daniel, walking to stand in front of him, Maddie at his side.

"Hey Danny," Sheldon said. "I didn't expect to see you here."

"Why?" Daniel asked.

Maddie piped up. "You hate stuff like this."

Daniel shrugged. "True." They both looked at him, waiting for him to say more, it seemed. "I really care about what happens with the refugee families," he said. "I want to help, even if it means sitting in rows in a crowded room."

Maddie whistled. "Wow," she said. "You do care."

Sheldon grinned. "Come sit with us. Looks like Ani is ready to begin."

"Thanks," Daniel said. "I'll find a seat when it really gets going."

He ended up sitting all the way in the back pew, right behind George and Mercy Jackson, Aveline's lawyer couple. Mercy turned and smiled at Daniel as he got settled. He nodded back, attempting a smile. His stomach was doing somersaults. Things were still awkward between them, though they had all attempted to be kind and polite to one another.

Last year, when Daniel was suspected of writing racist graffiti on George and Mercy's shop, George hadn't known who to believe. Daniel didn't blame him. The air of suspicion that had followed him for the last ten years had been heavy; it had been hard to see through it. And George hadn't known Daniel all that well. Not many people had.

Then Theresa came forward and told them all that Cam had committed the robberies, Cam had graffitied the shops in town. Cam had assaulted her.

Daniel took a long, deep breath, clenching and unclenching his hands. He was free of accusation now. He leaned forward.

"Are you coming to backyard night this week, George?" he asked.

George turned. "Wouldn't miss it," he said. "You?"

"I have two words," Daniel said. "Frankie's grill."

"I have two more," George said. "Lupe's molé"

"Lupe's making molé?" Daniel asked.

"That's the rumor."

Mercy shook her head. "You two. You can't tell me backyard night is about anything other than food."

"Oh, we talk some. Pray some," George said. He met Daniel's eyes. "But yes, a whole lot is about food."

Daniel settled back against the hard pew, feeling a little better. Maybe he could repair his relationships with the people of Aveline, one connection at a time.

Ani looked small and brave as she stood at the front of the church.

She was a stranger here, Daniel thought. He understood that. There were different ways to be strangers. One way was to be completely new, like Ani. Another was to be here for a long time, yet unknown. All the blanks people had in their minds about Daniel, they had filled in wrong. Dangerous, suspicious, malicious. He had almost started believing it about himself. He sometimes wondered if growing up with his parents would have taught him resilience, despite what others said about him. Maybe. He would never know.

It was brave for Ani to stand in front of all these people. Daniel pulled his attention back to her words.

"First things first," she said. A patch of gentle light filtered through the tall stained-glass windows to fall across her hair and face. "Yesterday, I received the dossier with the names and information for our families." There was a stir as people murmured and whispered throughout the big room. "And," Ani went on, "stay with me...there have been some pretty big changes."

There was silence. They waited.

CHAPTER SIX

Daniel listened intently. Ani tucked her hair behind her ears.

"We had thought that our refugees would be from Syria or Afghanistan. Instead, yesterday I learned that my organization has picked out four families from Venezuela to live in Aveline." Daniel heard exclamations from around the room, but Ani pushed forward. "The director and board think this will be best, as there is a strong need for placement for Venezuelan families. And this community, as you know, has a strong Latin American presence and grasp of the Spanish language." She looked at Francisco, who was sitting in the front pew with his parents and little girl. "Obviously."

People started talking again. Daniel smoothed his hands over his jeans and tapped his fingers on his knees. He wasn't sure what to think about this news. He watched and listened as people reacted.

"This may be simpler," Mercy murmured to George.

"Nothing is simple in this political climate," George responded. After a moment, he added, "But yes, you may be right."

The sound of many voices lifted and fell, lifted and fell. Daniel crossed his arms over his chest. Ani was standing quietly, watching the people in the room, biting her thumbnail. In the front row, Frankie bent his head to listen to something his mother was saying.

This was what had bothered Ani, Daniel realized, watching her. This change. She looked beautiful and strong as she stood there. But she was frowning. She started to say something a couple of times, but the room was too noisy for people to hear her. Daniel stood up.

"We should listen to the rest of Ani's presentation," he said, lifting his voice to be heard.

So many faces looked at him, so many sets of eyes. He sat down, his heart beating in his throat.

Ani smiled at him. She tapped a key on her computer, and photos of a man and a little boy showed up on the screen.

"We have a home for this family," she said. "Thanks to those who have come together to pay a year's rent for the family to get settled. Also, for the second family." She tapped the computer again, and the screen changed to a photo of a family with three small children. "We are still in need of homes for the third and fourth families, though we have at least one solid lead."

Lewis, a young Black man who had started a farming community in Aveline, stood up.

"I can confirm that I have space for a family," he said.

"One of the houses will be empty soon, and I can offer a position in our business if they happen to be interested."

Daniel watched as a smile lit Ani's face like a sunrise. She
grabbed her papers and leafed through them, looking at one
of them intently.

"Yes, I thought so," she said after a moment. "This family's
background is agriculture, and your place would be perfect.
Thank you, Lewis." She looked up. "You don't know what it
means for these families to come to a welcoming space. There
is a lot of work ahead. They carry trauma and need a lot of
support. It won't be easy, but if we weren't here for them,
they would have to bear this by themselves and might find
themselves swept like dust through the cracks in the system,
overwhelmed and overloaded by the stress of so many new
things."

Ani pressed a hand to her chest and took a deep breath.
Her face was flushed.

"On to the last family," she said, clicking to another photo,
this one of two adults and two children. "This one is
complicated."

Daniel stood.

"I want to help the last family," he said. "And I'm interested in buying a house to offer as a place to live. I've been
talking with Carlo about properties that are on the market,
and I think we're getting close."

The silence in the room was like an overly heavy blanket.
Daniel had hoped to see that smile like a sunrise again, but
Ani's face did not transform into a smile. It looked...blank.
She frowned, and Daniel felt heat rise to his own face.

This was what he had been preparing for; this was the new chapter of his life. He had been preparing for it. Learning today that the families were from Venezuela was a change, but it only meant that the Arabic Daniel had been studying was no longer necessary. He would have to brush up on his Spanish, but he had spoken it on and off since he was a child, and he was good with languages.

Still, no one spoke. "In conclusion," Daniel said into the silence, feeling totally out of his depth, "I can offer the last family a home."

Ani shifted her weight to her other foot, and Daniel remembered that standing this long might be hard for her, with her leg pain. Should someone find her a chair?

"Are you sure, Daniel?" she asked. "You haven't heard what the complication is. Do you have..." She trailed off, looking at Frankie.

Frankie spoke, swiveling in his seat to look back at Daniel. "I think Ani is wondering whether you have the resources for something like this."

Ani made a small sound but didn't correct him.

This was not the same response Lewis had received, and Daniel was bewildered. He had misjudged something here. There was a feeling like a bad cold in his chest. He wanted to bolt.

Over on the other side of the church, Carlo stood. "Amigos," he said. "I, uh, I think people might be forgetting their manners. I can share more about the work Daniel has done to ready himself for a land purchase, and I can vouch for his ability to do so. I know on the surface it may seem as though our beloved postmaster does not have the resources for this, but Daniel is full of surprises. He can follow through on his desire to help. We're in the process of choosing between two properties now."

People starting talking again. Daniel was still standing in his pew, staring at the photos of two little kids and two adults on the screen.

Focus on them, he told himself. Do not think about Ani's unsmiling face. Do not think about the fact that only one person in this room thinks you can do this.

A woman spoke up, her voice loud. Daniel recognized her from the post office, but she wasn't someone he knew well.

"I'm just wondering about background checks and things like that. Not to sound mean or anything, but how do we know what their history is?" She made a sweeping gesture that encompassed both Lewis and Daniel.

Lewis frowned and looked over at Daniel, eyebrows raised, lips twisted to the side.

"Which one of us do you think needs a background check, Ma'am?" Lewis asked.

There was more murmuring, like the buzz of bees in a tree. Daniel felt light-headed.

George stood. "I can speak for Lewis," he said, "and I'd like to remind everyone here that Daniel has been cleared of all charges against him. I want to apologize for any suspicion that my own actions may have caused."

Me too!" Theresa burst out, jumping to her feet. "This is all my fault."

From where he was sitting, Daniel saw Sheldon try to tug Theresa back into her seat. Maddie was stone-faced beside her mother. Mercy had her head in her hands.

This was Daniel's nightmare. Not only was the meeting becoming all about him and his reputation and past, but it was also bringing up painful memories for others. He should just leave. It was too much to ask for the past to not affect his future. Maybe the only answer was to disappear. He sank back into the pew and tried to breathe.

"All right, everyone," Ani said. She stood with her back straight and spoke with a clear voice. "Let's focus on the task at hand. In answer to your question--yes! We do extensive background checks on all our sponsors." She paused, looking at Daniel and Lewis and then at her hands. "I want to say that this amount of interest from people who want to be sponsors is absolutely a gift from God. We are ahead of where we thought we'd be, with homes offered for every family. I am so thankful for God's work in each of you, readying you for this."

She smiled and moved to unplug her computer. It seemed the meeting was over. "Oh!" she said. "One more thing. I am looking for a new apartment or suite, so let me know if you have any ideas. My budget is small, but I need to get out of the apartment I'm in currently."

Carlo turned and met Daniel's eyes, raising his eyebrows. Daniel nodded at Carlo. He knew exactly what the older man was thinking.

CHAPTER SEVEN

Carlo came to Daniel as soon as the meeting broke up, his wife Juanita at his side. Juanita put a hand on Daniel's arm.

"Don't be discouraged," she said. "Some things take time."

Juanita was as tiny as Carlo was large, but her presence was big, and she exuded kindness and peace. Daniel smiled at her.

"Thanks," he said. "I need..."

He paused. What did he need? He was nearly shaking from the effort of holding himself together after people discussed his abilities in such a public way. He knew his feelings weren't only about today. The memories were vast and deep. Daniel needed to get somewhere quiet. He needed light and water and motion.

"Let's go look at those houses tomorrow, then?" Carlo said. "And are you thinking what I am? Let's take a look at the old commune? It could house you, the family, and Ani if you wanted."

Daniel nodded. He was starting to freeze and could barely manage this conversation. Across the room, Frankie, Lupe, and Ani were talking together. Lewis and Sam were chatting nearby, faces serious, arms folded across their chests. Daniel saw people glancing his way and knew he couldn't talk to anyone else. Not now. He had nothing left.

"I'll see you in the morning," he said to Carlo, nodding at Juanita.

"Nine o'clock?"

"Perfect."

With that, Daniel was gone, slipping out of the room like a ghost.

He jogged all the way to the lake and to the dock where his rowboat was tied. He fumbled with the ropes and forced himself to slow down, to lift the loop over the hook and climb in. The oars fell into Daniel's hands, and then he was in his body again, straining with the muscles in his back and shoulders to move the boat away from land.

The sun was low in the sky, and the light across the water turned the surface into shades of silver and gold. Daniel closed his eyes to feel the cool spring air but immediately opened them again to soak in the light and color. He breathed, inhaling and exhaling with the strokes of the oars, finding a rhythm that brought his heartbeat back to its regular pace.

This was why he had always avoided people. They were

so hard to get along with, but then they seemed to think he was the difficult one.

Did he really want to do this? Did he want to get further involved with beings who could be so thoughtless? For ten years, Daniel had stuck mainly to himself, going from his apartment to his job without fail. He had joined the town band, but that was music; he hardly ever talked to the other band members.

Then last year, Sheldon had invited Daniel to backyard night and into that group of men. And after that, Theresa had come back to Aveline. Reesey was pushy, pulling him into her circle, into life. Daniel, against his better judgment, had grown hopeful. That baby hope died when Daniel saw that George didn't believe he hadn't vandalized the law firm.

Devastated, Daniel had gone to see his therapist for the first time in months. Lydia, who had been counseling Daniel since he was first diagnosed with autism, told Daniel that George's confusion wasn't surprising. George's life contained tragedy, loss, and betrayal, and trust wasn't automatic for him. Daniel hadn't really opened up to anyone, even his bandmates. Very few people knew about his life or his personal history. Lydia said that if Daniel wanted people to trust him, he needed to show them who he was.

"You can't trust what you don't know," she said. "You have to let them know you."

"I don't know how to do that," he had told her. "It's a skill I don't have."

"You may have to pretend at first," she said. "Try it for a while. I know it seems scary. Just tell people things. Try a year of freedom, where you allow yourself to do what you want and show people who you are."

"I don't think I've ever known what I want."

"You have the chance to find out. A fresh start."

She had crossed and uncrossed her legs, reaching over to the table beside her to take a sip of water. "Just give it a year. If, at the end of the year, people still don't know you and are still as," she glanced at her notes, "unrewarding, I think you said—"

"And opaque," Daniel inserted.

"—and opaque. If things still don't improve, you can go back to how they were. You can retreat into the world of stars and planets, or music theory, or whatever else."

Unrewarding and opaque. Daniel, after that meeting, would still use those words. But it wasn't time to retreat yet. He had agreed to give it a year.

He rowed and rowed, and slowly, his body began to feel like his own again. The sun went down, but Daniel stayed in the boat. Finally, in the middle of Lake Aveline, far from the lights of the town, he stretched out and lay his head back on the stern. The stars came out, one by one. The night was cold, but Daniel barely felt it.

The Pleiades. Orion. Andromeda. Venus, Jupiter, and Saturn in a long line. Daniel sought out the stars behind the stars, and his soul felt as though it was washing away the bog slime of human misunderstanding. Finally ready, he rowed back to shore. When he reached his apartment, he was so exhausted that he fell asleep in his clothes.

. . .

THE NEXT DAY, he woke with a start to his alarm. After a moment of fierce blinking, he heaved himself up to take a hot shower in his tiny bathroom. He had lived in this apartment for fourteen years, ever since he turned eighteen and aged out of the foster care system. It still didn't really feel like a home, but Daniel wasn't sure what home felt like. He dressed in jeans and a T-shirt with a plaid shirt on top, and a beanie, checking his reflection in the mirror. His beard was growing; it was nearly time for a trim.

Carlo was waiting in front of his real estate office, keys already in hand.

"Ready?" he asked. "Let's take my truck."

Daniel nodded. "Sounds good. I'm ready."

He had his head down as he dashed down the front steps in front of the office, zipping up his hoodie as he went. He only saw the woman at the bottom of the stairs in time to keep from knocking her over.

He reached for her arms to keep her from falling, then pulled his hands back.

"Sorry!" he said. "So sorry! I wasn't watching where I was going."

It was Ani, in a maroon-colored jacket zipped up to her chin, hands jammed in her pockets. Daniel saw again how pretty she was, with her long black hair loose around her shoulders and her eyes bright behind a pair of clear-rimmed glasses. She had a tiny nose stud and was wearing a beanie, salmon-colored again, nearly coral. It reminded Daniel of the color of the sunrise on the lake.

"It's okay," she said. "I wasn't really looking, either."

"You wore that color yesterday, too," Daniel said, gesturing to Ani's hat.

Her cheeks reddened. "I did," she said. "I wear it a lot. It's my favorite."

"Hi Ani," Carlo said from the steps. "We're heading out to look at properties."

Ani looked back and forth between them, ducking her head.

"About that...Daniel, I didn't get a chance to talk to you, but I'm really sorry about what happened yesterday."

"You don't need to apologize," he started to say, but Ani shook her head.

"No, please, let me explain. My question came across as so patronizing, and I'm such a newcomer here. I didn't know —Theresa told me a little of what the last years have been like for you, so I wanted to explain that Lewis and I have been talking about his farm as a potential home for weeks. That's why I was so eager when he spoke up. When you said something, it was a new idea, but I didn't question you because I thought anything..." she broke off, seeming at a loss for words.

This was excruciating. Daniel understood and appreciated her apology, but it was making him uncomfortable. He had to change the topic.

"Do you want to come with us?" he asked. From the corner of his eye, he saw Carlo turn quickly to look at him, but he ignored it and went on. "You can give us feedback on whether the properties are good for refugee families. It shouldn't take long. We're only going to two locations. We have room, right, Carlo?"

"If you don't mind sitting in the middle of the bench seat," Carlo said graciously, but he gave Daniel a strange look when Ani wasn't looking. "We should be back by noon."

Ani kept looking back and forth between the two of them.

"Really?" She glanced down at her phone. "I guess I don't have anything on until this afternoon, although I had thought of looking at a studio apartment that I saw online."

Carlo looked over at Daniel. Daniel guessed that maybe Carlo wanted him to say something about helping Ani in her need for a house. But it wasn't time for that yet. First things first.

"All right," Ani said. "That sounds nice. I can come. But are you sure you want me along?"

"I wouldn't ask if I wasn't sure," Daniel said.

"He means, of course we want you," Carlo said.

They stood there. Daniel was distracted by the pleasing contrast between Ani's hat and her black hair.

"What are we waiting for?" Carlo asked.

Daniel shook himself.

"You're right," he said. "Let's go."

CHAPTER EIGHT

A ni climbed into Carlo's old truck gingerly, pivoting on her right leg and using her arms to gain enough momentum to haul her left leg in. She had woken already sore after yesterday's long hours of standing and knew that she would need pain pills by the end of the day.

Was this wise? Ani hardly knew either of these men. But it was too late. Carlo had climbed in on her left and Daniel on her right. The truck wasn't very big. They were squished in like the sardines game Ani remembered playing as a youth. Carlo started the engine, but Juanita came running out of the realtor's office just before it pulled away. The windows were down, and Juanita stuck her head in beside Carlo.

"If I were you," she said to Ani, "I'd be wondering what I got myself into. But I can vouch for these guys. They're good ones!"

She gave her husband a loud kiss on his cheek, just above the line of his beard. It made Ani wonder whether the last-minute conversation had been an act of reassurance or warning for Ani. *This one is taken.*

Juanita didn't need to worry, Ani thought wryly. Carlo wasn't the one that caused a heightened awareness in Ani.

She felt heat rise to her face. *Where did that come from?* It was true, though. Ani could smell the fragrances of Daniel's laundry detergent and shampoo intermingling. He smelled like lavender and fresh air and something else that was just him, she thought. She was aware of his slightest movement. She found herself staring at his arm, lying along the window's edge. He tapped lightly on the side of the truck.

Carlo had said something, and Ani had missed it. "Sorry?" she asked. Honestly, her face was going to burst into flame. What was happening? She didn't even know Daniel, and he wasn't exactly charming. She must be genuinely lonely. That, or she was losing her mind.

"I asked if you've had a chance to explore much of Aveline."

"No, I haven't, really. I've been absorbed in meetings, both online and in person. And I had to spend a couple of weeks at a convention in L.A. last month."

"So that's where you went," Daniel said. "I wondered."

There was in the little truck. Ani wasn't sure what to say in response to that. After a few minutes, Daniel spoke again.

"My brain is different," he said. "I'm autistic. Years ago, they diagnosed me with Asperger's syndrome, but people don't use that term anymore."

"Yes," Ani said. "I've heard that."

Daniel blinked at her. "About me? Or in general?"

"I keep up with diagnostics because I'm in social work," Ani said. "I hadn't heard it about you."

"I'm surprised Theresa didn't tell you," Carlo said. "She likes to talk about how she and Daniel are in a special club."

Ani smiled. "Sounds like her." She really, really liked Theresa. The straightforward, beautiful woman was the same diminutive height as Ani, and because of the way she looked at Ani, holding back nothing in her gaze, she reminded Ani of her mother or one of her aunts. She had none of the caginess of American culture.

"I bring it up because I notice a lot of things that other people don't," Daniel said. "I always notice people's comings and goings--who is absent, who is around. Some people find it creepy, but I don't mean it that way. It's just the way my brain works."

Ani felt a slight breath of disappointment like a breeze along her shoulder and realized she had been flattered that Daniel noticed she was gone. But she also knew it was a vulnerable thing for him to share.

"Thank you for telling me," she said. After a moment, she added. "I didn't find it creepy."

Carlo cleared his throat. "You'll get to see two beautiful parts of Aveline today. These properties are some of my best."

"Oh," she said. "That's wonderful."

It truly was beautiful here. The new green of spring ran over the hillsides, and wildflowers were growing in ditches and fields. Ani took deep breaths of the fresh air blowing through the open windows of the truck.

"Have you talked to any of the families yet?" Daniel asked.

"Not yet," Ani told him. "They're in orientation in San Diego." She glanced at Daniel's face and found him looking back at her. His eyes were light hazel, with faint lines spreading from the corners. He had a nice face. A kind face. Tanned from the sun, with golden highlights in his hair... she looked away. She was staring. *Pull yourself together, Ani!*

"We're here," Carlo announced. "First stop."

"We're going to look at two properties?" Ani asked as she stepped out of the truck on Carlo's side. He held out a hand to help her down. She accepted it gratefully and looked around, walking to the edge of an embankment to get a sense of the space. They were on a heavily forested ridge, under some tall firs. It was lovely, with light filtering through the trees and falling on the large house in the distance.

"Tell me about this property, Carlo," Daniel said. "Do your realtor thing."

The two men started walking toward the house, and then Daniel paused and turned back to let Ani catch up, smiling at her. They fell into conversation about the pros and cons of this property, especially regarding housing a refugee family. Ani was thankful for the practicality, especially since her heart had decided to revert to being fourteen years old. She chimed in when she had thoughts or when they asked her questions, really trying to think through the possibilities of the space.

There were two buildings; a large main home for the family and a smaller mother-in-law cottage that Daniel could live in. There were pros and cons. The pros were the wide spaces, the beauty, and the quiet. This would be a refuge for a family new to America. The cons were the remote location and maybe the depth of the forest around the home. It would be dark in the winter. The house was also massive.

"The size of the house seems a little overwhelming for a family who has most recently lived in a refugee camp," Ani said. "I would almost suggest that you live there, Daniel, but the cottage is too small for the family."

"Ah," Carlo said. "I hadn't thought about it being too big. But I can see what you mean."

"All in all, not terrible, but not perfect," Daniel said. "And you can't see enough of the sky for stargazing. Let's see the other property, Carlo."

They climbed back into the truck, and Carlo turned it around between the trees.

"That house would be too intimidating even for me," Daniel said, peering out at the two-story building. "I'd be rattling around in there, losing things as soon as I put them down. Walking in circles."

Ani laughed.

"You may really like the next property," Carlo said.

"Where is it?"

"Over near the university, still in the hills, but it was logged in the early part of last century. Still plenty of trees, but not as dark. It's really close to Lewis's farm."

"Oh, that would be amazing!" Ani said.

Daniel turned to look at her.

"I think it would be good for two of the families to live close together," she added.

"It's an old commune, a farming experiment, with three homes and a large garden," Carlo added.

"I told Carlo that I needed to be able to see the sky," Daniel said. "I always have to see the sky."

CHAPTER NINE

Ani gazed out through the windshield as they drove. Carlo sang softly in Spanish, occasionally tapping on the steering wheel. Then, after a while, he began to sing Moon River, and Daniel joined in with the harmony. There was something so beautiful about the light coming through the dust on the truck windows and Daniel's soft, rumbly tenor mingling with Carlo's deep bass. It made tears come to Ani's eyes. She dabbed at them with the back of her hand, trying to be subtle about it, but Daniel noticed and looked at her with concern.

"I'm sorry, did my singing bother you?"

She laughed, surprising herself. "Bother me enough to make me cry?" she asked. "No. Your voices are beautiful, and the day is perfect."

"Oh," Daniel said, turning and settling back against the seat. "That kind of crying."

"Did you hear that, Danny?" Carlo asked. "Ani thinks we

sound beautiful. Ani, have you heard our band play? I'm the guitarist and lead singer, and Daniel plays bass and sings. George plays trumpet, and"

"You have a band? Well, that explains why you sound so good," Ani said.

"Thank you," Daniel said. "You should come and see us sometime."

The road beside the lake hugged the shore closely, and Ani turned her face to gaze out across the water. The sun was reflected in a million sparkles on the lake's surface. Little gusts of wind whipped the water into tiny white peaks. It was chilly with the truck windows down, and Ani pulled her sweater sleeves farther down on her wrists.

Carlo turned up a road on the left, heading away from the lake, and the truck thundered along for a while before he pulled up to a gate and punched in a code. The gate swung open, and Carlo drove a few more yards before pulling the truck over and cutting the engine. He immediately hopped out, but Daniel and Ani just sat there for a moment, in stunned silence. They looked at each other.

"Well, this is something," Ani said.

Daniel got out of the truck and turned to offer her a hand. Ani had planned to get out on the driver's side again, but it felt too awkward to turn him down, so she scooted over to his door and took the hand he held out. She stepped down carefully, but they were on a slope, and her leg gave way a bit. She stumbled into Daniel. He put an arm under her other elbow to steady her, his face showing concern.

"You got it?"

Ani felt a bit breathless. He was very close. "Yes," she said, pulling back.

She turned away to hide her face and to look at the view again. The property was stunning. It stretched along gentle hills, scattered with trees that had large, reaching branches. Moss dripped from tree limbs. Three houses were scattered around a hollow, with a meadow and an old overgrown vegetable garden between them. The hills were absolutely covered with wildflowers.

"This isn't even as beautiful as it gets," Carlo said. "The wildflowers are at their full strength in another week, and the jacarandas come into bloom in May."

"Wow," Ani breathed. She didn't know what else to say.

"Ready to explore?" Carlo asked.

Ani followed behind as Daniel nodded. He looked in every direction, his eyes wide. She wondered if he felt the same way she did. As they began to walk, Ani turned to look behind them, and there was the lake in the distance, shining through the trees at the bottom of the hill. The town of Aveline was tiny and perfect beside it. What a view!

"Lewis's property adjoins this one," Carlo said, slightly out of breath from the uphill walk. "But there are five more acres before you get to his fence."

"It would be excellent to have land adjoining Lewis's land," Ani said.

Daniel turned to look at her. "You said that before. You think so?" he asked.

"Yes," she said. "Two of the families could be close together. But this property has one too many houses."

Carlo glanced at Daniel again.

"Can you show us around?" Daniel asked.

Carlo shook the keys to make them jingle. "That's what we're here for," he said.

They spent the rest of the morning in exploration. Ani didn't know what had happened to make these people leave, but the homes they had created were beautiful. They were warm, hand-built, full of light and details that made life special, like outdoor benches or flower gardens. One of the houses was a good size for the family. The other two were smaller, with two cozy bedrooms each, tiny living rooms, and lovingly constructed kitchens which were small but had plenty of space for organization—cabinets and drawers and hooks on the walls.

After a while, they all wandered in different directions. Ani went back to the house furthest down the hill, drawn back by something she couldn't name. She opened the short gate and stepped into the garden, walking up the path and through the front door. The house was a dream, with a living room that had windows opening up to a view of the lake. One of the bedrooms had a window that was sheltered by the curving branches of a tall tree. The other also had a view of the lake and a little door onto a patio with an outdoor shower and tub. A weathered wooden wall protected the bathing area from the eyes of anyone who might be nearby. Ani went back inside. The soft colors on the walls, the light coming through the windows, and the overgrown garden made Ani dream of having this kind of home, this kind of life, something she had never before considered. Ani was a city girl, a focused girl. She was an immigrant, an only child, driven to serve, to work, to keep moving.

She had never imagined the pull that a yellow kitchen with tiny handmade drawers could have over her. She leaned on one of the countertops, chin propped on her hands, giving in to the daydream entirely for several minutes. Finally, she shook herself and headed back up to the biggest house to find the others.

The real question was whether the big house was appropriate for the family that Daniel would sponsor. Ani thought it was. It was big but not too big, bright and welcoming, as all of the houses were. It could use some work--they all could--but Ani assumed Daniel knew that. She walked through the rooms one more time, looking at closets and checking the bathrooms. There was no question. This house would be a great place to welcome a refugee family.

CHAPTER TEN

C arlo locked the houses up while Ani made her way back down to the parking area. Daniel was already leaning against the passenger door of the truck, arms crossed over his chest. Ani's leg ached from hip to ankle, sending little shivers of pain up her spine. She knew she was limping slightly and would be making phone calls this afternoon from her sofa, her leg propped in front of her. She looked up to see Daniel watching her with concern. He moved to offer her an arm, but she shook her head.

Rather than feeling annoyed, which Ani often did when people offered unsolicited help, she felt a flash of longing. It was rare that people could show their concern for her without making her feel like a child. Somehow, Daniel managed to express compassion for Ani's disability without making her feel small. How did he do it? And why did he have this effect on her? She would have to keep her distance.

Ani had set her life course long ago. All of her living situations were temporary, and there was no use getting attached.

"Well?" Carlo asked after he had jogged down to meet them. "What do you think?"

Carlo was looking at Daniel, but Daniel turned to look at Ani. "What do you think?" he asked. "Does the house look like it will work for the Loria's?"

"It looks perfect," she said. "But isn't the property too big? What will you do with the extra house?" Her face flushed as she realized she was asking a question that was none of her business.

Carlo turned to look at Daniel. Daniel nodded.

"Well," he said, "when Carlo first told me about this property, I didn't even think I would look at it because I didn't want the extra house. But then at the meeting, when you mentioned that you needed a place to stay, both of us had the same thought. Ani, what if you moved here, too?"

For a few moments, Ani wasn't sure if she had heard correctly.

"What?" she asked, finally.

"You're looking for a new place to live," Daniel said. "You can pay me a little bit of rent and keep the place up, and you'll be really close to two of the families. And Lewis." Daniel put a particular emphasis on Lewis's name, and Ani frowned in confusion, but her attention drifted over to Carlo when he started talking.

"We could draw up a contract that includes a lowered rent," he said.

"You could stay in that house," Daniel said, pointing at the one Ani had fallen in love with.

Ani closed her eyes. She wanted to scream 'YES!' but had she even heard right? She opened her eyes again. The men were still there, and yes, they were looking at her, waiting for her to respond. Yes, Daniel had offered her a place to live, a home that she had looked at in a sort of wistful, I'll-never-live-somewhere-like-this way. She stared over at the house and then back down at the view of the lake and town. Was there anything wrong with accepting something like this?

Time. She needed time.

"This would be the most generous thing I had ever heard of," she said, "if you weren't already buying land to help a family you haven't even met." Her words drifted away as she lost her train of thought. She imagined living here, on this land, with the Loria's and their complicated immigration case. It would be helpful to be so close. She looked at the wildflowers that covered the hills.

"I need time to think," she told Daniel, turning to look at him. He was gazing back at her.

"Of course," he said. "Take as much as you need."

"But there is a time constraint," Carlo said, "because I need to know whether you are going to purchase this property, Daniel."

"Oh, I want to buy it," Daniel said. "The houses are good, and there is plenty of open space for stargazing. Hopefully, Ani will move in, but if she doesn't, we'll find someone else. Now that I've seen it, I can't let it go."

"There shouldn't be any problems," Carlo said. "It's been listed for nearly a year."

Ani was grateful for this. It meant she would be able to consider Daniel's offer without any thought that his decisions rested on her. They were quiet on the drive home. Ani's leg throbbed, and her mind was racing. Daniel had pulled a piece of modeling clay out of his pocket and worked it into shapes with one hand. He looked up and saw her watching him.

"It helps me think," he said. "Want to try?"

She smiled. "Sure."

He handed her half of the lump of clay, warm from his hand. She rolled it into a ball, once again aware of him beside her.

Daniel and Carlo started singing, and to Ani's horror, tears began to run down her cheeks until she was actively weeping.

"I'm sorry," she said, as Daniel handed her some tissues that were in Carlo's glove compartment. "I think I'm just overwhelmed. It's been a tough week, and I don't know how I'm going to handle this new refugee situation. I don't speak much Spanish."

Carlo smiled. "I do," he said. "And so do many of the people in this town."

"I'm working on mine," Daniel added.

"Your Spanish is great already," Carlo said.

"But I'm learning more," Daniel said. "Don't worry, Ani. You're not alone. We can help."

CHAPTER ELEVEN

W hen she reached her apartment and closed the door behind her, Ani stood there for a moment, staring at the ugly beige walls. This apartment really was depressing, though Ani felt guilty even thinking it, knowing how many people were displaced throughout the world.

Had Daniel really offered to let her rent that beautiful house? Was it okay for her to say yes? Ani felt teary and overwrought. Why was she so emotional?

She let out a breath, went to the kitchen to splash water on her face, and then grabbed some hummus and flatbread from the fridge. She set the bread and a few spoonfuls of the hummus onto a plate, peeling an orange and laying the pieces on one side, then heaping some dark, oily olives onto the hummus. She felt shaky, like she just wanted to sit down and cry, but her workday wasn't over. Arranging the food calmed her a little, and she took it to the living room with her, laying the plate on the table beside her couch. She had two calls to make.

She settled into the couch cushions with a giant sigh, hauling her bad leg onto the ottoman and kneading the tired muscles with her fingertips. Tears stung her eyes again. What was it about the morning that had unlocked so many emotions? Was it being with the men who were already close to feeling like friends? She had felt uncharacteristically safe, chatting with them and listening to them sing. Their voices were so beautiful, harmonizing together. For as many ugly things as there were in the world, there were so many moments of sheer beauty.

Ah, Ani thought. That was it. Opening her heart had always been risky because if she let the good things in, the sorrow came rushing along as well. She didn't like it. She didn't open her heart all that often. Music was sneaky, though, music and beautiful landscapes. She did the best she could to shrug the feelings away.

She picked up her phone and pressed Amanda's cheery photo icon.

"Ani!" her boss said when the call connected. "How are you? How did you take the change?"

Ani grimaced, though she also felt instant comfort at the sound of Amanda's familiar voice.

"You can probably guess."

Amanda laughed. "Yeah, I can guess."

"My mom thinks it will be good for me."

"I love your mom."

They both laughed. Ani took a bite of her food and closed her eyes. She was hungrier than she had realized.

"Other than that," Amanda went on," how are things in Aveline?"

Ani smiled at the thought of the people of Aveline. "Surprisingly good," she said. "This might be the most loving community I've ever met. They're really, really excited to welcome the families."

"That's good to hear. No more incidents like the one from last year?"

Last year, in the middle of a rash of hateful graffiti, there had been some words scrawled on walls about refugees taking jobs. She knew, though, that the person responsible had been arrested.

"I have gotten a total of three angry letters," Ani said. "But I offered to talk to the letter writers, and it seems to have gone a long way toward making them feel better about our project."

"Did anyone take you up on the offer to talk?" Amanda asked.

Ani wrinkled her nose. "No," she said. "I wish they would. I have armfuls of statistics."

"I bet you do." Amanda cleared her throat. Ani could hear her typing and knew, as she took another bite of pita and hummus, that her boss was sitting at a desk while Ani curled up on her sofa. Ani was thankful for her own comfort. It was a perk of the job.

"I wanted to talk to you about the Loria's," Amanda said.

"Yes...the problem case. Spill it." Ani was fairly certain she knew whwat the problem was, but she wanted to hear it from Amanda's perspective. There was a reason that Amanda was the new director of their organization, despite her youth. She had a straightforward warmth and wisdom that set everyone around her at ease.

"Okay," Amanda said. "They're a wonderful family, very tight-knit. They really love each other. They're adjusting well to the center, but they had a terrible journey from Venezuela, full of anxiety and danger. None of that is the problem, however. It's Maria and Leo."

"They are not the parents," Ani said.

"Right," Amanda said. "You got it. They are the children's grandparents. And they claimed to be parents on their paperwork. That's how they got in. So two things, they lied, never a good thing with DHS, and as you know, asylum seekers cannot sponsor grandchildren."

Ani made a tsking sound that reminded her immediately of her own mother. "It's such a stupid rule," she growled. "It's from this modern western idea that the nuclear family is the true family. You know how much harm this has caused. In many places in the world, the grandmother is like a second mother!" She sighed. "Sorry. I know you are aware."

"I know it, and you know it. Not everyone sees it that way. Fortunately, there was a sympathetic officer, and one of the children was sick, so he let them in without looking too hard at their paperwork. But it's going to be a fight to get them asylum status. We need all of our skills for this one. We will really need to fight."

Ani closed her eyes, imagining the hearing.

"I have one more thing to tell you," Amanda said. "Don't freak out."

Ani's eyes snapped back open. She popped an olive in her mouth and massaged her leg, which was aching terribly.

"Do the words 'don't freak out' ever work? Never mind. Let me guess. The families are actually from Burma."

Amanda chuckled. "No. Still Venezuela. But you know how we thought they would arrive in Aveline in two months?"

"Ye-es..." Ani said, not liking where this was going.

"We have them all here in San Diego, and we are ahead with the paperwork. Not only that, but the org is feeling that some of these families are more vulnerable and need to be in a stable place right away. They all have children, as you've seen."

Ani kneaded her leg, closing her eyes. She thought about all that needed to happen before the town was ready for the refugees.

"Anddd..." she said. "You had better say that they have given us extra time to prepare because they know we need it."

"They will be arriving in one month," Amanda said.

For a moment, there was total silence because Ani couldn't get words out of her mouth. But then whatever had stopped her lungs let up, and she shrieked. "What???"

"You said you wouldn't freak out," Amanda said.

"No, you told me not to freak out, at which point, I promised exactly and precisely nothing."

She sighed and let her head fall back on the couch cushions. "Ahh, Amanda, this is insane."

"I know," Amanda said, sounding genuinely empathetic. "You have to understand that we're crunched right now. And because you let us know that you have housing for everyone, Rita decided to move you up in the queue."

"But you have authority over Rita! And having housing is not the same as being ready!"

"I rarely pull rank over Rita, who is very, very good at her job, Ani. You can do this. I believe in you."

Ani took a deep breath, ready to launch into a tirade.

"Oh, look at that! I've got to go, Ani."

And she ended the call. Ani was left staring at the phone.

CHAPTER TWELVE

Ani couldn't quite take it in. This assignment was falling to pieces around her. She dialed her mom.

"Hi, sweetie," her mother said. "This is a welcome surprise."

"Hi Mama," Ani said. "How are you?"

"I'm fine, but you sound terrible."

Ani sighed. "Thanks," she said. Her mother wasn't wrong though, Ani was exhausted. And it was only partly the walking, which was actually good for her. Before this assignment, Ani had been sitting at a desk for too many hours of the day. She needed consistent exercise to stay limber and strong.

It was the emotion. That's was what was tiring. Changes and emotion. The way the case was flying in different directions without Ani having any control over it at all.

"To what do we owe the honor of this call?" Ani's father asked. He was using his joking voice.

"Oh, are you both there?" Ani asked. She had imagined

talking with her mother alone. But her father was often around, now that he was retired. She shrugged. Oh well. They would both get an earful.

"I needed to get your advice on something."

Ani's parents were silent, and Ani could practically hear them rubbing their hands together, giving each other glee-filled glances. She grinned despite her worry. Her parents loved it when she asked them for advice.

"Go ahead," her mom said in an overly casual voice.

"I got an offer today, and I'm wondering whether I should accept it."

"Go on," Ani's father said after a moment. Why was Ani finding it hard to tell them about this? She was making it a bigger deal than it needed to be.

"You know how we have sponsors for the families?"

"Yes," her mother said.

"We have one sponsor who is buying a property specifically to house one of the refugee families. There are three houses—one for the family, one for him, and he's offering to rent me the third."

"Put us on Facetime," Ani's mother said. "I want to see you."

Ani did so, waiting for the video feed to turn on. When it did, she smiled. There they both were: Ani's father with his thinning hair and spectacles, and her mother, so beautiful with her silver and black hair.

"Why the hesitation?" Ani's mother asked.

Straight to the point. Ani was not at all ready to confide the new, strange attraction she had to Daniel, this quiet postmaster of a small town. She could barely understand it herself, it wouldn't lead anywhere, and her parents certainly had different hopes for her future. Ani sighed, remembering her last conversation with her mother. She had been rather eager to set her up with Francisco. They certainly had relaxed their hopes of an Iranian or Armenian doctor.

"I guess because there are only three homes on the property. The new family, this house of this man, whose name is Daniel, and the little house that would be mine."

Her parents gave her the exact same look, and Ani burst out laughing.

"You two are spending too much time together," she said. "You're starting to look like twins."

"Don't change the subject!" her father said. "Why did you say his name like that?"

"Daniel? Like what?"

"There! You did it again. You gave it a special caress," her father said decisively.

"I did not! You're imagining things."

On the screen, her mother had turned and was staring at Ani's father.

"She's right, darling. You are imagining things. Ani has feelings for the pastor of the town."

"What?" Ani shrieked, in much the same that she had shouted at Amanda earlier. She put her face in her palm. "If you two are not going to be sensible, I'm going to take back my request for advice," she said.

Her mother's eyes widened in alarm.

"Okay, sweetheart, no need to be abrupt. Tell us more."

So Ani told them about the whole situation. The dream house, the proximity to the other family, the view of the lake. How it seemed perfect, but almost too perfect, as though there was some reason she shouldn't accept such a wonderful gift.

"It sounds excellent," her mother said, after Ani was done speaking. "I say go ahead. You don't need to worry about propriety since you are not under the same roof. And you will not be the only people on the property."

"Well, I wasn't actually asking for permission," Ani said.

Her mom rolled her eyes, and her dad laughed.

"Okay, prickle face," he said. "Do it!" He blew a kiss, murmured something in Armenian that Ani didn't quite catch, and then headed out of sight of the camera.

"What did he say?" Ani demanded.

Her mother smiled. "Something for me."

Ani's parents had grown up in Iran and mostly spoke Farsi together, which Ani spoke as well, but their mothers had sung and spoken to them in Armenian. Sometimes they used it as a love language that Ani barely understood. She felt a familiar sensation from being a child, of being an only child on the outside of her parents' love. Not remembering Iran well, not speaking the language of her grandparents. Not being actually Iranian. Not being "actually" American.

Logically, she knew she was actually all these things, Armenian, Iranian, and American, but these were the feelings of being the kind of immigrant child she was. And there was no protection, apparently. Not even spending her life with other immigrants could make her feel as though she was on the inside of something. She had learned Arabic and Pashtu, she spoke English and Farsi fluently. She even knew a tiny bit of French.

And she would still be on the outside of her new Spanish-speaking community. What loving words would she miss this time?

Plus, she wished her parents had told her not to do it. Why did she wish that?

Ani told her mother goodbye and blew her a kiss. Then she went to make a cup of tea, wincing as she limped toward the kitchen. If only there was a bathtub in this apartment deep enough to make a difference. This one was so shallow that Ani couldn't really soak her leg thoroughly.

She had a vision of the outdoor bathtub and shower at the little house on Daniel's new property. The tub was clawfoot and massive, with a circular opening above the protective walls. She imagined that at night, one could soak one's sore leg in a hot bath and look at the stars.

She had wanted her parents to say it was a bad idea because she didn't want to fall in love with the house, she realized. She was scared of loving things too much, afraid of all the longing it could bring.

CHAPTER THIRTEEN

Daniel put the finishing touches on his corn salad, garnishing it with chopped cilantro. His apartment had one single countertop, covered with bottles and dishes because the few cupboards were full. It meant that he had to prepare something simple for backyard night. It was too hard to cook complicated food in the tiny kitchen.

He covered the salad bowl with plastic wrap and looked around for his jacket. He found it slung across the chair in the living room and shrugged it on, thinking about his new house. After ten years of living in a small apartment, the thought of the new kitchen was a dream. He remembered walking through it, opening the hand-crafted cupboards, finding space for every necessary thing, even little nooks to tuck away spice bottles. There was a sink and stove out on his porch as well, in case he wanted to cook out there.

Daniel had been only half-living for most of his life, hiding, keeping his head down. At first, he had hidden from bullies and angry foster parents, then it was well-meaning neighbors who couldn't really see him and never tried to include him. But this was the year he had promised to try freedom. To try connection. To choose life. Well, buying this property was choosing life, that was certain. Could something so beautiful really be his?

He left his apartment and walked up the road with the salad bowl tucked under one arm. The acreage was farther from town, which meant more driving, less walking. That was a negative point. But Daniel, though he had tried, had been unable to come up with any other marks against it. He had put an offer on it the very day after seeing it.

Carlo had checked with him more than once. "Are you sure, Danny Boy? Should you think about it a while longer?"

"I know exactly what I want," Daniel told Carlo. "I want this property."

Carlo started the paperwork.

Now Daniel was on his way to backyard night to announce his good news to the others. He also had a couple of questions for them. He pushed through Frankie's gate and found that he was one of the first people to arrive. Frankie's eleven-year-old daughter Rosa was playing in the yard, jumping from paving stone to paving stone. Frankie stood at the grill, Sam by his side.

"No fire tonight?" Daniel asked as he laid his salad on the table.

"I got started late," Frankie said. "Had a last-minute meeting with Ani and thought this would be faster."

Daniel fumbled with the bowl at the mention of Ani's

name. It landed harder than he meant and clattered. Both men looked up.

"Sorry," Daniel muttered.

He took a seat, and Sam drifted over, clapping Daniel on the shoulder.

"Hey there," Sam said.

"Oh, hey, Sam," Daniel said. Dang it. He had forgotten greetings again. "What was the meeting about?" he asked Francisco.

"I'll fill you in when everyone gets here," Frankie said. "It concerns all of us."

Daniel watched as Rosa jumped from stone to stone, attempting bigger jumps, one-footed jumps, spinning jumps. He envied her freedom. And then he wondered what was stopping him from joining. So he got up and followed her lead, jumping from one paving stone to another. Rosa laughed when he began. Before long, without any discussion, the play evolved into a copying game, where Rosa made a certain kind of jump and Daniel had to imitate what she did.

When Sheldon and Carlo arrived, Daniel was attempted a full twirl between one stone and the next. Sheldon and Carlo stood frozen just inside the gate, staring at Daniel. He landed the jump, and Rosa clapped and cheered.

"Yes," Sheldon said. "I can see why you would be concerned, Carlo. Danny? You all right? Carlo says you're behaving uncharacteristically. He thinks you're not yourself."

Daniel was annoyed with the question because he was trying to focus on Rosa's jump. She had taken points away on previous turns because of slight differences in posture or direction, and he needed to pay attention.

"Maybe," he said, "neither of you knows what is 'characteristic' of me." And then he attempted the jump, a complicated affair including a last-minute flick of the back foot. Sheldon and Carlo stood there for a moment longer, then went to chat with the other men.

After a while, George arrived, Lupe came out to collect Rosa, and Daniel joined the other men, pulling his chair close to the fire in the chilly spring evening air. Frankie started the meeting with a simple prayer.

"Be with us; help us to see each other through the layers of joy and trials."

The men helped themselves to the food. Daniel opened a soda, took a sip, and then ate a bite of sausage with his corn salad. He sat back with a sigh. It was good to be here.

He was happy about the changes that were coming, but it was nice to have things that were the same, like backyard night with these men, the branches of the trees black against the dusky sky overhead.

"Next week, we may be indoors again," he said.

George nodded. "Rain."

"What do you think our weather will be like for the new families?" Sam asked. "What's the weather like in Venezuela?"

"Tropical," Frankie said. Daniel nodded. He had been researching.

"It will be an adjustment for them," Daniel said, "but by the time they get here, it will be close to summer."

"Speaking of which," Frankie said. "I have news that Ani

said I could share tonight, especially since she knew I was going to see you, Dan."

"Oh, I don't like to be called Dan," Daniel said.

Frankie blinked at him, then turned to look at Sheldon, which annoyed Daniel because he was the one who had spoken.

"You can call me Daniel or Danny if you really must shorten my name," Daniel said. "Carlo started that one. Those are the names I like."

He could have gone into it more. The teasing and hurt from foster homes, the way the first thing they had always done was shorten his name to Dan, until he didn't even know who he was anymore, didn't know who had a claim on him, who could name him. But Frankie didn't need to know all of that.

Frankie nodded and took a sip of his beer, blinking fast. "Thanks for telling me," he said.

"For telling all of us," Sam added.

Daniel nodded.

"So as I was saying," Frankie continued, "Ani told me something important today, which is that they have moved the arrival date up. Our families will be getting here a month earlier than we thought." There were exclamations from around the fire. "Ani talked with Lewis, who said that was fine, and our rental is nearly ready. The other house too. Daniel, your house is the only questionable one."

"Questionable?" Daniel asked.

"Because you haven't bought it yet."

"Oh." Daniel looked at Carlo.

Carlo had a large bite of food in his mouth. He held up a finger while he chewed, then spoke. "We've made an offer, and no one else has. No one is living there now, so the current owners may be fine with us moving in before the sale is finalized."

"So then, we just need to furnish the new family's house," Daniel said. "And my house. And Ani's house, if she decides to move in."

Exclamations again. Sam sat forward in his chair, and Sheldon choked on a sip of beer, needing Carlo to pound him on the back while he tried to get his breath back.

"Did you just say Ani's house?" Sheldon asked.

Carlo explained. "There are three houses on the property. Daniel has offered one to Ani because she is looking for a new place to live. She's taking some time to decide."

"She's seen it?" Sheldon asked.

"She came out to look at the houses with us the other day," Daniel said.

George, Sheldon, and Sam were all staring at Daniel.

"What?" Daniel crossed his arms over his chest, not sure what their faces meant.

"Who are you?" Sheldon asked, grinning. "What is happening to you?"

CHAPTER FOURTEEN

"**W**hat do you mean?" Daniel asked, frowning at Sheldon.

"I mean, you are pretty much turning your life upside down--buying land, sponsoring a family, playing with kids... all without warning and out of the blue."

"Are you interested in Ani?" Sam asked, breaking into Sheldon's tirade.

Daniel was feeling uncomfortable with their eyes and questions directed solely at him. He didn't know which statement to address first, so he answered the last question asked.

"You mean, romantically? Me?"

Sam nodded.

"I don't know," Daniel said. . "But it wouldn't matter if I was because I'm pretty sure she's interested in Lewis. Which reminds me...can we invite Lewis to backyard night?"

"Actually, I have invited him in the past," George said. "He's been busy, but he's interested."

"Let's get back to Ani, though," Sheldon said. "Why do you think she's interested in Lewis?"

"Because of things I've learned about people over the years," Daniel said. "You guys wouldn't understand because you're not autistic, and it all comes so naturally to you. I'm always observing, always trying to see and memorize peoples' tells and little things they do that will be a clue to how they feel. Once I learn them, I never forget."

Never get hit twice by the same person. That had been his motto when he was younger. The first time was a surprise, but he should have learned how not to get on their bad side by the second.

"Are you ever wrong?" Sheldon asked.

Daniel shrugged. "Sometimes. But I'm right a lot, too. I wasn't wrong about Cam."

Silence fell on the little group. Sheldon's face grew stiff.

"How are things going with all that?" Frankie asked. Sheldon glanced at George.

"He was refused bail, which is good. Hopefully, he'll be sentenced sometime this summer, and we can all put it behind us."

Daniel shifted on his chair. "Sorry," he said. "Maybe I shouldn't have brought Cam up."

Sam shook his head. "It's okay. We were talking about this as a family the other day. It's good for us to have to say his name and talk about the effect his actions have had on our family and our town. It was all such a secret for so long."

Sheldon was nodding. "For too long. And you paid the price for it, Daniel. You have every right to talk about it."

Daniel didn't know what to say.

"Well," he said finally. "That might help me answer the first question. I don't think my behavior is out of the blue. You know what has happened recently to change things for me."

Frankie was nodding. "You've been absolved. You have a clean slate."

Sheldon sat forward with his elbows on his knees. "May I just point out that this is the most you've ever spoken on backyard night?"

Daniel smiled. "You may point that out," he said. "That's what I want to talk about." His smile fell. It was hard to say it out loud. "For years, people suspected me of doing terrible things, and nothing I said could change their minds. Even when the police said it probably wasn't me. I know because I got a lot of letters."

"You did?" Sam asked. "I didn't know that."

"I didn't tell anyone," Daniel said. He shook his head, feeling the familiar sick feeling in his gut. "I don't want to talk about the letters. But my question is about now—I want the years back. I can't get them back. But when I try to live normally, people still question me. I think maybe they always will. How do you find the courage to do things even if you know you will be misjudged?"

"Are you talking about what happened at the meeting?" Frankie asked.

"Yes and no--it happens all the time. I decide to smile at someone, but then they look at me with what I think might be fear. Or I want to talk more, but then people mention that too. I just... I want to be free."

The men sat and looked at Daniel and then at each other.

"I want to apologize," Sheldon said. "I don't think I realized how hard this had hit you. Maybe because you were quiet about it." He sat back and glanced up at the sky. "My opinion is that you shouldn't worry about what people think about you. I don't."

"Yeah, me neither," Sam said. "Why would you worry about what other people think?"

"Well," George said, stretching out the word and leaning forward with his arms crossed. "I think you maybe are approaching that from your personal experience, which is not the same for everyone. I understand what you're talking about, but caring about what people think has a different weight if you've been judged for something you honestly have no power over. Like a disability. Or your race. And if those judgments have serious consequences, like they have in Daniel's life."

Daniel nodded, his eyes on George. He hadn't thought of how this linked to George's experience. "Yes," he said. "That's it."

"For me, it doesn't matter where I go. You have had a lot to deal with in this town, Daniel. For me, it's better to be here, where people know me. I'm safer here. I don't know if people are friendly to Black people everywhere I go. It's the unseen, unspoken things which are sometimes the most dangerous."

"What do you do about it?" Daniel asked. His heart hurt to hear about George's situation. It was true, Daniel could move somewhere else, and at least for a while, people might not suspect him of anything. George carried his difference on the surface. There was no hiding it.

George sat back in his chair. He glanced up at the leaves overhead, then took a sip of his drink.

"I try to think about what people would have done who had it worse than me. There are so many people who have been oppressed but have never given up the freedom of their souls. They have not allowed people to put a stamp on their inner beings. I take my inspiration from them. Even people who were kept from reading and writing, considered stupid. They knew. They knew they were not stupid. And some people were consistently defiant and full of dignity, even in the face of those kinds of judgments. You need freedom. Freedom from the tethers of others. But it is not an easy freedom. It comes from deliberate choice."

Daniel felt the weight of George's words hit him. A deliberate choice to be free. George's opinion came from a deep, experienced place. A different place from Sheldon or Sam's advice to just ignore what people thought. A different place from Daniel, even with his disability. George's son, Zion, had been killed by police because of mistaken identity. They had taken Zion's ultimate freedom, the freedom to be alive in the skin he was in. But George, despite the pain, still believed that the soul could be free.

"Thank you," Daniel said. It was such a small thing to say in response to something that was shaking Daniel to his core. The thought of a deliberate choice to live free.

"For my part," George said. "I'm sorry for the fact that I

was one of the people who didn't know whether I could trust you."

Daniel stood up, then, and walked to George, who stood as well. The two men hugged.

"Thank you," Daniel said. "I've admired you for so long, and I hated that you were hurting and that you thought I might be the one who had hurt you. But I don't think you did anything wrong. You only knew what the police said. And it was such a violent thing. I'm still sorry it happened. Still sorry I couldn't stop it somehow."

They stood like that for a long while. When George backed away, there were tears on his cheeks. "That's the terrible thing about injustice," he said. "It multiplies. I harmed you with my doubt and fear as people have harmed me with their doubt and fear. All we can do is respond with love and freedom."

CHAPTER FIFTEEN

Early the next morning, when Daniel was still sitting at his table, drinking coffee, his phone rang. It was Carlo.

"Hey," Daniel said.

"Good news!" Carlo said, his voice too loud for the hour. Daniel winced.

"Really? Tell me," he said, holding the phone farther away.

"The owners of the property approved your bid!"

Daniel was speechless for a moment. He looked around the dark, plain apartment that had been his home for nearly a decade.

"Really? Already?"

"Yes. And they agreed to let you move in as soon as you want."

"You're really good at your job," Daniel said.

Carlo laughed. "It helps that you have a nearly perfect credit score," he said.

Daniel nodded, though Carlo couldn't see. It was true. He'd had a high school teacher who had emphasized good credit and how to achieve it, and Daniel had taken this very seriously. He'd just never had anything to use his good credit on before.

"It's my day off," Daniel said. "Can we go today?"

"I don't see why not," Carlo said.

"Really? It really is my house?" Daniel had a sense of wonder at the idea, as though someone had told him he owned the moon. It seemed nearly as likely.

"Yes, and it's bare of even a stick of furniture. I would say we have our work cut out for us. Especially because of the news we heard yesterday. We only have a month."

"We should go and make a list of needs and repairs. I'm going to call Ani and see if she wants to come with us!"

"Again?"

"Of course. We need her help with the list. And if she decides to move in, she'll need to make one of her own."

Ani sounded sleepy on the phone, but she woke up when Daniel told her what was happening.

"Really?" she asked. "You can move in before everything is finalized? That's so good. I was worried about that part. Whew, that's the last major piece. Now we just have to figure out school and jobs and..."

"...furniture," Daniel finished. "We don't have any furniture."

"Yes, that's something," Ani said.

"We're going out there to make a list of needs and repairs," Daniel said. "Do you want to come?"

"You and Carlo?"

"Yeah."

"Sure... I guess this other work can wait. And I need to give you an answer about whether or not I'm going to move in. Maybe seeing the house again will help me." There was a little silence. "That is, if the offer still stands."

"Of course it does," Daniel said. He smiled, thinking that seeing the house again might convince Ani to say yes.

"Maybe if we have time, we can drive over to see Lewis and his property."

"Yes!" Ani said. "Perfect!"

Daniel didn't know Ani all that well yet, but he was pretty sure she had excitement in her voice. He nodded to himself. She was interested in Lewis.

"Let's meet at Carlo's office at 9:00," he said.

Daniel got dressed and paced his apartment, thinking. They needed help. Not just three people with ideas. This was a serious project. He picked up his phone.

By the time 9:00 rolled around, Daniel had assembled a caravan—nearly a fleet—of helpers. These were the professionals, the people of Aveline who knew about houses and construction, the needs of refugee families, decorating, or just style. Sam and Katie, Theresa and Sheldon, Maddie, George, Mercy, Juanita, and Carlo were all there. That meant there wasn't enough room in Carlo's truck for Daniel and Ani, so Daniel brought his car.

Ani was the last to arrive at Carlos's office. Her eyes widened as she saw the people gathered there. She turned to look at Daniel.

"Everyone is coming?"

He nodded. "We're going to need help to get the houses ready in time, so I invited the others. Ani nodded, her eyes still wide.

"They all had time, last minute?"

Theresa had arrived at Ani's side. "He may have applied some pressure," she said. She hugged Ani.

"Although we're also just wild with curiosity about this property," Katie added, hugging Ani as well.

Sheldon shifted from foot to foot, then said, "I have to get back to the store. Can we make a move?"

"Yes, Sheldon is a man of great importance," Sam said. Theresa elbowed her brother, and Daniel grinned.

"He is a man of importance," Daniel said.

"Thank you, Daniel," Reesey said, shooting Sam a look.

"I'm just saying," Sam said as he climbed into the driver's seat of his car, "Shel's not the only one with a store."

"Food or hammers?" Sheldon retorted. "That's what you have to ask yourself."

Amid the laughter, everyone got into the various vehicles they had arrived in, and Daniel and Ani were left standing on the sidewalk. Daniel noticed what she was wearing for the first time; jeans and a sweater with a mauve scarf tied around her black hair. She was so very pretty.

"Are you okay with riding with me?" he asked.

Of course," she said. She followed as Daniel walked to his car and held open the passenger side door for her.

"Wow, what a great car!" she said when he slipped into the driver's seat.

"Thanks," he said. "I restored it myself." Daniel's car was a 1981 Volkswagen Jetta, hunter green and fitted with dark green leather seats and beautiful trim, inside and out. He loved his car. He assumed he would get to drive it more often now that he was moving out of town. He shifted smoothly and pulled away from the curb.

"I don't think I pictured you as a car guy," Ani said. Daniel looked at her in surprise. For a moment, he was flattered by the idea that she pictured him at all, but he reminded himself that she liked Lewis.

"Car guy is a pretty vague term," Daniel said. "It encompasses everything from a guy who likes new cars with their terrible solid colors and lack of metal, to someone like me, who likes to restore a perfectly beautiful older car and drive it forever."

Ani laughed. "That's true. I would definitely be more surprised to find out that you liked new Mercedes Benz's or something like that."

Daniel made a face.

"I'll tell you a secret," he said as they left the town behind and turned onto the lake road. He glanced over at her and caught his breath. Ani's hair was dancing in the breeze from the partially opened window, and her profile was all outlined in light. For a moment, Daniel could hardly believe he had such a beautiful human sitting in his car.

"What's the secret?" she asked.

Whoops. It had left his mind entirely. Daniel tried to reorient.

"Right. Well, ah, yes. I'm going to buy a jeep. It will be

good for living out of town and doing gardening, and hauling extra people around. I'd love to get an old truck, but it wouldn't have a big enough cab."

"You're all about buying new things right now," Ani said.

Daniel looked at her but couldn't tell what she meant by the comment. Was it sarcastic? He didn't think so. He hoped not. He answered her sincerely.

"It's been a long time coming. Have you heard about what happened ten years ago?"

"I heard that you were accused of some things that you didn't do."

"Yes." He nodded. Outside the car, the sun was very bright. Would it really rain next week? It didn't seem like it at the moment. He looked at the trees and the sun on the lake. Above, a large eagle swooped to pick something off the surface of the water. A fish, maybe? Or a snake? How should he explain this to her?

"I lived pretty small after that, always worried about the attention of people because attention wasn't always neutral or benign. Now, I'm trying to be more free, trying to figure out what I want, and then do it. I want to host a refugee family. I want to buy this property. And I want to buy a jeep. Or maybe a truck."

When he glanced over at Ani, she was watching his face. He noticed again how large her eyes were.

"Those are very freeing things," she said. "You seem to be off to a good start."

"What about you?" he asked. "What do you want?"

"What do I want?" she asked.

"Yeah," he said. "Sometimes it's hard to tell, right? For a long time, I never even asked myself, but then my therapist and Theresa both told me that I should start paying attention. So, every time I thought I wanted something, I either wrote it down or did it. After some practice, I'm starting to learn what things I like and how to tell what I want."

He looked up again to find Ani staring at him. He turned his eyes back to the road, unable to interpret her look. He went back over the words quickly to check for offensive statements but couldn't recall anything that would offend.

Maybe she was just thinking. They drove in silence. After a while, Daniel turned onto the road that led to the property, breathing in the fragrance of the pines clustered around the gate.

Finally, Ani spoke. "Thank you for telling me that. I don't think I've ever realized it before this conversation, but I don't think I know how to tell what I want, either. Reaching for it right now feels like reaching into a blank space. There's nothing there."

Daniel pulled through the gate, which the others had left open, and found a place to park. He could see the others walking around his new property, gesturing and talking. Suddenly Daniel realized what he had done—the variety of opinions he would hear today. He shook his head at himself, laughing under his breath, turning to smile at Ani. She was biting her lip, also staring at the people in the distance. She had pulled her hair up and fastened it while they parked, and she wore the glasses with the clear plastic frames.

"I think there are things in that blank space," he said.

"Maybe you have to search around a little to find them. But let's go, or Sheldon will commandeer the whole day. Oh! And I invited Lewis, so he should be arriving soon, too."

He hoped that news would cheer her up. And Ani did smile at him in response, so Daniel thought it might have worked.

CHAPTER SIXTEEN

Ani could smell a mixture of bay and eucalyptus leaves as soon as she opened the car door. The scent brought her back to her mother's house in San Francisco, the slender bay tree in their little courtyard, and the giant eucalyptus trees clustered in the parks and streets of the city. The fragrance felt like home.

The air was warm and still, with gathering clouds. In the distance, a shaft of sunlight filtered through, lighting the water of the lake. Gravel crunched under their feet as Ani walked toward the houses with Daniel at her side. Two large dogs bounded toward them. Ani froze.

"It's okay," Daniel said as the dogs reached them. He bent to pet them. "This is just Sirius and Remus. They belong to Katie and Theresa."

"They won't bite?" Ani asked.

"Never," Daniel said. He looked at her. "Have you been bitten?"

"Yes," she said. "When I was a child. In Iran. Just a street dog who he didn't like the leg brace I had to use back then."

"That's terrible," Daniel said. He was all the way down now, on one knee, and both dogs were licking his face, their entire hindquarters wriggling until they knocked him all way onto his butt.

Theresa was striding toward them, her face stern.

"Don't let them do that!" she said. "We're trying to train them to be more gentle!"

Daniel's face broke open in a wide smile, and Ani felt a little thud in her chest at the brilliance of his smile and the way it rearranged his often serious face.

"Sorry!" he said. "They're irresistible."

"Well, resist them," Theresa commanded. "Sirius, Remus! Come." The dogs ceased trying to climb onto Daniel's head and went to Theresa with their heads down. "Sit," she said. "Lay down. Roll over." The dogs did exactly as she said, and Ani's shoulders relaxed a little. She glanced at Daniel to see him looking at her as he stood and brushed himself off.

"Hey," he said. "Come meet them. As you can see, Reesey has them under control."

Up at the houses, Sheldon cupped his hands around his mouth and shouted. "Hurry up, you three! We don't have time for this."

"Hold on a second, Sheldon!" Daniel called back. "You know very well that Raj runs that store better than you do!"

Theresa gasped. "You did not," she said.

"Ani was bitten by a dog and is quite understandably afraid of these two," Daniel told her.

Theresa's face changed quite drastically from fury to sympathy. "Sheldon!" she yelled. "Start with the others. We'll be there in a minute!" She turned and held a hand out to Ani.

"Come," she said, "they're really calm now."

Ani took a step forward, breathing deeply as she did so. She still felt the stone of terror that always seemed to sit in her belly when there were dogs around, but she could also see the sweet faces of the dogs as they sat, panting, their bodies completely relaxed. She took another step forward. Daniel held a hand out as though to help her, and when she took it, there was a jolt of recognition. *I know you,* her body and heart said. But that was ridiculous. Ani took four more steps and let go, all swirly inside from fear and attraction.

"You can touch them," Theresa said. "They're really soft."

They were both mutts of some kind, and really very cute. Their sides shook as they panted. They were so doggish, in the best dog ways, not mean, in the bared teeth, feral eyes way. She put a hand on the nearest dog's head, feeling the soft fur under her fingers. She fondled his ears and pet the fur on his neck. Theresa was right. He was soft. It was nice.

She spent a bit of time petting both dogs, and when she looked up, both Theresa and Daniel were smiling at her.

"They seem nice," she said when it seemed that they were both waiting for her to say something.

"I hope you can really get used to them," Theresa said in the strange, direct way she had. "If you're in our inner circle, they're basically always around."

"Am I in your inner circle?" Ani asked, laughing. She half

expected them to say no, that they were just joking. But they both stared at her.

"Of course you are," Theresa said. "You can't understand what these families mean to us. You're in the inner of the inner circles." Daniel was nodding emphatically beside her.

"Oh. Wow," Ani said. She felt an unexpected weight in her chest at Reesey's words. It wasn't an unpleasant weight; it was the kind she got when she watched a gorgeous sunset or had a really good talk with her mom on the phone. She had helped many refugee families get settled into their new communities, and no one had ever told her she was in their inner circle.

"Let's go," Daniel said. "Before Shel explodes."

"He really will," Theresa grumbled as the three of them began walking up the hill, the dogs loping and frolicking beside them. "And then you know who gets to clean up the mess."

"I know you love it," Daniel said.

Theresa grinned--a brief, brilliant smile that illuminated her already stunning face. "I really do. He's so funny when he's dramatic."

Ani was relaxing in their banter when she realized that Daniel was totally comfortable with Theresa in a way that he didn't seem to be with anyone else. She knew enough about their history to know that they were long-time friends, both autistic, and that Theresa had always known that Daniel was innocent and had always believed in him. What would it be like if Daniel was like this with everyone? How much had he lost, how much had they all lost, by suspecting him because he was different?

When they reached the others, Ani realized that the dogs were still right on her heels. They sat at her feet, gazing up at her. She felt a little off-kilter. Daniel was watching her.

"They really want to be liked," he said. "They'll keep trying until they think you have fallen for them."

"Do they do this with everyone?" Ani asked, leaning forward to gingerly pat them between the ears.

"Not everyone," Daniel said. "They seem to know the good ones to choose."

Ani looked up at him quickly, but he was looking over at Carlo. Was that a compliment? She couldn't tell. She scratched the dog called Sirius a little harder, and he responded by leaning hard on her side. Thankfully it was her stronger leg. She stroked his head, and he looked up at her with what could only be called adoring eyes. Remus pushed his head against her other side, also wanting attention, until Sam came over and scolded them both.

"Let her go," he said. "You two are completely shameless. Just big babies."

Ani laughed. Then Carlo clapped his hands together.

"How do you see this going?" he asked Daniel.

Daniel turned to Ani. "What do you think?"

Ani was a little startled at being the center of attention, but she pulled herself together quickly. "What are we trying to accomplish?"

"We want to know about immediately necessary repairs.

And make lists of things to buy to furnish the houses," Daniel answered.

"Well, I'd suggest the people who know the most about repair form a team and go from room to room, and everyone else can make a list of needs. Between all of us, we should be able to make the home the most welcoming it can be." She felt a twinge in her chest at the thought of the family. She often felt this way, thinking about the families who had left everything they knew to come somewhere that they hoped would be safer. It was such a massive, world-altering thing to do.

"Anything we should remember?" Mercy asked.

"They've been through a lot," Ani answered. "Seen things no one should see, especially not children." She paused. Should she tell them? Yes. They were officially all in this together.

"What I know about the Lorias is that they are going to have trouble with immigration. They seem to be grandparents and grandchildren, rather than the parents and children they said they were when they entered. This likely means that these children have lost their parents, either back in Venezuela or on the way. It is a treacherous trip. They need to heal. And we are learning about what that means. Trauma is not stored only in the thoughts, but in the body, so we need to think of every single thing that can bring wellness to the body. Think of the senses--music, beauty, light. Think warm and simple, not fancy. Fancy will just be overwhelming."

She felt heat rise to her face as she realized how long she had been talking. But everyone was watching her intently and nodding along.

"One more thing, before we start," she said. "Even all our best efforts cannot change the sorrow and horror they have experienced. That will be with them forever. We can only accompany them on the journey."

She realized there were tears on her face and quickly swiped at them. She felt someone beside her and realized it was Katie, putting an arm around Ani and giving her a little squeeze.

Sam spoke up. "Okay, let's do it. We have important grocery store celebrities who have to get back to work." Everyone laughed, and Sheldon scowled.

"I think we should all make a list for Daniel, too," he said. "The man doesn't know how to furnish an apartment."

Daniel nodded. "It's true. But I've also never really tried."

"What do you mean?" Katie asked.

"I mean, I've only ever existed in a place," Daniel said. "I haven't make a home."

Ani waited, but he didn't say anything more. When she looked around at all the people watching him, she didn't blame him. It seemed like a vulnerable conversation for a big group. She would have to ask him more about it later. Not because she was worried about him, but because it was awfully similar to how she thought of herself.

CHAPTER SEVENTEEN

T he big group broke into teams soon after that. Sam called for Carlo, Theresa, George, and Frankie to look into building projects and repairs. Katie and Juanita walked down the hill to look at the gardens. That left Sheldon, Daniel, and Mercy to walk with Ani and think about comfort design for a refugee family at the big house. Ani had her phone out to take photos and make notes, and at the entrance to the house, she paused to write a note about the wobbly stones on the front path.

She heard footsteps behind her and turned to see Lewis. She smiled. It was always nice to see him in his customary Carhartt overalls and gold wire-rimmed glasses against his black skin. Lewis wore his hair natural and quite tall, with the sides shaved, and he had a longish beard. Theresa and Ani agreed that Lewis was the hippest farmer they had ever met, and Ani had felt a bit flustered around him before she got to know him and found him to be funny, wry, and down to earth. She was glad he was going to be hosting a family. He seemed well suited for it, especially with his success at running a gardening community for five years. Lewis had a knack for people. Everyone liked him.

"Sorry I'm late!" he said, reaching out to touch Ani's elbow on one side and put an arm around Mercy on the other. That was another thing about Lewis. He was effortlessly affectionate in a non-creepy way. Ani had accidentally remarked on it one day, and then wanted to sink into the floor. Lewis had laughed and told her it was the result of growing up in a gigantic family.

"I'm one of seven," he said. "We have different ideas of personal space."

Ani thought of her childhood as an only child with a disability. She couldn't imagine having six siblings.

"You're not that late," she said, smiling at him. "We're just getting started."

Sheldon and Daniel paused on the front stairs of the house and looked back to see Lewis. An expression crossed Daniel's face that was so strong, Ani felt she should recognize it, but it was gone before she had a chance to pin it down.

"Hey Lewis," Sheldon said, coming close for a fist bump. "Maybe you should join the gardeners. You'll have ideas for sure."

"No!" Daniel said in a loud voice. They all stared at him.

"Wouldn't it be better if you take the chance to learn what your family needs to feel at home?" Daniel asked.

"Yeah, that's true," Lewis answered, rubbing a hand over his hair.

"Perfect. You should walk with Ani," Daniel said.

He turned and started walking up the stairs again.

Ani and Lewis looked at each other, and Lewis's face seemed as puzzled as Ani felt. She looked at Mercy, a couple stairs above, and saw her shaking her head.

"Daniel's an odd bird," Lewis said as they started up the stairs together.

"That's not all that's going on," Mercy said, but she didn't elaborate.

Ani actually felt a little disappointed as the day went on. She had hoped to spend time with Daniel at the house and finish the discussion they had started in the car. Instead, they split into two teams. Daniel tried to insist that Mercy join him and Sheldon, but Mercy gave him a direct stare and told him to stop being controlling.

So Mercy, Ani, and Lewis walked through the house together. Ani could see its potential. It was a large, airy house, similar to a craftsman, with large windows and delicate edging around the ceilings. The floors were hardwood, in good shape. There were two bedrooms in the back of the house, with a living room and kitchen in the front. It looked as though there had only been one bathroom to start, but someone had added one beside the back porch.

"Curtains," Mercy said. "We need curtains."

They were in the smaller of the two bedrooms, and Ani was typing on her phone as rapidly as she could.

"Yes," Ani agreed. "And beds. We obviously need beds for everyone, probably two twin beds in here. But I would guess that the Loria's will end up sleeping in one bed, at least in the beginning, so we need a kingsize bed in the big bedroom."

"Really?" Lewis asked. "Should I get a kingsize bed as well?"

"Definitely," Ani said, "since your family also has two kids. Also, the government requires us to have bedframes in the bedrooms, but I find it's important to buy frames that are designed to be low to the ground. I wish whoever was in charge of setting the requirements for sponsorship houses knew that most people in the world aren't used to sleeping way up high in the air."

The meaningless rules around the acceptance of refugees were annoying to Ani. She got it--she really did--organizations and government groups were trying to prevent the risk of abuse, to make sure no one was sleeping on a dirty mattress on the floor while their sponsors accepted grants to pad their pockets. But some of the rules were cultural and unnecessary.

"I never would have thought of that," Mercy said. "That sleeping up high would make things less comfortable."

Ani smiled at her. "That's why I'm here. And it's a small thing, really. But the whole experience will be one million small changes, and coming to a new home is such a physical experience. It's part of what we were talking about in overcoming trauma. Things being low to the ground feels safer for people who are used to living low to the ground. So we'll do what we can."

"Do you have any good recommendations for beds?" Lewis asked.

"Yes!" Ani said. "I can send you some links."

They continued to walk through the house, making their list. They needed some couches and recliners, lamps and rugs for the living room, and a table and chairs for the kitchen. They also decided to get a low table and floor cushions as well. Ani wanted warmer colors on the walls. Lots of pillows and rugs and some toys. Not loud ones that took batteries, but perhaps a few boxes of lego. Her list grew longer and longer. She loved preparing for families, dreaming of what would be welcoming and helpful, and she felt flushed with happiness, even though she was overwhelmed by all that needed to be done.

But every time they got close to Daniel, he caught Sheldon by the elbow and pulled him into another room.

After the fourth time this happened, Mercy crossed her arms.

"Something's going on with that boy," she said. "What has gotten into his head?"

Lewis grinned. "If I didn't know better, I would say that our postmaster is matchmaking."

Ani looked between herself, Mercy, and Lewis. "Match-making...you and me?"

Mercy gave a peal of laughter. "Well, not me! I'm happily married to a man my own age, thank you very much."

"But..." Ani felt flustered and also sad for some reason that was hard to identify.

"Don't worry," Lewis said. "I'm not after you."

"But, well, don't take this the wrong way...I mean, you have a very handsome..self...and beard..."

Lewis and Mercy were laughing so hard they could

barely stand up. They didn't jump in to help Ani at all.

"Yes?" Lewis said, gasping. "Tell me more!"

"You know what I mean!" Ani said. "You're a great person...uh, I'm making this worse."

Mercy stopped laughing and wiped her eyes. "Stop it, Lewis, you're embarrassing her." She patted at her hair. "Don't mind us, Ani, we're just being ridiculous, but you trying to let Lewis down easy is maybe one of the sweetest, most hilarious things I've ever seen." She went into a fit of laughter again. Lewis was shaking, he was laughing so hard. When Mercy was able to pull herself together, she went on. "It's obvious that you and Lewis have no spark. You and Daniel, on the other hand, are very sparky."

Ani frowned. "Obviously not, if he's trying to hook me up with someone else."

Mercy shook her head, still chuckling. "There's no telling what he's got in that head of his. And who can help him sort it out? Maybe I need to have a word with him."

Ani looked at her with alarm. But just then, Daniel and Sheldon came into the room. Daniel's eyes darted between Ani and Lewis. A strange sound came from Lewis, and he turned to look at the window, pretending to examine it. Ani knew he was laughing again. She sighed.

"All set?" she asked. Sheldon nodded. Ani took the plunge. "Daniel, can you take me to look at the little house? I want to have another look at it."

Daniel's face cleared. "Sure," he said.

Ani ignored Mercy's whisper of "Yes, Ani!" as she left the house with Daniel.

CHAPTER EIGHTEEN

Ani and Daniel walked down the path together, toward the little house that Ani was already starting to think of as hers. Her leg had begun to ache, but she didn't want to retrieve her cane from the car until she had to. Clouds had covered the sun, and Ani shivered in her jacket.

"I wanted to keep talking about what you were saying in the car," she said.

Daniel looked over at her. "Which part?"

"Well," she said, trying to think of how to word it. "How did you figure out what you wanted? That's the hardest part for me. I feel like I can see every side to every issue. I'm always trying to think of what's best for everyone."

"Can you give me an example?" Daniel asked in his deep, soft voice. Ani stumbled over a loose stone, and Daniel moved closer to steady her with a hand on her elbow. Sometimes Ani hated it when people jumped in to help her, but Daniel's way was so unassuming and straightforward that she almost didn't notice. She needed balance, and there it was, not needing to be congratulated or adored.

"Like right now," Ani answered. "I'm trying to decide whether I want to move here. But all I can think is that maybe I will be a burden to you, and maybe it will be good for the family to have me here, but perhaps my mother wouldn't like it, and is it too nice when I have devoted myself to serving others? Will other people be jealous if I have such a nice place?"

Daniel frowned while he opened the little wooden gate that led into the yard around the house. The gate was knee-high and didn't seem capable of keeping anything out. Its solitary purpose seemed to be cuteness. And it was adorable. Ani loved it on sight.

"That's all going on in your head? Every time you make a decision?"

"Yes. Usually, it's fairly straightforward. Either my choice will hurt or help someone, so I always go with help. But with something like this, I can't even get through the piles of questions to begin. Let alone knowing what I want to do."

They were at the front door, and Daniel unlocked it so they could step inside. The little house was even lovelier than Ani remembered. The garden was overgrown, but Ani could see herbs poking through the weeds. The outdoor bathtub and shower were desperately in need of cleaning, but they were well built.

"Look at this," Daniel said, walking over to the shower. He turned a crank, and the covering over the space receded. "If it's clear out, you can pull the roof back." Through the garden,

Ani could see the view into the hills. It was stunning—all of it.

They wandered back into the kitchen, which was bright and sunny, built with handmade shelves and stone countertops.

Daniel opened and closed the drawers. A couple of them were stubborn, and one didn't want to come out at all.

"I'll have to get Sam to look at those," he said.

He straightened and looked at her.

"I think maybe your stakes are too high," he told her. "You need lower stakes."

"What do you mean?" she asked him. He had such kind, direct eyes. He spread his hands on the countertop and looked at them, rather than her, as he answered.

"Some things aren't good or bad, harmful or helpful. Maybe you could just ask yourself, do I like this? Make the question that simple, not about hurting or helping anyone. Lower the stakes."

She bit her lip and looked out the kitchen window. A branch of bougainvillea tapped on the side of the house, waving at her. Ani had always felt that she was made to serve. It was only in the last few years, now that she had built her career around service—and loved it so much—that she had realized she didn't know what to do with the rest of herself.

"Do you like this house, Ani?" Daniel asked.

She nodded. "I love it."

"Then you should come and live here. If you decide later that it's not good for you, you can move out."

Ani watched his hands because his eyes were still on

them. As she watched, he moved one hand to grasp hers and squeeze it. She inhaled. She had more questions for him. She really wanted to ask why he was trying to throw her and Lewis together.

Instead, she just turned her hand to squeeze back and said, "Okay. Thank you. I'll take your offer and move in."

She looked up just in time to catch his sudden, gorgeous smile. Oh, goodness.

There would be time for second-guessing later, she thought as they walked back up the hill. Time for worrying about what her parents would really feel once they saw the space, or the consequences of living so close to one of the refugee families, and whether she would ever get a break. She stopped to look back at the little house. It was so pretty. Daniel stopped to look as well. Almost as an afterthought, he said, "Oh, right. See the big tree there? Beside the house? It's a jacaranda. It should bloom next month."

A small flame of happiness kindled inside of Ani. She liked the house very, very much. And she was going to live there. Just because she wanted it. And there was a jacaranda tree in the yard, which would be all over purple by the time she moved in.

The others were leaving the other two houses, and all of them ended up walking back down to the vehicles together, the dogs nearly wild with joy at being a part of such a big group of humans. Ani was smiling at their antics when Mercy joined her.

"Did you ever figure out what Daniel is up to?" she asked.

Ani laughed. "No. I'm afraid to ask." She really actually was afraid to ask, but she wouldn't tell Mercy that.

"I almost forgot to tell you what was on my mind today. I wanted to invite you to my house for women's circle."

"Women's circle?" Ani asked. She felt a spike of unease. "What's that?"

"Kind of what it sounds like, but better. We eat together, maybe read something from the Bible or a book we're into at the moment, pray for one another. We talked about it last week, and we would love to have you. Please come. You are very welcome. Reesey will be there, as well as other women you know."

Ani didn't know how to answer. She had one million things to do before the families arrived, and she always felt shy in groups. But Mercy was so kind. And if Theresa was there, Ani would have one more person she knew. But she had to be honest.

"You know I'm not going to be here very long, right? I mean, I'll be here for the next six months or so while we get the families settled, and then I'll be off to help another group of families."

She glanced at Mercy to find the older woman looking at her.

"Yes, I know," Mercy said. "At least I know that's what you think is going to happen."

They were interrupted by footsteps as Theresa caught up to them. "Are you inviting Ani to women's circle?" Theresa asked.

"I am," Mercy said.

"Are you going to come?" Theresa asked, peering into Ani's face. One of the first things Theresa had told Ani about autism was that she usually stood too close or too far, rarely in between. Right now, she was very close.

"I would like to," Ani said. "If I can manage the time." She shook the handful of papers that people had given her. Some people had texted lists to her instead of writing on paper, so she had work ahead, compiling everything and then setting appointments to get the jobs done.

"Well, you won't be working on that by yourself," she heard. Ani turned to see Daniel behind her, with Sam by his side. "We'll do it together," Daniel said.

Ani gave a short laugh. "I guess I don't have any more excuses," she said. "Can I come once? I really am a bit of an anxious soul, and I don't want to commit to something that I'm not going to be able to continue."

"Oh, you'll be right at home," Theresa said, at the same time that Mercy said, "Of course."

The ride back with Daniel was quiet. They were both absorbed in their own thoughts. Ani thought that Daniel seemed unusually still. He wasn't tapping or humming or anything like that, just gazing out through the windshield and taking the curves smoothly.

Ani didn't mind the silence. She knew what was bothering her, creeping at the edges of her awareness. She massaged her leg absent-mindedly, thumping her thigh with her fist where the nerve often pinched.

Saying yes to something she liked. Resting more. Going to a circle with other women. These were good things, but there was a door in Ani's mind that she didn't want to be opened. These things threatened a crack in the door. Could someone who had seen the things Ani had seen ever be normal? She knew the answer was yes and no. This was something that she taught, thought about, studied, and tried to work through with her clients.

But Ani knew the dangers of becoming too still; she knew the sharp line of terror that could overtake the nights. She had felt the tilting toward despair. The usual answer was to keep things dull and busy. Too much beauty or space threatened her fragile balance. And yet, like she had told Daniel, she was finding the cracks in her method. A great sense of loss had started to overwhelm her days as she found that the things she had chosen, the ways she had avoided feeling, simply left her empty. The loss felt like a cloud. Ani didn't know where to go from here, and a sense of hopelessness began to rise in her throat, choking her.

After Daniel dropped her off, she unlocked her door, looked at her beige apartment, and lost it. She sank to the floor, sobbing, her leg feeling like fire because she hadn't wanted to use her cane in front of all her new friends. She thought about the stories of horror that refugees had told her. About her own start to life, leaving Iran. The doctors who had mocked her shriveled leg. She knew the cruelty of people. And she knew that when the despair overwhelmed her, all she could do was sleep. She got up, stumbled to her bed, and lay there curled up until she slowly drifted off.

CHAPTER NINETEEN

At times in the following days, Daniel felt like he could hardly catch his breath at the rate of life change. He moved out of his apartment that week to be present at the new property for construction and purchasing. He was very often close to being overwhelmed and carried his modeling clay everywhere so he could keep his hands busy and soothe his crowded mind. He alternated between the post office, which was beautiful in its dull familiarity, and the property, which was terrifying and wonderful.

Lewis came over often to help with the garden and talk through their shared preparations. Daniel went to visit Lewis's land as well, to gather ideas and help out. The farm was a sight to behold, with Lewis's volunteers and staff working hard at the spring planting. There were new seedlings in many of the beds, a sprinkling of green over the dark brown earth. Lewis had a program for youth rehabilitation that gave him four volunteers each season. He had staff from another refugee program, and now he was making space for the family he was sponsoring, the Mendozas. His workshop was a mess of drawings and plans for the new gardens they were putting in, as well as a building that would house natural dying and herbalist workshops.

"How do you do it all?" Daniel asked, feeling slightly stunned by the activity going on at the farm.

Lewis laughed. "I have no life," he said. "And I have a business degree. Two things that will ensure any farm's success. I've had to develop a green thumb after growing up in the city. My mom loved houseplants, but that's about as far as I got into gardening. Now I'm drawing on knowledge from generations of indigenous farming and the farming of my people in this country. It's healing and challenging." He paused, looking around. "I do know I have to stop working so hard if I ever want a family."

Daniel's ears perked up. "You do want a family?"

"Yes, eventually."

Daniel tried to think of how to be subtle. "Ani seems like someone who would want a family, too."

At that, Lewis threw his head back and laughed, long and loud. It was infectious, and Daniel found himself grinning, though he wasn't sure what was so funny. Lewis just shook his head and said, "You keep trying to lead yourself down this particular road, my friend. Let's see where it takes you."

Daniel would have asked more about what Lewis meant, but they were interrupted by one of the volunteers, and Daniel left soon after that, heading back to his own land to see how Sam was coming along with the repairs. There weren't too many things to be done. Some stairs needed repairing. Some plumbing. A few doors didn't open well any longer. Katie was there, too, scrubbing out the kitchen cabinets in the big house.

"When is your furniture coming?" she asked, from where she sat.

"Ani, Juanita, Sheldon, and I are going to IKEA tomorrow," Daniel said. "I've promised Sheldon we'll go to the flea market and thrift stores as well."

"Oof. I can't believe you're taking Shel. That's going to be a long day." She sat up and looked at him. "Will you bring sensory help?"

Daniel smiled at Katie. He knew Sam's wife had always been supportive of Theresa since she told them she was autistic. It was really thoughtful of her to think of how hard a full day of shopping would be for him.

"Just the basics," he said. "I think we'll be okay. I'll sit some of the stores out if I need to."

Katie nodded and went back to cleaning. "You should give this place a name," she said. "We just keep calling it Daniel's place, or the new property."

Daniel thought about that. A name. "That's a good idea," he said. "I've never had a home with a name before. Oh, actually, that's not true. The group home had a name."

"I don't think we want a name like that," Katie said. "Let's think of something creative."

"Let's wait until Ani is with us," Daniel replied. "She may have some ideas."

Katie lifted one eyebrow, but all she said was, "Yes, let's ask Ani."

The shopping expedition went as well as could be expected. Daniel skipped all the thrift stores and flea markets in preparation for IKEA, sitting in the car while Sheldon took enough time to go through each flea market stall with a magnifying glass. Ani seemed flustered, coming out of one store with Sheldon gesturing wildly beside her. "Magic takes time! If you want the magic, you need to take the time!"

"I don't know if I want the magic," Juanita muttered.

They did find a few dressers, one sofa, and some tables at the flea market. Then they drove to Billers to go to IKEA. Although Sheldon was bossy, it was good to have him there. He organized them into teams to find things in the store, and naturally, he knew where everything was and highlighted pathways on the store maps for them, so they didn't get lost. Daniel and Ani found mattresses and bed frames, pillows, and duvets, while Sheldon and Juanita shopped for sofas and chairs as well as kitchen and bathroom apparel.

Daniel appreciated being paired with Ani. She was so still and calm, looking at tags and prices. Smiling at him when he bounced on the mattresses. Her stillness, the way she held herself together, seemed to cancel out some of the noise and busyness around them in the giant store. He really liked her dark hair and eyes, the way her hands moved when she talked, like small birds flying in front of her. Sometimes she became very quiet, and her face seemed turned in on itself. Daniel was trying to learn to read her signals, to memorize them, but it was hard because she was so self-contained. There was one that look was becoming familiar, though, and it would often settle onto her face immediately after they laughed at something or Ani had told him that she liked something or noticed a pattern or color was beautiful.

"Can I ask you a question?" Daniel asked as they walked away from the bedding section.

She seemed to come back from far away.

"Yes," she said.

"It's okay if you don't want to answer. Are you sad right now? I'm trying to learn your facial expressions."

Her eyes widened, and she looked at him. Her eyes catching his nearly took his breath away. She was so beautiful. Maybe the most beautiful person he had ever seen. She would be a great partner for Lewis, he reminded himself. Lewis was a lucky man. Daniel noticed that she was limping a little. She had her cane with her, but it had been another long day of walking.

"Do you want to sit for a minute?" he asked her. He checked the list Sheldon had given them. "I think we're nearly done. Just need...lamps."

He found a sofa, and they sat.

Ani rubbed at her forearms as though she was cold. Daniel waited, hoping he hadn't offended her.

"I am sad," she said. "Although that isn't the whole story."

She met his eyes again. "I'm actually really happy," she said. "And sometimes, when I'm really happy, I feel sad."

"Why?" Daniel asked. He pulled his modeling clay out of his pocket.

Ani sighed. "I'm not sure how much I can explain right

now," she said. "But I have seen a lot of very, very sad things in my life. Evil things that humans do to one another. So sometimes, when I see something really beautiful or funny or good, an image comes to me of the sorrow of the world, such a contrast, and makes me sad. I feel heartbroken. I feel guilty. That's all. I'm just a bit of a mess, and I don't know if I will ever be okay." She put a hand over her mouth. "I'm sorry, I didn't mean to say all of that." She smiled at him, but the look he was now able to store away as 'sad' was still in her eyes. "You're just really easy to talk to."

Daniel felt a little bloom of happiness in his chest when she said that. It was a good thing to be easy to talk to. But he felt heavy as he thought of her sadness.

"Let's go look at the lamps," he said.

She nodded and stood, but just before they started to walk away, Daniel did something crazy. He stepped very, very close to Ani and opened his arms to offer a hug. She froze for a second, then squeezed her arms around his rib cage and turned her face into his shoulder. He wrapped his arms around her and laid his cheek on her shiny black hair. They stood like that for a few moments, rocking back and forth a little. When Daniel pulled away, there were shiny tears on Ani's face. He used the pads of his thumbs to gently wipe them away, then stood back, feeling flustered.

"I'm sorry that you have seen such sad things," he said. "And that beautiful things remind you of those sad things. It doesn't seem fair."

"Thanks," Ani said, choking out a little laugh. "If there is anything I've learned, it's that fairness does not apply to this world. Thank you, though. That means a lot."

Things were quiet and calm between them then, as they looked through the lamps, pointing out the ones they liked to each other. Ani had said that soft, warm light had been shown as helpful for post-traumatic stress. Daniel picked out a few lamps for his home on top of the ones for the big house and insisted that Ani pick some out for her house. She chose a standing lamp for her living room and a little bedside lamp for her bedroom.

When they got to the checkout area, Sheldon and Juanita had just arrived.

"You go sit," Daniel told Ani and Juanita. "Shel and I will check out the stuff."

They bought all of it and then went out to the truck and loaded it up. Daniel felt tired and overwhelmed, ready for a meal and sleep. In the car, Sheldon turned to Daniel as they were all riding along in silence.

"How do you have the money for this?" he asked. "Or did I not realize that postal workers were paid six figures a year?"

Daniel snorted. Though it was true that he had saved a lot of money because he never spent anything, this kind of money didn't come from his work.

"I have a lot of savings and excellent credit," he said. And that was all he said. Someday, maybe, he would tell them the whole story. Carlo knew it. For now, he thought he was opening just about as many inward doors as he could handle. There was a lot of sorrow behind the story of his money.

Daniel thought of what Ani had told him. About how she

felt like she was a mess because of all she had seen. He had felt the same way for so long. It sometimes seemed that there was one place for people who were put together and well, who hadn't spent their lives being shipped from home to home because people couldn't stomach them, who hadn't lost their caregivers. And Daniel didn't fit in that place. Was there a place where he and Ani fit? Where people struggling with so much loss could come together and be well?

It was what he was hoping for, in this year of freedom, with this new family. He hoped he would find a place where broken people could belong.

CHAPTER TWENTY

"Tomorrow's the day, isn't it?" Mercy asked as she took Ani's coat and ushered her into the house. Ani inhaled the smells of food cooking and something else, maybe scented candles.

"Yes," she said. "I move tomorrow, and the families arrive. Everything is happening at once!" She looked around as she followed Mercy into the house. "You have a lovely home." In the living room, Katie was curled up on the sofa, and Theresa was sitting on the floor, playing with a little white dog.

"Thank you," Mercy said. "Lucy and Dorothy are just finishing up with food in the kitchen. It's Dorothy's week to cook. Have a seat and tell us how these last days of preparation have been."

"Hectic," Ani told her, settling into a chair that didn't look like it would swallow her. Katie looked perfectly comfortable on the sofa, but Ani was a lot tinier than Katie and didn't want to fall asleep while being drawn back into the couch cushions. There was a gorgeous painting of Nelson Mandela on the wall and a little gallery of artwork beside it. Ani recognized some of them. Others were new to her. She wanted to examine them more closely. "I almost didn't make it tonight."

It was women's circle night, and Ani had come up with seventeen different reasons not to be here, but in the end, she didn't want to face Mercy's disappointment, so she came.

"I'm excited, though. I think we're ready."

"I'm excited, too," Theresa said.

Ani noticed that Theresa had clay on the collar of her shirt and a smudge under her arm. She smiled at her friend. The dog walked over to sniff at Ani's leg, and she tensed up involuntarily, then forced herself to relax.

"This is Boo. She's new to us," Mercy said. "George and I have been feeling a bit lonely in this big house by ourselves, and we finally decided to get a dog. She's a Maltese mix from the shelter in Billers."

Boo walked back over to Theresa, who leaned all the way over and let Boo lick her face.

"Ugh, Reesey," Mercy said.

"It's how she says hello," Theresa replied. "Mercy brings her to the office, which is pretty cute. Only in Aveline would you go to see your lawyer and end up playing with a puppy."

"Well, we can't leave her here all day," Mercy said. She didn't say anything for a moment. "But it is pretty cute."

"Zoe texted to say that she and Ingrid are on their way," Katie announced, looking at her phone.

"And Faith should be here any minute," Mercy said. "Let's wait for them, and we can eat when they get here."

Lucy came into the living room with another woman that Ani gathered was Dorothy. Lucy held a platter of food, and Dorothy carried a bottle of wine.

"Here, get into this, everyone," Mercy said, "while we wait."

"Ooh, wine before dinner," Theresa said. "Yum."

"No thanks," Katie said when Mercy offered her a glass.

"What?" Mercy said. Ani didn't understand the sudden silence that fell between the other women.

"You don't want wine, Katie?" Dorothy asked.

"No," Katie said, and her words were all choked. Then Mercy's daughter Faith arrived with the cold air of the evening swirling in with her, and between greeting her and questions for Katie, there was a lot of noise, and people were laughing and crying. At some point, Ani gathered that Katie was pregnant and that she and Sam had been trying for a while.

Ingrid and Zoe arrived in the chaos, and Ani sat in her chair and soaked it all in. She felt separate from the group, but not in a bad way. She had always hovered on the edges of things, but here she felt scooped into the laughing, chattering, melodious voices of the women. Zoe and Theresa had louder voices than everyone else, and every once in a while, a squawk or shouted sentence would rise above the rest of the noise. Ani couldn't help smiling.

Finally, they all began to calm down, and many of the women wiped tears from their cheeks. Ani found that she was crying, too. She didn't even know why, but the little warm fire in her heart gathered fuel, and she felt that she was hovering close to it, warming her hands and feet.

"Well," Mercy said. "Between this and our families arriving tomorrow, we have a lot to talk and pray over."

When Mercy prayed, it was as though the tiny fire leaped higher inside of Ani's heart. Mercy prayed for wellness for Katie's body and the baby within her, and for the refugee families that would arrive tomorrow.

"Let them be covered in love and peace," she prayed. "Help us to be your hands and feet to our dear new families in their new homes. Cover their grief, comfort their losses."

Oh, goodness. Ani reached for one of the tissues from the table beside her. Mercy said 'amen,' and others reached for tissues too.

"Mercy keeps us well-stocked," Zoe said in a stage whisper to Ani. Ani smiled at the other women, feeling a bit shy. She knew Zoe was a philosophy professor and writer at the university, and she felt a bit star-struck by her. Looking around, she felt more than a little star-struck. It was a group of such powerful, talented, lovely women. Who was she? The little lame girl who had been teased so badly for her accent when she first arrived in San Francisco. The young woman with a limp. She shook herself and went to the place she always went when she started to have these feelings. She was a servant of the Most High. She served well. She had worth.

But for the first time, she questioned this automatic answer to the question of her worth. What else? Did she have worth besides her service? A small, desperately lonely place inside of her wanted to collapse into tears and cry for years. She shook herself.

Mercy was speaking.

"Has there been any... what do you call it?"

"Nonsense?" Faith offered.

"Pushback?" her mother finished.

"To having refugees?" Ani said. "Yes, of course. There always is. We've had some letters. Frankie has been fielding them, mostly."

"The poor reverend," Faith said.

Theresa burst out laughing. Ani looked at her, not understanding the joke.

"Don't mind Faith," Mercy said, her voice wry. "She doesn't understand the more ornate parts of Francisco's spiritual practice and can never help pestering him about it."

"I don't pester him," Faith said. "I never talk to him. I just call him the reverend. If he's going to walk around with a clerical collar, it's the least I can do."

"Tell us about the letters," Katie said.

"I'd rather not, actually," Ani answered. "They're pretty terrible. People can't seem to understand that people running from danger are no threat to their livelihood or safety."

"It's what they've been told," Ingrid said.

"That's no excuse," Zoe flashed at her.

"I didn't say it was!" Ingrid said. "They can think for themselves. But it's what's going around right now."

"It's what's in the air," Ani agreed. "Never mind that. The main thing is that this town voted to let our families in, and they're on their way. Every time this happens and people have their fears put to rest—nothing bad happens...no monsters descend on us at night—it carves a path for the future. I have to hope in that. And there are far more supportive people in this town than there are detractors. I'm actually going to have a hard time leaving."

"You're leaving?" Theresa demanded, looking horrified.

"I always leave," Ani said. "It's part of my job. I told Mercy..." she felt a bit panicky, had they not understood?

Mercy shook her head. "You're welcome at this circle as long as you can come," she said. "Theresa is just shocked, right, Reesey?"

"Right," Theresa said. But she exchanged a look with Mercy that Ani didn't know how to interpret. Ani started to sink into sadness again.

Just then, Dorothy called them all to the table. Ani shook off the sadness. The rest of the evening was a blur of food and chatter. There was Dorothy's cream of broccoli soup and fresh bread, the sound of cutlery on ceramic bowls, the bright paintings and textiles on Mercy's walls. Lucy's sticky rice and mango dessert, which left Ani feeling very full. They read a little from the Bible together, and somehow Ani finished up the night with Boo curled up in her lap.

ANI WAS out of bed before the sun was up the next morning. Everything was happening at once. In the morning, she needed to move into her new house, and in the afternoon, the refugee families were arriving from the center in San Diego. It was beyond hectic for both to be happening on the same day, but Sam had discovered a mold situation in Ani's roof at the new house and had been working non-stop to replace the ceiling. He had finally finished, just in time, so everything in Ani's apartment was packed up and ready to go. Just as Ani finished her first cup of tea, the doorbell rang.

She found Daniel and Lewis standing outside. She glanced at the clock. It was only 5:30 in the morning.

"You two are up early," she said.

"We told you we'd be here," Daniel answered. She glanced at him and then away. He looked rumpled in an early morning way, his hair still slightly damp, and it was too much.

"To be honest, we're always up early," Lewis said. "Daniel works at the post office, and I'm a farmer."

"And we don't want to do this without you," Daniel said, unintentionally setting the little fire ablaze in Ani's heart.

She turned so they wouldn't see the look on her face. "Let's start with the kitchen," she said. "This way."

Lewis nudged her with his elbow as he went past. "He doesn't want to do this without you," he whispered, and she gave him a hard, narrow-eyed look." He laughed, then started stacking boxes.

The tiny dingy apartment had come furnished, so all Ani really had were her own boxes of things. Dishes and food, clothes, her office stuff, and the knickknacks and bedding that came everywhere with her. The knitted blanket her mother had made for her. A few wall hangings and paintings. It didn't take long to pack the truck, and as they left, Daniel turned to look at the apartment, his face showing his distaste.

"Good riddance," he said. "This place is all wrong for you. You're much lovelier than these gloomy rooms."

He left first, and Ani glared at Lewis again. "He needs to stop saying things like that," she said.

Lewis raised his eyebrows. "Or does he?"

Ani growled, shaking her head. "This is not how this is going to go, Lewis," she said. "You need to stop. We have to focus today."

"Oh, I'm focused," he said. "I'm focused on how much lovelier you are than these gloomy rooms. I do not promise that I will stop anything."

She moved toward him to smack him, and just then, Daniel came back. He saw Lewis laughing and Ani playfully hitting him, and his face fell. Then he carefully rearranged it. "I'll be in the truck," he said. "When you're ready."

He ducked back out. Lewis's face grew serious. "When are you going to tell him that this," he gestured back and forth between the two of them, "is not a thing."

"I'm not," Ani said.

"If you don't, I will," said Lewis. "And that is a promise."

CHAPTER TWENTY-ONE

As with Carlo and Daniel, Ani was surprised by how comfortable she felt, sitting between Lewis and Daniel in Lewis's truck. There was something about these two. Their calm presence, the way they laughed without a hint of mockery or malice. Daniel's offer of a hand to help her climb in. She found herself relaxing, settling into the ease of their company. She was not on high alert as she so often was, checking for her own safety. It was not easy to be a woman in this world. Not easy to be a disabled Iranian woman in America.

Lewis had music playing, and there was an early morning quiet as they drove. Ani thought about Lewis's words and the misguided sweetness of Daniel trying to throw her and Lewis together. She remembered all the puzzling things over the last few weeks, the times his eyes had gleamed when she mentioned Lewis or his farm. The times he had told her that Lewis was coming over and then gotten out of the way. She glanced at Lewis. There was no question that Lewis was a beautiful man. He was tall, muscular, and his smile was captivating. But Ani could barely feel his presence as he drove; he was neutral, nearly invisible to her awareness, whereas every square inch of her right side was pinging, sending alarms to tell her that Daniel was nearby.

And the truth was that Daniel was just as off-limits to her as Lewis was because Ani was not available. She was not seeking a relationship, she was not receiving potential matches from her mother, she was not looking. Period. Ani had work set out for her; she had a vocation that didn't include a man who was settled, dug into a specific place.

Besides all that, Ani knew that men didn't really think of her that way. Something about her limp and cane transformed her into their cute little sister. She had dated before when friends or her parents had set her up on dates, but it had never worked out. And none of her crushes had ever seen her as more than a friend.

None of this mattered, though. Daniel deserved to know that she wasn't interested in Lewis, so he didn't waste time matchmaking.

"Daniel," she said, and her voice was a little too loud in the enclosed space. Lewis glanced at her as he turned the music down.

"Yes?" Daniel said when she didn't say anything else.

For all of Ani's resolve, she could not help noticing his deep, gentle voice. She took a deep breath, glancing at Lewis briefly before continuing.

"You know nothing is going on between Lewis and I,

right?" she said.

She felt the way Daniel's muscles tensed immediately. Lewis laughed and kept laughing even when Ani nudged him with her elbow.

"What?" Daniel asked. He was flustered, and for a moment, Ani felt bad about making him feel uncomfortable. But, she told herself, this needed to be cleared up before it got any more awkward. Like ripping a bandaid off.

"There is nothing between us," she repeated. "We don't feel romantic about each other at all."

She looked at Daniel. He was staring at the road. Through the windshield, the sky was a motion of color, the pink and violet of sunrise. The lines of Daniel's face were perfect to her, like his brown eyes and long eyelashes. He swallowed once, twice, three times.

"I thought...you seemed so glad to see Lewis, to live near him," he said.

"I know," she said. "I thought I should tell you so that you can stop your matchmaking efforts."

"Yes," Lewis put in. "They weren't exactly subtle." He was still laughing.

Daniel made a small sound of distress, and Ani nudged Lewis again. This time he stopped laughing.

"I was glad," Ani said. "Because I'm dedicated to these families, and I thought it would be perfect for them to live so close together."

"I can't ever seem to get things right," Daniel murmured, as though to himself.

Ani felt terrible for hurting him. It would have been worse if we let it go longer, she thought.

"That's not true, Daniel," Lewis said. "You get things right. You see clearly when the rest of us are fumbling. To tell the truth, the line between friendship and attraction is one of the hardest things to read. For everyone, not just for you."

Ani could see a muscle in Daniel's jaw still working.

"Hey," she said, reaching out to put a hand on his wrist. "Don't take it badly. I get things wrong all the time."

Daniel looked at her and nodded, trying to smile, it seemed, and failing.

"I never understand why people tell you not to feel bad because they also did something wrong. It's like saying there are so many wrong things in the world—here are more!"

Lewis turned onto the gravel road that led to the houses. Ani watched the trees, their dark branches against the light sky.

"I think we do that because getting things wrong is human," she said finally. "It's like saying, hey, I'm human too. We're in it together. That's what I'm saying to you."

Lewis put the car in park. In front of them were the three houses and the next part of Ani's life.

"Thank you," Daniel said. "You're going to be a good neighbor, I can tell."

Lewis laughed again. "Come on, you two, we have no time to mull this over. Aren't our families coming at noon?"

Ani jumped. "Yes!" She climbed out after Lewis, taking time to stabilize herself before reaching for her cane. The guys were pulling boxes out of the truck bed. Daniel handed her one that she could carry under one arm, and she hauled it to her new house.

It didn't take long. Ani didn't have many possessions. In fact, the truck was unloaded so quickly that Ani could start sorting her things in the bedroom. She hung up the dresses in the closet and put away her T-shirts and pants. Daniel had placed the plastic tote that read, 'Bedroom, linens' on the floor near the bed, so Ani put sheets and her duvet on the bed. She lit a scented candle to help with the smell of new ceiling paint mixed with the mustiness of a house that had been closed up for a long time. But the floors were clean and shining, and the windows sparkled. Daniel had done a lot of work to prepare for her arrival. With the bed made and her mother's afghan on top, the room looked like home. Ani breathed in the scent of the rose candle and looked around, blinking back tears. This room—this house—was beautiful.

She went to the kitchen, where she quickly sorted her food and dishware into drawers or onto shelves. Ani would have liked to sink into one of the chairs in the living room, put her leg up, and soak in the peace of her new house, but there was so much more to do before that would be possible.

She closed the front door behind her and walked up the hill toward the big house. Lewis and Daniel were sitting on the front steps with Katie, who had arrived a short while ago to put the finishing touches on the Lorias' house.

"I think we're all set here," Daniel said. "Katie brought flowers and welcome signs."

Ani checked her watch. "Then it's time to go," she said. "We have work to do at the church."

The plan was that the four refugee families would come first to the church and meet everyone before going to their respective homes. Ani had gone back and forth about this plan many times. Was it best to have a big introduction first? Or let the families settle in and get some rest before all that? In the end, Amanda had convinced her.

"There are so many things these families need to start rebuilding," she told Ani and Frankie on a video call. "To begin, they need order, clarity, and transparency. They're coming from a country where lies were everywhere. Some had secret agendas against them. And they have been confused for months because DHS doesn't always tell them what's going on. There are surprise interviews, or they find things out after everyone else. So I think being as clear and orderly as possible, from the very beginning, will be the thing that helps them settle in the most."

The plan was a welcome lunch at the church first thing, with the sponsors and helpers for each family. Then they would drive to their homes and settle in during the first week.

"Each family has someone who has been practicing their English," Amanda told them. "But we will have an interpreter there and available if you need them later."

"We have a lot of Spanish-speaking residents in this town as well," Frankie had said, smiling at Amanda, "but I guess you know that already." Ani sat stone-faced, still troubled by the fact that she wasn't going to be able to communicate easily.

"This is it!" Lewis said from his place on the top step at the Lorias' house. "It's happening. I can hardly believe it."

"Let's go," Katie said now. "I feel so nervous. It will be good to get to work at the church."

CHAPTER TWENTY-TWO

Daniel paced back and forth in the church kitchen while Katie, Frankie, and Lupe put the finishing touches on the welcome lunch.

"Can you do that somewhere else?" Katie asked after Daniel bumped into her for the third time.

"I'll stop," he said. "Put me to work."

"Nearly done," she said, "but you can chop up the cilantro."

With Lupe helping, Katie had figured out how to make pabellón criollo, Venezuela's national dish, to welcome the families. The kitchen was full of the rich smells of cumin and sautéed onions, roasted peppers, and fried plantain. While Katie fretted over it, Lupe insisted it was simple.

"Just black beans and rice," Lupe said, "but with stewed beef and fried plantain. Not so hard."

"It's more that any one of these women could probably make this dish with their eyes closed," Katie said.

"Yes, Mija, but how many times did they serve it in the immigration center?" Lupe asked.

Katie smiled and nodded. "You're right. I hope it's passable. It's more symbolic, not something that needs to be perfect," she said. "I'm hoping it will communicate that they are welcome as they are, with all of themselves, and that we won't try to change them."

"We will be richer for having them as they are," Francisco said.

Sam had come into the kitchen while Katie was talking. He walked over to her as she finished sprinkling chopped cilantro on the beans, and put an arm around her. "They'll love it," he said. "You did a good job."

They heard a voice from the church sanctuary. "They're here! Everyone onto the front steps!"

Daniel looked at Katie. "I thought you said it would be half an hour!"

"I thought so," she said. "They must have a fast driver."

She pulled off her apron and laid it on the countertop, then walked to the front of the church behind Sam and Frankie. Daniel followed, feeling a peculiar twisting in his stomach. Nerves, he realized. He was nervous.

Ani stood waiting with the others in the bright sunshine on the front steps of the church. A bus that was like a tour bus, but painted a dull gray with the letters DHS on the side, pulled into the church parking lot. Daniel stood a little straighter, feeling as though he was waking up. This had been a theory, a vague future. Now it was really happening.

The door to the bus opened, and Ani walked down the

stairs, gripping the railing on one side. The others followed slowly. The first person off the bus was a child, a girl of about eleven or twelve, Daniel thought. She paused in the bus doorway for a moment, looking a bit stunned by the large group of people waiting for her. Then she smiled and walked forward with impressive composure, taking the hand that Ani offered her. A younger boy jumped down behind her and turned to hold his hand out to the woman behind him. The woman took his hand and carefully climbed down. Oh. This was Daniel's first sight of the Lorias--his family. The grandparents seemed even older than their photos had let on. Ani turned and briefly met Daniel's eyes. She had recognized them, too.

After a few moments, everyone was off the bus. Ani made a motion of welcome and told them to come into the church. Frankie translated, and as a group, they all walked back up the steps and poured into the church foyer. They kept walking, back to the room where church suppers and food giveaways happened. Frankie told everyone to take a seat, and when all of the families and sponsors were seated, Ani stood up.

"Welcome," she said. "We have been looking forward to meeting you and are so happy that you are here. I know this might all be overwhelming," she said. "There are a lot of names to remember. So let's take it slow. We don't have to remember everything right away. There is no test. We'll get it; let's be patient with ourselves." She smiled and paused to wait for the translator, who had accompanied the families, then went on.

"I will introduce each family. Please stand while I tell everyone your names. Then, I will let you know who your support team is." She waited again for the translator.

Daniel had been practicing his Spanish, which was already pretty good because of his years with a bilingual foster family. He could understand most of what the translator said, but the Spanish was rapid and in a different accent than he was used to, so he needed to concentrate. He felt a fizz of excitement at the thought of all the practice he would get at home now. There was nothing Daniel loved more than acquiring a new skill. He pulled his attention back to Ani as she began to introduce the first family.

This was one of the families in the bungalows that the church and sponsors had rented and prepared. Francisco and his mother, Theresa, and Sam would be the primary contacts for these two families, with Sheldon, Katie, and Mercy also offering help where they were needed.

Ani introduced the parents as Jose and Alejandra Perez, and the children as Jose Jr, Sebastian, and Claudia. The boys were five-year-old twins, and the baby looked like she was a little over a year. Daniel was distressed at the thought of fleeing a country with children so small. The boys looked around with big eyes, though they kept their hands wrapped around their father's legs. The baby had her head buried in her mother's shirt. The parents looked exhausted. Jose said a few words about how thankful they were to be here, and then they sat down.

The next family was a single father named Luis Diaz and his eleven-year-old son, Javier. They would stay in the smaller of the bungalows, just a block away from the church.

Next, Ani introduced the family who would be living on Lewis's farm. Lewis stepped forward to wave when Ani told them that their support people would be Lewis and herself. The Mendozas were a very sweet family. The father was named Manuel, the mother Juliana, and the seven-year-old daughter was Layla. Daniel saw a smile flash over Manuel's face when the translator told him that they were living and working on Lewis's farm.

Then it was time for Daniel's family to be introduced. Ani began to speak, but the girl who had been first off the bus stood up.

"I have practiced English," she said. "Can I introduce my family?"

"Yes, of course!" Ani said, though she looked surprised. She glanced at Daniel with a smile on her face. He smiled back at her. He liked this kid already.

"I am Valeria Loria," the girl announced. "I am twelve years old. This is my brother, Gabriel. He is eight years old. This is my abuela, Maria, and my abuelo, Leo."

Behind her, Maria leaned forward, speaking rapid Spanish that Daniel couldn't quite catch, but he did hear Valeria reassuring her grandmother. "No, Abuela, it's okay. We can tell them. We are home now."

Ani smiled again. "You will be living with Daniel, and I will be close by. We are your support people."

Daniel stood and waved at the Lorias. Valeria and her brother waved back, but Maria and Leo just looked at him.

Fair enough, Daniel thought. They must be exhausted and nervous.

Ani spoke again.

"This week is for getting used to your new houses and forming friendships with your support people. And, most important of all, resting. You must be exhausted after all you have gone through. I know that the immigration center is nothing like home. You may begin to settle in. This is your place, and we are your new family."

There was applause when Ani finished. She blinked, then smiled and gave a mock bow. Daniel saw a few of the newcomers dabbing at tears. And then Lupe was next to Ani, telling everyone in Spanish that lunch would be served immediately. After a moment, the translator translated Lupe's words into English, and everyone laughed. The mood shifted. Then Frankie stood and prayed in both languages.

"Father of all, thank you for the families you have brought to our town," he said. "We love them already. Bless them at every moment. Thank you for food and love. Amen."

Ani appeared at Daniel's side.

"Ready?" she asked. They were supposed to eat together with the Lorias. Daniel glanced over at the table where their family sat. There were two empty chairs, and the girl named Valeria was staring hard in Daniel and Ani's direction. She grinned when Daniel met her eyes. He smiled back. He really liked this kid.

Daniel held out his arm to Ani, and she looked at it for a moment, then linked her arm through his. Daniel felt a wave of happiness as he guided her to the table and pulled out a

138

chair for her. She sat, and he pulled out a chair for himself next to hers, smiling at the older couple and then at the children. They were here. This family that Daniel had been preparing for—they were actually here. Finally, they could begin their lives together.

He knew there would be difficulties. For one thing, the grandparents seemed frailer than he had imagined, and he was pretty sure that as a part of the sponsorship, they were supposed to have jobs. But there would be time to figure out the practicalities. For now, Daniel just wanted to soak the moment in.

He introduced himself again in Spanish.

"Soy Daniel," he said. "And this is Ani. We are so happy that you are here. How was the bus ride?"

The kids started up a patter about the size of the bus and how comfy the seats were, not like Venezuela, moving between Spanish and English fluidly. Daniel was happy to note that Gabriel spoke English as well, though not quite as confidently as his sister. The pair would be starting school soon, and having a grasp of English already would be extremely helpful for them. He murmured translations to Ani whenever they switched back to Spanish. The grandparents were very quiet, watching and listening, looking around with wide eyes.

The food came, and as they began to eat, Leo exclaimed aloud to Maria. She looked at Daniel. "This is our food," she said.

"Yes," he said. "Our friends made it to welcome you."

"Gracias," she said. "It tastes like home."

Daniel realized then, as he watched Maria eat, that as much as they welcomed the families and told them they were home, these people had lost their home. Home was where they had come from, not where they were going. He took a bite of food and prayed the first of many prayers for love, comfort, for strength for all of them.

CHAPTER TWENTY-THREE

Once the welcome lunch was over, it was time to go home. Ani sat on the front steps of the church with the kids while Maria and Leo helped Daniel sort out the luggage. Sam pulled up next to the bus in his truck, and they loaded all the bags into the truck bed. Then Daniel, Ani, and the Lorias piled into Daniel's new SUV, a second-hand ten-year-old Jeep Cherokee he had purchased the week before.

Ani noticed Maria peering at their bags in Sam's truck with a worried look on her face.

"Will you tell your abuela that we're all going to the house, and Sam will meet us there with the luggage?" Ani asked Valeria.

Valeria, however, was thoroughly absorbed in a conversation with her brother and didn't hear Ani. Daniel was the one who translated. Maria nodded, settling back into her seat with her arms clasped around her stomach.

Ani looked over at Daniel from her place in the passenger seat. Both of the adult Lorias had refused to sit in the front, leaving the space for Ani.

"It seems that you have downplayed your linguistic abilities," Ani said.

Daniel looked surprised. "I told you I speak some Spanish," he said.

"It sounded perfect to me," Ani said.

Daniel snorted. "It's far from perfect," he said as he turned the jeep onto the street to follow Sam's truck. "But I'm good with sounds, in music and language. It helps."

The sun was bright, even under the trees, and this was the Lorias' very first trip together in the jeep with Ani and Daniel. The first of many, hopefully, a thought that made Ani smile. She liked firsts. She twisted so she could see behind her. The kids had their faces pressed to the windows. Maria watched the buildings go by, and she seemed fragile, her hands trembling slightly. But she smiled at the exclamations of the kids, who called out in excitement over things they saw. Ani wished she could understand them. It was usually her job to understand and translate, and she found the difference hard to take.

As they drove through a small stand of Redwood trees, Maria made a soft exclamation, leaning so she could see better.

"What did she say?" Ani asked, her curiosity overcoming her.

"Abuelita said that she never in her life thought trees could be so tall," Valeria said.

Ani nodded and smiled at the older woman. "Tell her I understand," she said. "I remember my first time seeing them. I felt like an ant."

Valeria translated, and the older woman chuckled.

"We will have to take a trip to one of the ancient groves," Ani said. "These are not even the biggest trees. They can be enormous, so big it would take many people holding hands to reach around them."

Valeria translated again, and Maria made a sound of surprise. She turned to Ani and patted her hand, speaking swiftly.

"She said, 'You and I will go and be the tiniest of ants,'" Valeria said. "*Pero, Abuelita, yo quiero ir tambien.*"

Ani thought she understood this. She had been frantically studying Spanish, but the conversation went too quickly for her most of the time. She felt a little better at having understood at least one phrase today. And she noticed that Maria's hands were no longer shaking.

They had left the redwoods far behind and were on a curve where the lake was visible below, under a sweep of oaks. The sunshine was softening in the late afternoon, and everything was golden.

"*Que hermosa,*" Leo murmured.

"*Si, que magnifico,*" Maria said, tucking her hand into his.

"'They say it's beautiful," Valeria said. "I think so too."

When Daniel pulled into the gravel driveway, the kids bounced up and down in their seats, excited to see their new home. Leo was talking at full speed, but the car was too noisy for anyone to hear him. Ani felt a little concerned about all the emotions building in the jeep. Everyone needed to rest, but she knew they had hours of work ahead to get the Lorias settled into the house. Daniel had hardly said a word since they started driving.

He stopped the jeep in the parking area, and they all climbed out. Sam walked down from where he had parked his truck, up by the big house.

"I'm going to have to head back soon, guys. The others need my help at the houses in town."

"Sure, let's unload now," Daniel said. He jogged up the hill to help, leaving Ani standing with the Lorias, who were looking around with their mouths agape. Standing with the lake at their backs, Ani's house was the closest on the right. Behind hers, up the hill, was Daniel's. The big house was on the left, across from Daniel's place, separated by a grass slope, still abundant with wildflowers, and the fenced-off overgrown vegetable garden.

"You're going to live in that house," Ani told Valeria, pointing. Valeria translated for the others. "I live down there in the little one, and Daniel lives up there."

It seemed like a month had passed since Lewis and Daniel had turned up at her front door that morning. For a moment, Ani thought longingly of her bed, but she was far from able to rest yet. They were just getting started. Sam and Daniel finished unloading, and Sam waved goodbye before he climbed in his truck and drove away. Daniel walked down to where they all stood.

"Ready to see your house?" he asked.

Ani felt a rush of something like relief. Daniel's presence was a reminder that she wasn't alone, and that even if things got emotional and difficult today, Daniel would be there. It felt a little like...counting on someone? It was dangerous territory.

Valeria and Gabriel cheered at the idea of seeing their house, and Ani once again noted their emotional state: over-excited and possibly on the verge of exhaustion. They needed to get everyone settled as soon as possible, or there would be tears.

"I'll speak in both English and Spanish," Daniel said. "I was thinking about it on the way here. I don't want Valeria to have to do all of the translation, so I'll just go back and forth so Ani can be part of the conversation." He repeated what he had said in Spanish.

Ani smiled. "And I'll keep working on my Spanish lessons," she said, sighing.

"You'll get it," he told her. "You're so smart."

"That's something, coming from you," she said. It was becoming more and more apparent to Ani that Aveline's post-master was brilliant. The realization raised so many questions about his occupation and life choices. However, now was not the time to ask.

Daniel smiled at her, then turned to the family. "Welcome to our little haven," he said, gesturing to a sign that Theresa had painted for them; a painting of a flowering jacaranda tree with the name of their home painted in large, clear letters. "Ani and I decided to name this property 'El

Refugio,' because this is a haven for all of us. We want you to see everything, but we can go slowly if you need. You must be tired."

Tired and wired, Ani thought, watching Valeria's wide eyes. Daniel led the way up the hill.

CHAPTER TWENTY-FOUR

Maria leaned on her husband as they walked, and Daniel came close and offered her an arm.

Maria shook her head at him, smiling, and murmured something.

"She said they always walk together," Valeria told Ani. The older couple walked arm in arm, both short in stature, with graying hair and clothes that were well-tended but had been around for a long time. They looked like love, to Ani. Like resilience.

She quickly retrieved her cane from the front porch as they passed her house. She had left it behind in the rush to get to the church.

"Oh," Valeria said. "Do you have a...injury?"

Ani blinked at the intensity of the word. An injury seemed grave and action-oriented, unlike Ani's experience of an often tired and aching leg, which put a strain on the tendons and nerves in her hip. Valeria must have heard the word in her travels as a refugee, in the camps, or groups of travelers. Ani's heart went out to the girl. She had been through so much already.

"One of my legs doesn't work as well as the other one," Ani told Valeria. "It's been that way since I was a little girl. Sometimes it just gets a little tired, and then a cane helps."

"Like Abuela. But she uses Abuelo for help."

Ani laughed. "Yes, like that."

Daniel led the way up the hill to the house, with the grandparents walking behind him, Ani, Gabriel, and Valeria following behind. Ani smiled at the boy, who had grown quiet since they began the walk, clutching a stuffed bear. He looked at her seriously and didn't smile back.

Ani tried to see it all through their eyes.

The house was lovely in the afternoon light, a wooden home that was a little random in construction, as though there had been many additions over the years. What it lacked in continuity, it made up for in artistry. There was a large veranda where Mercy had insisted they place a couch so the Loria's could sit and look at their view. The meadow between Daniel's house and the big house was a carpet of wildflowers, and the jacaranda trees had just begun to bloom their vibrant purple. After two cold and rainy weeks, the weather was starting to get balmy and warm, and the steps to the house were flanked by California poppies.

"*Que bella, que bellisimo,*" Maria kept murmuring, and she paused to cup a poppy in her hand. Purple lupine rippled in the grass before the house, and at the bottom of the stairs were beds of lavender and a few rose bushes. Leo bent down and broke off a sprig of lavender for his wife, handing it to her before they followed Daniel up the stairs. Tears pricked behind Ani's eyes.

Inside the house, Ani and Katie had placed vases and bowls of flowers everywhere. They had gone back and forth about this, wondering if it would be overwhelming for people who had been staying in a government facility for months. But Venezuela was tropical, and flowers would have been a way of life for the Lorias. Ani felt that to make this house feel like home, they needed more beauty than even seemed necessary.

There were little signs that said *'Bienvenido a vuestro casa,'* or *'Bienvenido al Refugio,'* as well as 'Welcome home,' and 'Welcome to El Refugio,' in English. The Lorias exclaimed over each detail, and now there were tears on everyone's faces. They went from room to room, looking at the two bedrooms, the living room, the kitchen, the veranda, and the back porch. Ani and Daniel had tried to furnish the home simply but beautifully, with lots of color and space. The kids' room had bunk beds and a shelf of books in English and Spanish, as well as some toys and art supplies.

"For us?" Valeria breathed, looking at a box of watercolors.

'Si,' Ani said, smiling at the awe on Valeria's face. "For you."

They ate dinner early, after bringing everyone's luggage to their rooms. There wasn't much. Just a backpack each-- only what they had been able to carry. Around the table, they talked about what would happen next. Daniel had thrown together pasta for dinner, and Ani kept getting distracted by how good it was, but she tried to explain the next steps as well as she could. The conversation went slowly because of the need for translation, but the time allowed Ani to watch each person.

"Daniel and I can help with grocery shopping," she told them. "We'll show you where things are and help you learn your way around town. We're here whenever you need us."

"How will we get where we need to go?" Leo asked.

"We'll drive you at first," Ani said. "And then we need to work on getting you a car."

"And licenses," Daniel said. "For Leo and Maria."

Maria shook her head. "I don't drive," she said.

"Oh, okay, just for Leo."

Refugees were so vulnerable, Ani thought for the millionth time in her life. What if these four didn't have anyone to help them? Many refugees were just dropped in a city somewhere and expected to figure life out, but they were vulnerable to liars and thieves. And if Leo was the only driver in the family, his safety was so important. His family wouldn't be able to function without him.

"I can't wait till I can drive!" Valeria declared. "Then I can take everyone everywhere!"

Ani smiled at the girl. This family did have a future. And they had Ani and Daniel. It was no good to focus on the obstacles, the haters, or the people Ani couldn't help. She had work to do, right here.

"Also," she went on. "We'll start the process of getting you two in school. I think you'll like the school here, and they look forward to having you."

That was when Gabriel burst into tears, throwing his fork down and sobbing into his hands. He had been bouncy and excited all day, looking into every cupboard, smelling flowers, trying to climb over fences, but it seemed he had hit the wall. He said a jumble of words mixed with sobs. Ani did not understand. She looked at Daniel.

"He says he doesn't want school," Daniel told her. "He wants his Mama and Papa, and he wants to go home." Daniel kept translating for her in a low voice while the Lorias spoke to one another. They were all crying now.

"We cannot," Maria was murmuring, with tears on her face, while Gabriel climbed in her lap like a toddler and pushed his face into her neck. "We cannot go home. We can never go home."

"They are tired and overwhelmed," Ani said to Daniel.

He nodded.

"We will wash the dishes and then go," Ani said. "You need to rest."

"No, no," Maria said. "You have cooked for us, and you have prepared everything in the house. We will wash the dishes after the children go to bed."

Ani tried to argue, but Maria had such a fierce look on her face that Ani backed down. The older woman was exhausted, but she would not budge. Ani knew how vital a sense of control was when you were rebuilding a life.

"Okay," she said. "We'll go. We'll see you in the morning."

Maria shuffled Gabriel to Leo's lap and walked Ani and Daniel to the door.

She asked Daniel something, gesticulating between Ani and Daniel. At first, Daniel wouldn't translate. After Ani asked him three times, he finally told her what the older woman had said.

"Can I ask why you live in two separate houses when you are married? If you are in trouble, maybe you can ask the reverend for help."

Hearing, Ani understood Daniel's deep blush. She felt heat rise in her own face.

"We are not together, Abuela," Daniel told Maria. "We are only friends."

Maria leaned back and crossed her arms over her chest, looking back and forth between them. "That is not fooling anyone," she said. It was even harder to get Daniel to translate this, and they waved a short goodbye and left before any more embarrassing things could be said. Ani felt the cool night air on her hot face and felt a rush of relief that they had made it through the day. She said goodbye to Daniel and walked slowly, gratefully, to her bed. It was soft and fragrant with her favorite fresh sheets, and she could see stars through her window as she drifted off to sleep.

CHAPTER TWENTY-FIVE

Daniel was surprised by how quickly they fell into patterns of life. The first few days were a bit startling as he woke in his new house and realized there were people around who needed him. He felt torn between the desire to leap up and find out if everyone was okay, and resistance to the idea of so much change. So he did what he knew how to do. He went small, really small, and focused on the next steps.

He went up to the big house and found the kids sitting on the steps with mugs in their hands. The sight was beautiful, and a warm feeling bloomed in his heart.

"Did you sleep well?" he asked in Spanish.

"We did," Valeria answered. Gabriel nudged her. "At least, for a while," she corrected. "Gabriel had his nightmare, and Abuela had to wake up and sing to him. But then we went back to sleep, and the bed was very soft, so we slept all through the rest of the night, and we woke up when the sun did."

Daniel had to concentrate to follow all her words, but kids were often easier to understand than adults when speaking, and it was all pretty clear. He wanted to know more about the nightmare, but Gabriel was biting his lip and staring into the middle distance, so he decided not to ask quite yet.

"What are you drinking?"

"Hot chocolate," Valeria answered. "Abuela found the ingredients in the kitchen, and she added cinnamon, just the way we like it. And cream. Yummy. I don't even know the last time we had hot chocolate. We used to have it all the time when we were little at home." She looked at him with wide eyes. She seemed somehow both younger and older than she was. "I hope it is okay that we used what was in the kitchen. I told Abuela I thought it was okay."

"Of course," Daniel answered, leaning on the railing. "Everything in there belongs to you."

Gabriel's eyes grew big, and he took another sip of his drink. Valeria nodded.

"That's what I told her," she said. "But she had a hard time believing me. She says it's too good to be true. We haven't met very many nice people since we left home. Well, some people were polite, and they gave us things. But not like neighbor and family nice. Do you know what I mean?"

"I do," Daniel said. He might not have before he met Francisco and started hanging out with the others. 'Neighbor

154

and family nice' really was different from 'polite nice.' "Is it okay if I go in?" He asked.

Valeria looked startled. "Yes! There is some hot chocolate for you, too. And I think Abuela is making breakfast for all of us."

Daniel tried to make some noise walking into the kitchen so he wouldn't startle Maria, but she still jumped when he said her name. She was standing at the stove, stirring something that smelled delicious. Daniel's stomach woke up.

"Ah," she said. "Here you are. Where is Ani?"

"I haven't seen her yet," Daniel said.

"You will need to get her," Maria said. "I am making breakfast for everyone."

"You don't need to do that," Daniel said.

A voice came from the living room. "Yes, she does," said Leo. "Maria has not been herself since she lost her kitchen and her ability to host people. Trust me. Give her this."

"I'm making perico and sliced oranges," Maria said. Her words faded to a mutter as she went to the cupboards to pull out dishes, setting a stack of six plates on the countertop.

"I will go find Ani!" Gabriel announced, then disappeared out the open front door.

Maria and Valeria froze and looked at each other, mouths open. After a moment, Maria dabbed at her eyes and then went back to cooking.

"He hasn't been doing very many brave things since before we left," Valeria said. "Since before Mama and Papa died."

Daniel nodded. He really did want to hear the story of

how they left, how the parents died, and what needed to happen for them to heal. But he also didn't want to ask. The air in the room felt fragile. Maria gripped her spoon like a lifeline.

Valeria was poring over a book written in Spanish, and Daniel looked at it with her for a while. There were some words he didn't know, and he got her to translate. Sometimes she didn't know the English word and had to try to explain it in Spanish. They laughed a few times when the explanations were too hard.

Maria brought them coffee, very strong and bitter, and then started to lay the table with plates covered with a mixture of eggs, tomatoes, and peppers, flanked by buttered toast and sliced oranges. Daniel's mouth watered. They heard the slamming of the screen door, and Gabriel marched into the room, smiling. Ani was right behind him.

Daniel inhaled at the sight of her. Her black hair was shiny and loose, and she wore a mauve sweater and a pink scarf. Ani looked brilliant and clear. She made everything else in the room look faded.

He started to remind himself that she liked Lewis, that her heart wasn't available. But then he froze. No, they had told him yesterday that it wasn't true. What did that mean? What would he do with the way he felt if he couldn't brush it away?

Leo came into the room then, and they all pulled out seats around the large round table that Daniel had found at the flea market. It was heavy and solid, a family table.

Daniel found himself taking in this new family, thinking

with a tiny bit of panic about how this was only the first of many meals in this house. Focus on now, he reminded himself. You can't inhabit the future. The grandparents were lovely and slight of stature, and the children sparkled. They seemed eager to eat their grandmother's food. Gabriel kept sneaking small pieces of egg. How long had it been since Maria had a place to cook?

Leo offered a prayer of thanks, and they began to eat. There were appreciative murmurs and exclamations as everyone tasted Maria's food.

"You call this perico?" Daniel asked. "As in parrot?"

"Yes," Maria said. "But we should have some arepa to go with it. And I don't have the ingredients for that. You said you would take us shopping?"

"For international ingredients, we will need to go to Billers," Daniel said. He was translating for Ani, and when he said this in English, she frowned at him.

"That shouldn't be," she said. "We should ask Sheldon to order stuff in. Our new families must be able to buy their food here."

"Excellent idea," he told her, and then turned to Maria. "We can go shopping later today." The older woman smiled at him. She had deep brown eyes, and a face seamed all over with lines. Her hair was silver and tied into a bun at the back of her head. She wore clothes that looked like somebody's cast-off clothing; they didn't fit her very well.

Daniel pulled out his phone and started to make a list.

grocery store

clothes shopping

"Also," Maria went on, "do you think we could grow some food here? We always had gardens at our home in Venezuela, and there are so many things you can grow. It is a waste to buy when you can just put seeds in the ground!"

Daniel added another thing to his list:

seeds

He'd been thinking about the garden and how to go about planting, but knew almost nothing about gardening. Hearing that Maria really wanted to plant vegetables was more motivation to learn.

"Aren't you going to work?" Valeria asked.

Daniel took another bite of food and closed his eyes. Maria had used simple ingredients, but the result was so, so good. "I have a lot of vacation and sick time saved up, so I used it all for your arrival," he said. "I don't have to go back for four more weeks."

"Wow," Ani said, sitting back and shaking her head. "I haven't been here very long, but I can tell it's going to be weird for people if you're not at the post office." She looked at the Lorias. "Daniel is the town friend who is always there for people to come and talk to, at least during business hours."

Daniel smiled and nudged her.

"We all have to get used to change," he said. "Including people at the post office."

The following days took on a kind of pattern. After they woke, they ate breakfast together in the big house. Daniel got Maria the ingredients she needed for arepas, a sort of Venezuelan fried bread. Together with Ani, Maria gave Sheldon a list of ingredients she wanted him to stock at

Green's. She had asked the other families what they wanted as well. Then she expressed shock that Jose, and not Alejandra, was the cook in his family.

"Abuela is very old-fashioned," Valeria confided to Daniel. "It's okay, the world is changing very quickly, and sometimes she can't keep up."

After breakfast, they would have a brief family meeting and discuss the day. Within the first week, Ani had the kids registered in school. The plan was that Daniel would drive Valeria and Gabe, starting Monday of next week, and once they felt comfortable, they would take the school bus.

Ani made the first appointments for all the families to meet with Mercy Jackson and a friend of hers in immigration law.

They often prayed as they started the day. Daniel sometimes felt emotion swelling in his throat during the prayers of the Lorias. They overflowed with thankfulness for small things, like the orange California poppies or the new frying pan that was better for arepas than the first one. They prayed for friends back in Venezuela. They thanked God for the jacaranda flowers and the hills in the distance. Daniel thanked God for his continued grace to work with others. He had not expected this to be so simple. Normally he was not very good at being with other people, and the ease had come as a surprise. Ani was quiet during prayer, but every once in a while, she prayed in Farsi. When Valeria asked her about it, Ani told her that it was the language she had first prayed in.

"It feels like the language of my heart," she said.

CHAPTER TWENTY-SIX

On the weekend, Daniel began planning the garden beds with Maria. They sat on the veranda in the soft Saturday afternoon sunshine, looking at seed catalogs and thinking about what the garden layout should be. They talked about trellises and climbing plants, lettuce beds, and all the different kinds of peppers Maria wanted. Ani spent the day visiting the other families, returning home to sit around the table with them that evening. She was full of stories about how everyone was.

"Manuel dove right into farming at Lewis's place," she said. "I think Lewis is having trouble coming up with things for him to do. They're going to be able to expand the farm this year. And the Perezes, in town, are doing well. They're going to wait a while before putting the twins in kindergarten. Javier Diaz will start school at the same time as you, though," she added, looking at Valeria and Gabriel. At eleven, Javier was just a year younger than Valeria. Valeria made a face.

"You don't like Javier?" Daniel asked.

"I like him!" Gabe said.

"He thinks he knows everything," Valeria said.

Daniel met Ani's eyes and hid a smile. He could imagine how the girl who knew everything herself felt about this.

On Sunday, the whole Loria family was rigid with nerves about the kids starting school the next day. So, even though Daniel was eager to see how the other families were doing, they decided to stay home and rest, rather than go to church. Daniel made lunch, and they spread blankets on the grass, chatting about what the kids could expect at school, trying to set their hearts and minds at ease. Daniel had formed an immediate bond with Valeria, who was now his partner in crime, helping with his Spanish, translating words he didn't know, adding to her English vocabulary daily, and helping him understand the rest of her family. Gabriel, on the other hand, was going to take more time to warm up. He moved from hyper to painfully shy indiscriminately and seemed suspicious of Daniel most of the time. He was calmer with Ani, whom he seemed to adore.

"You know where to go," Ani said, "because of the tour we did. And you know your teachers."

"And our language assistants," Valeria added.

"Yes," Ani said. "But you'll barely need them. You're already doing so well."

Daniel lay back on the grass and looked at the sky. He didn't have much to say. He had loved and hated school. Loved it because of learning. Hated it because of bullying. He hoped that kids were kinder these days.

The next morning, after a lot of discussion, Daniel and Ani drove the kids to school, leaving Leo and Maria to rest at home. Maria still seemed so frail and tired, and Ani was worried about the constant barrage of new things in her life. She had advised Maria to stay and clean up after breakfast, then take a break, rather than accompanying them. Finally, Maria agreed to rest when Daniel told her Lewis was coming to help with the garden beds later in the day.

Daniel felt as nervous as a parent, or so he assumed—he'd never been a parent--watching Ani walk Valeria and Gabe into the school. They'd done all they could, and it was up to the kids to settle in.

Lewis was just pulling in when they got home. There was a moment of awkwardness as they all looked at each other, and Daniel remembered his wildly inaccurate assumptions. He had prided himself on his ability to read people by learning and memorizing their habits, despite his autism. How had he got it so wrong? Ani mumbled an excuse and left. Daniel and Lewis walked up to the garden plot. Finally, Lewis lightly elbowed Daniel.

"Don't do that," he said. "It's in the past, and it wasn't a big deal."

Daniel looked at him, seeing his smile and straightforward gaze. He wasn't hiding mockery or offense, it seemed.

"Okay," he said. And that was it. They spent the afternoon blocking out the beds with Maria's input, and replaced the sagging, rusted fence with new chicken wire. They even started building one of the beds, but soon it was time to leave and pick up the kids.

"I'll come back tomorrow," Lewis said.

"You sure?" Daniel asked. "You have time?"

Lewis laughed. "I decided a while back not to sign up for things I don't want or can't afford to do. So you can trust me when I offer help. I'm into it! And Manuel is so good at farming that I'm finding myself with more free time since he came, not less."

Daniel stared at him for a moment. He wanted to ask more about the philosophy, but Ani was at the jeep waving that they really needed to go. "Well, thanks a million," Daniel said. "I wouldn't be able to do this without your help. I mean, I would, but it would take ages to learn."

"You're welcome," Lewis said. They bumped fists, and Daniel jogged down to the jeep to join Ani.

The kids were noticeably exhausted when they climbed into the car. Dinner was muted, and they responded to questions about the day with brief answers. Everyone went to bed early. The days continued in this way all week. After breakfast, Ani and Daniel would drive the kids to school. Then, Ani did various work; scheduling, phone calls, visits. She often sat on her porch with her laptop, under the jacaranda tree, where Daniel could see her. Lewis came over and helped with the garden. They finished constructing a few of the beds and hauled in soil to fill them. Leo and Maria helped, and Lewis told them what he knew about composting and soil health.

"I'll haul some compost over before you get started with planting," he told Daniel. "You'll need to mix it in. Once you have a good pile of your own, you should add compost before every planting, and rotate your crops so you don't deplete the soil of the same minerals again and again."

Gardening was fascinating to Daniel. He was much more used to studying the cosmos than the composition of earth and soil. Fungi networks, micro-bacteria, and soil structure were all new to him. They mulched the beds to let them rest before they broke the compost in.

In the afternoons, Daniel and Ani, or sometimes Daniel and Leo, picked the kids up from school. They continued to be tired during dinner and were more likely to squabble or refuse to talk than they had been the first week. Gabriel, in particular, seemed affected, but Daniel noticed shadows under Valeria's eyes as well.

"Is this normal?" he asked Ani one afternoon. They were in the jeep, on their way to pick the kids up.

She took a moment to answer. "Well, how do you feel?" she asked finally. "After a full day of trying to get to know this family and me, adjusting to this new life?"

He thought about it. His mind felt incredibly busy lately, thoughts rolling around like marbles.

"Tired," he answered.

"And this has been your town, your country, for a long time. Yes. It's normal. I feel for them, but the only way to get through this is to adjust, slowly, bit by bit."

She was chewing on her nail as she said it. Daniel resisted the urge to reach out and touch her hand. He had more and more moments like this, finding himself gazing at the side of her face or a strand of wayward hair. It was all he could do not to rest his hand on her shoulder or tuck her hair behind her ear for her.

Stop staring, he would remind himself. Staring was one of the first things he had learned was off-limits when he was a boy and would get smacked or beat up for looking at people too long. He looked back at the road and switched on the turn signal to steer into the school pick-up zone.

That evening, Ani pushed a little harder to talk about school around the dinner table.

"How has it been?" Ani asked. "Real answers."

Gabriel stared at his plate. Maria had cooked again, a dinner of black beans and rice and chicken. It was rich with flavor, and the rice was cooked to perfection.

"It has been good," Valeria said.

They waited. "Any more details?" Daniel asked.

Valeria looked at her grandmother.

"You don't have to worry about sounding ungrateful," Ani said softly. "The most important thing about getting used to all of this is being honest about what you're feeling. You can be thankful and be having a hard time. Both are possible."

Valeria quickly wiped a hand over her eyes.

"I think I will like it someday," she said. She spoke so quietly that Daniel had to lean in to hear her. "But it is very, very different from school in Venezuela, and I miss my teacher. I miss the feeling I had there when I was getting ready for school. This school is big, and the lights are very bright. The teacher doesn't hug me. My old teacher was my friend."

Ani nodded. Daniel felt completely out of his depth, but Ani didn't seem intimidated by these revelations.

"It's a big change," she said. "It must make you miss home. What was the best part of the week so far?"

Both kids seemed to think it over. Gabriel spoke first. "My class has a lizard. I like it."

Maria made a face, and Gabriel laughed.

"I like band class," Valeria said. "My teacher said I can try out a few instruments and then decide what I want to play."

Daniel sat up a little straighter. "You like music?" he asked. After a moment, he realized that all four of the Lorias were staring at him.

"Are there people in the world who don't love music?" Leo asked.

Daniel laughed. "Strangely enough, yes. Or at least, some people don't care about it. Do you play an instrument?"

"Yes," the older man said. "I play guitar. And my wife sings."

"In Venezuela," Maria said, "the children grow up dancing. Sometimes they dance before they know how to walk."

"We have been surprised that there is no music here," Leo said.

"But there is music!" Daniel said, shocked. "We have a town band. The Aveline Swing Band."

"Daniel plays in it," Ani asked. "I've never heard him play, but I have heard him sing." She grinned at him.

"You're a musician?" Valeria asked, leaning forward.

"I am," Daniel said. "I play bass and sing, like Ani said." He sat and looked at each of the Lorias. They were weary.

They had lost so much and had so much ahead of them. It was so obvious, now that they were talking about it—they needed music.

"Tomorrow is the town meeting," he said. "After church. We can talk about music. We need to play music together. You can teach us how to dance."

"No one can teach me how to dance," Ani said, laughing.

"I take that as a challenge," Leo said.

"And you," Daniel went on, looking at Valeria. "What instrument do you think you want to play?"

"Well, I'm still trying different ones out," she told him. "But the one I like the most is the trumpet."

"Wow! Really?" Daniel asked. "My friend George plays trumpet. He's in our band, too. I'll introduce you, and you can talk to him about it."

Gabriel jumped up and mimed trumpet playing. Maria waved him back to his seat. The air was light around the table again, and Daniel crossed his arms over his chest and thought about music, how it had changed his life. He knew that they had stumbled onto something important this evening. That night, Daniel dreamed of playing bass while Leo spun Ani around the dance floor and Valeria soloed on trumpet. He woke up smiling.

CHAPTER TWENTY-SEVEN

Nothing in Ani's new life was more blissful than sitting at the little table in her small garden, her teapot and a glass of strong tea in front of her. Spring was fully upon Aveline now, and Ani watched as butterflies and bees came to visit the flowers. She had roses and climbing clematis blossoms, there were pots of lavender and mint flanking her doorstep, and the jacaranda tree was in full, glorious bloom. Every morning, she woke in her comfortable bed and lay there for some time, gazing at the sky as it grew light through the window with the view of the valley sloping down to the lake.

Sometimes she could barely believe her good fortune. She had taken her mother on a little video call tour of the tiny home with its excellent small kitchen and garden. She had shown her the outdoor bathtub and the jacaranda tree. Ani's mother, Maryam, appreciated it just as much as she did, if not more. Any private reservations Maryam might have had about Ani living so close to Daniel had disappeared with the first glimpse of the lake view, and she was already planning a visit.

"This is a blessing from God, Ani," her mother said. "You cannot take it for granted or feel bad about having so much beauty. You must soak it in. Sit in it and let it wash over you."

Maryam knew Ani too well. She knew Ani's propensity to rush into hard things and push away comfort in order to bring some sort of balance into the world. It never worked. The world didn't work that way, and Ani was not the arbitrator of justice.

But Ani had never been able to think clearly about pleasure and rest. It had worked for her to spend her life for others, partly because when she slowed down and tried to enjoy things, the sorrow began to leak in. Recently, though, what had worked before seemed to be breaking. She had started to wear herself out, and she was too young to be finished. Something needed to change.

Ani had always resisted her mother's advice, but this time was different. She was simply unable to get herself up from the table and rush around. She wanted to sit and listen to the birdsong. She was soaking it in, whether she wanted to or not.

Today was the Sunday service and the town meeting, and Ani had planned to make at least three calls before leaving for church. Instead, she sat idly drinking tea, watching hummingbirds at the feeder that Daniel had installed for her. She didn't know how much time passed, but she glanced at her phone she realized she only had half an hour to get ready. Whoops! She was still in her robe after her shower. *Oh my, Ani,* she thought. *You're really getting into this.*

She found a pair of leggings and an embroidered lilac tunic and pulled them on, then laced boots onto her feet. She looked at herself in the mirror, deciding to tie just a bit of her hair back and leave the rest of it down. It was long, well past her shoulder blades, and she didn't often leave it down because it was thick and hard to detangle. Today felt special, though. The first town meeting since the refugees arrived would be a celebration of sorts. She put on some moisturizer, lipstick, and the tiniest bit of silver eyeshadow. Her lashes were too thick and dark to need mascara, so she never bothered with it. After tying on a fuchsia-colored scarf, she was ready.

Ani was driving by herself today, since she needed to be at the church early to plan the meeting with Frankie and some of the other sponsors. Daniel would follow with the Lorias, and Ani had promised to sit with them during the service. Then they would have the town meeting at the Aveline Café. They had rented out the whole big front room and pooled money for a catered lunch. Ani couldn't remember whose idea it had been, but she heartily approved. She loved the café.

She filled her water bottle and went out to her car, singing. Ani had always been too shy to sing around other people, but everyone else was eating breakfast up at the big house, so she let loose. She was taken aback, therefore, to walk around the Jeep, heading for the Jetta, and run straight into Daniel's chest. Without thinking, she reached out to balance herself by gripping his arms. She was frozen for a moment, staring at the top button of his shirt. Her head was level with his chin. She dropped her hands.

"Sorry," she tried to laugh, but her voice cracked. Oh, this was humiliating. She could feel heat rushing to her face. "I didn't realize you were out here."

She didn't want to look at him, but he didn't say anything, and after a moment, she had to see what was going on.

He was staring at her. Oh, dear. All she could think to do was run away. She gave him an awkward little pat on the arm and then went to open the car door. As she did, he finally spoke.

"I've never heard you sing before," he said. "Your voice is beautiful."

Ani couldn't believe it. She gave a short laugh as she sank into the driver's seat. *That's* what Daniel was thinking? Not that she was clumsy or weird? But that her voice was beautiful? Daniel was unlike any man she had ever met in her life. She couldn't quite believe he was real.

"That's because I don't normally sing in front of other people," she told him. "You caught me."

She waved goodbye, still feeling horribly embarrassed, shut the door, turned the key in the ignition, and drove away. All of it seemed to take an hour. She just wanted to get away and give her hot face some air. But as Ani looked in the rearview mirror, Daniel was still standing there, watching her drive away. She shook her head. She knew he didn't mean anything by his words—he was just direct and honest and without guile. But the combination of his strong arms (and, to be honest, rock-solid chest) and the compliment, was going straight to her heart. He was too much.

Don't think about him, Ani, she told herself. *You can have the house for now, but he is not for you.*

And the tiniest, most rebellious part of herself asked, *But why not?*

Mercy pulled up in the church parking lot right after Ani did, and they walked in together.

"How are things at El Refugio?" Mercy asked.

"Things are...good," Ani replied. It was true. Things were very good. They were better than Ani would expect after just two weeks. At the same time, she knew better than to believe that they had gotten through the hardest parts. "I think we're still in the honeymoon period."

"Mmm," Mercy said, nodding as they got to the church hall, where the others were waiting. "Well, honeymoons happen to help you get through the next thing."

Ani laughed, but she felt a pang of nerves at the same time. What would come after the honeymoon?

CHAPTER TWENTY-EIGHT

Frankie and Sam were already set up at one of the round tables, and Mercy and Ani joined them. After a few minutes of small talk, Theresa showed up with takeout coffee —one for each of them.

"I have good news!" she announced. "Sheldon has found a supplier for plantains, so he'll stock them regularly now!"

Ani looked up and caught the look on Francisco's face as everyone else made sounds of appreciation. She grinned.

"I've been living here for eight years," he said, scowling. "And have had to shop for plantains in Billers."

"Don't be like that," Mercy said. "Besides, did you ever ask Sheldon to stock them.?"

Francisco smiled. "No, I didn't even think of it."

"Well, Maria has been to Green's four times in two weeks to ask," Ani said. "And if she can't make it, she tells Daniel to ask. She doesn't take no for an answer."

Theresa nodded. "Sheldon is dreaming in Spanish, the words, '*Quiero plantanos ahora, por favor!*'"

They all laughed. Ani took a sip of her coffee and closed her eyes. It was delicious.

"Wow," she said. "Where did you buy this?"

Theresa looked surprised. "At Ingrid's coffee shop," she said. "Have you been?"

"No," Ani admitted. "I've been rather single-minded since I got here."

"Oh, but you have to reap all the benefits of Aveline, too. Let's go together."

Ani smiled at Theresa. "Okay."

"This week is women's circle," Mercy added. "Another benefit of living in Aveline."

"Ooh, yes, are you coming again?" Theresa asked.

"I would like to. If I can manage it, I'll be there."

"Where is Lewis?" Mercy asked.

"He couldn't come this time," Ani said. "We'll need to figure out a way for him to get to the meetings. He's bringing the Mendozas later. But I have updates from both him and Daniel for today."

"Well, then let's pray and begin," Francisco said. He prayed for them all in his sonorous voice, and Ani felt her muscles begin to relax. She realized she was holding tension in her neck because of all that needed to happen for the families to settle in. The beauty of her new home made her forget that she was actually working very hard right now; none of this was easy! She let the prayer flow over her, reminding herself again that this was God's work and he needed to make it flourish.

After the prayer, she heard from each of the people around the table about how their families were doing. In some cases, she had advice or questions.

She also filled them in on how Daniel and the Lorias were, as well as giving bits of news from Lewis. All in all, Ani was pleased as she wrapped up. Of course, there were some nightmares and moments of confusion. A couple of parking tickets for the new drivers. But mostly, things were going smoothly.

Next, Mercy filled them in on the legal status of the families and how things would go from here. "Three of the four cases are straightforward. The immigration lawyer, Barry, couldn't come in today; he's all tied up with a surplus of work. But, as we all know, Daniel's family has complications. Barry and I are putting a case together. It's turning out to be quite intriguing but also troubling. This country has quite a history of dismissing the value of the family outside of the nuclear setup."

"Can you explain that in terms I can understand?" Sam asked, smiling faintly.

"Ah," Mercy said, sitting back and crossing her arms. "Around the world, family is much more than father, mother, and children. In many families, a grandmother is no less of a mother than a mother. Something in the settler history of this country disrupted this, however, so that those in authority felt that a grandparent or an aunt was not a good family member for a child to live with. As a result, many indigenous children were taken from families that were not defined as families. It is similar in the African American community. I myself was raised by my grandmother while my mother got her degree and then worked to form her own company."

"I see," Sam said. "Yes, that is different from the way we tend to think about family as white Americans."

"You can just ask the question, do you find it strange if more than one generation lives under one roof?"

"I remember people making fun of immigrant families when I was a kid," Theresa said. "Saying there were a hundred people in a house. They thought it was crazy that grandparents would live in the same house as the parents and kids."

"Many people would think it was crazy that they did not," Ani said softly. Her mother had grieved so heavily over the death of Ani's grandmother, mere months before she was cleared to join them in the United States. Maryam had longed for her mother to come and live with them.

Ani herself wondered if there would be a point when her parents would come to live with her. She knew that if she ever settled down, got married, and had kids, her mother would want to move right in and take care of her grandchildren. But that couldn't ever happen if Ani continued with the work in front of her.

"What this means for us," Mercy continued," is that we have to tap into our current awareness that we've made mistakes in trying to force people into culture changes, especially surrounding family structure. Is the government ready to acknowledge that the grandparents are often the best placement for children? So...we are deep in research, looking through cases and precedents to find when the law has admitted wrong-doing in separating an extended family."

"And how is it going?" Francisco asked.

"To be honest, it's heartbreaking work," Mercy said. "We're wading through stories of too many children taken from the people who loved them best and placed with strangers. How anyone thought it would be beneficial for them is beyond me. I hope we can prevent it happening here and now."

CHAPTER TWENTY-NINE

The church service went a long way toward reviving Ani's tired spirits. The songs, the sounds of people praying around her, the awe on Valeria and Gabriel's faces as they sat between Daniel and Ani in the pew. This was the first time Ani had ever had the experience of going to church with families in her program. Although many of the Syrian refugees who came to America were Christians, Ani's last two assignments had been with Muslim families, and Ani had helped them find a mosque for their worship.

Of the Venezuelan families, two were Catholic, and they had attended the Catholic Church over by the university. But the Lorias and Mendozas were both Protestant and had decided to come to Francisco's church.

"We'll stay if Maria likes it," Leo said. "She is the boss of the family." He laughed at the fiery look on his wife's face.

Francisco translated for himself, delivering the message in a mixture of Spanish and English. When Ani glanced over at Daniel partway through the sermon, she found his gaze on her. She looked away quickly, feeling silly about how much his eyes affected her, hazel and fringed with dark lashes. He probably had no idea how handsome he was. He didn't act like he knew. She darted more glances at him. He was facing the front, now, fully immersed in what Francisco was saying, so she could look at him without being seen. He had slightly curly sandy hair and that short beard, with high cheekbones. Full lips. What was it that was so appealing about him? She couldn't tell. Ani had seen hundreds, maybe thousands of handsome men in her life. She had never been this drawn to someone.

And with that, they were standing to sing, and Ani realized she hadn't absorbed even one sentence of the sermon. What was *wrong* with her? This was the worst crush she had ever had. And it was utterly impossible for anything to happen between them.

When the service was over, those who hadn't been part of the welcome committee seemed curious about the newcomers. A few came to greet the Lorias. Ani was thankful that everyone didn't rush over. The people who did come were kind and gentle, some English speakers and some fluent in Spanish. Daniel translated their welcomes to Maria and Leo as needed. Gabriel and Valeria came back from children's church, bubbling over with excitement. Valeria, in particular, seemed enamored by her teacher, Zoe. Zoe from women's circle? Ani wondered. She knew Zoe was a philosophy professor—did she also teach children's church? Ani realized she thought of Sunday school teachers as grandmothers, not modern young professors like Zoe.

After chatting, they walked to the Aveline Cafe for the meeting. Ani tipped her face up to feel the sun on her face and stumbled over a broken piece of pavement because she wasn't watching her feet. She felt Daniel's gentle hand on her shoulder, helping to steady her. Ani's heart went into a staccato rhythm. *Honestly.* She turned to thank him, but couldn't meet his eyes.

Mercifully, they had arrived at the cafe by then, and there was plenty for Ani to attend to as she greeted the other families and helped everyone find their seats. Then the food was coming out, and she was very much preoccupied with a bowl of cream of spinach soup that sent her tastebuds into a state of delight. Today, Katie had stuck to serving her regular cafe specials. Ani didn't know how the others liked the food, but everything was a hit at her table.

"Katie is a good cook," Daniel said in response to the continued exclamations of enjoyment from Leo and Maria.

"That is one of the biggest understatements I have ever heard," Ani said emphatically.

When lunch and dessert were over, and Ani was looking sadly at her empty cake plate, Francisco stood to speak.

"It has been two weeks since we saw your bus pull up," he said, turning to look at each of the new families, "and we are still so thankful to finally have you here. We dreamed of you and prayed for you for so long."

Ani felt her heart fill with warmth. It was such a simple, lovely thing to say. Some small part of her was opening, after being so closed for so long. She couldn't tell if it was good or bad, to feel open like this. In some ways, it seemed like heartbreak in the making. It felt dangerous. It also seemed as though there was nothing she could do to prevent it. Ani watched and prodded at the feeling during the rest of the meeting, waiting to see what it would become. It remained, a small bloom, while the families shared how their first weeks had been. While the light turned soft and made shadows of garden plants on the walls. While Ani snuck glimpses of Daniel, and while he stood to share his idea of making music together. They agreed on a future lake party with a concert from the town band, and committed to giving more thought to regular jam sessions once everyone was settled and things had slowed down.

Valeria rode in the car on the way home with Ani. Ani could tell that Valeria was fizzing with the kind of excitement that could tip into overwhelm. To be honest, Ani felt the same. She had two matching anticipatory emotions going on. One, she couldn't wait to get home. The thought of her beautiful little space waiting for her was such a good feeling. And two, though she had just left Daniel, she couldn't wait to see him again. She automatically started to scold herself for the thought, but then wondered why she was bothering. She was never going to do anything about this crush, never going to act on it. What harm could come from letting herself think about Daniel if she wanted to? In a way, it was completely safe. He wasn't looking for love, and she wasn't going to be around for all that long. She almost didn't hear Valeria chattering away behind her.

"I wonder what kind of food Abuela will make for us tonight?" the girl was saying. "Oh, look, there is Daniel in the garden! I will go help him."

Ani smiled, catching sight of Daniel as well, sitting in the golden light of the late afternoon, in a white t-shirt and Carhartt overalls, sifting through dirt. She watched and waved as Valeria ran over to him. Then she went into the house to see what Maria was up to.

Ani was exhausted and expected the older woman must be as well. They could certainly order pizza for tonight. But when she arrived in the kitchen, Maria already wore an apron, and her sleeves were rolled up. She was making *arepas* and wouldn't hear of anything else, even in Ani's broken Spanish. So Ani set the table and then went out to the garden, humoring her desire to be close to Daniel.

The last rays of sunlight were falling on the garden, and the lake was very blue in the distance. Ani could hear birds and smell fresh earth. She knew there were challenges ahead, but for now, contentment was seeping into her bones.

"What are you doing?" she asked. "Can I help?"

Daniel eyed her clothes. She hadn't changed after arriving home. "You'll get dirty," he said. "Do you want to run to your house and change?"

Ani didn't want to go anywhere. She wanted to sit here and savor this feeling in her heart, this light, as she watched Daniel digging the garden bed, pausing every once in a while to reach down and break up a clod of earth. His arms were sinewy with each lift of the shovel.

"I'll just watch," she said. "I can help next time."

Valeria was over at another garden bed, pulling out the tiniest of weeds.

"In answer to your question," Daniel said, "I'm double-digging. Digging Lewis's compost deeper into this bed to help the soil."

It was mesmerizing. Ani sat on a patch of grass and could feel herself almost sinking into sleep, listening to Daniel talk about what he had learned about soil. But then something broke into the piece; Maria yelling as she ran to the garden.

She was talking a mile a minute, and Ani lifted a hand to her heart as it began to thud heavily. She stood. What had happened? Was it Leo? Gabriel? Maria came into the garden and pointed a finger at Daniel, shrieking at him. He answered in soft, conciliatory tones, but she didn't stop shouting. Valeria went to her grandmother and pulled on her arm, to no avail. After a while, Daniel seemed to freeze, no longer answering, just staring at the ground. He began to rock back and forth slowly, tucking his hands under his arms. Ani felt helpless. She had no idea what Maria was saying.

"Can you please tell me what is happening?" Ani asked. "Daniel. Daniel!" He didn't answer. He didn't seem capable of it. He had squeezed his eyes shut tight.

"She had already planted some seeds in this garden bed," Valeria said. "She is very upset. Abuela says at that the border, white men took her seeds from home, even though she cried, and now Daniel is taking her seeds again. She found them at Sheldon's store and bought them with her own money. She says he is the same as the men at the border."

Finally, Daniel spoke. "I didn't know," he gasped. "Tell her I didn't know."

Maria was still yelling, on and on. It was testing even Ani's ability to stay present. Valeria pressed close to her grandmother's side and began speaking quickly, in low, urgent tones. Her grandmother answered in rapid Spanish and then burst into tears, holding her hands to her face, wailing.

Ani went to the older woman and placed a hand on her shoulder. Maria pulled away, looking at her with a defiant, tear-stained face, and Ani saw in the older woman's face how displaced and exhausted she was after being brave for so long. She kept pointing at Daniel and saying something Ani could not understand. Daniel was shaking his head back and forth now as he rocked. His eyes met hers, and there was a wild, trapped look in them that pierced Ani's heart.

"Valeria," Ani said, taking control. "Your grandmother must rest. Take her back to the house."

Valeria nodded, her face miserable. She linked her arm into her grandmother's and pulled. Finally, Maria allowed herself to be led out of the garden, and the two of them began to trudge back up to the big house.

Ani felt stunned. Though she had expected some sort of emotional outburst, this one had come so suddenly, out of seemingly nowhere, about something so benign. It took her breath away.

"She is not really talking about you, you know that, right?" she said suddenly to Daniel. He was still rocking back and forth, sitting in the dirt. He put his head between his hands.

"No, no, no," he moaned repeatedly.

Ani felt helpless again. She knew what this was. He was having a meltdown. He had told her about these. And to be honest, she wasn't autistic, but she didn't think even she could have withstood that level of accusation without crying.

She put a hand on his shoulder.

"Daniel," she said softly. "What do you need?"

He shook his head, mute. He still hadn't said anything besides no.

"Can you go lie down for a while?" Ani asked.

He glanced at her, and she saw that his face was shiny with tears.

"Daniel," she repeated. "Let's go to your house. I think it would be good for you to get a little time alone. It's been a long day."

She saw him take a shuddering breath. Then another. Then he nodded and stood, brushing his hands over his pant legs. He was bent half over, panting. Then he stood all the way up and turned to go. She made to follow him, but he held up a hand to stop her. He still didn't say anything, but she understood. She watched as he slowly walked to his house, half bent, like an old man.

CHAPTER THIRTY

Ani didn't know what to do with herself once she was left alone in the garden. In the growing dusk, she gathered the tools and put them in the shed that Daniel had built in one corner. She shut the gate behind her. Then she went to the big house to see if she could help the Lorias.

The house was dark, and the whole family was huddled on one of the sofas. Maria was weeping loud, gasping sobs while Leo held her. She held up a shaking hand, pointing her finger at Ani, and said something Ani couldn't understand. The meaning was clear, though. Maria didn't want Ani there.

Ani walked back out to the kitchen and found two plates covered in plastic wrap. Tears were stinging her eyes. After a moment, Valeria joined her. "I made these for you and Daniel," she said. "I didn't want you to be hungry."

She turned to go back to her family, but just before she

walked away, Ani caught sight of a look of heartbreak on the girl's face. She put a hand on Valeria's shoulder to stop her.

"Hey," she said. "What is it?"

Valeria's voice wobbled as she answered.

"I really liked it here," she said, her voice nearly a whisper. "But it's not my abuelita's fault. Those men were cruel to her, and she does not understand that everyone is not the same."

Ani tried to understand what Valeria was saying, and it came to her in a flash, suddenly.

"Honey. We're not sending you away because of this," she said. "And even if Maria is having a hard time today, she will feel better later."

"Are you sure?" Valeria said, looking up from under her cloud of curly brown hair. Her eyes were large and damp. "I don't think you understood everything she said to Daniel. She said cruel things."

"She is hurt. Daniel understands that. This is part of healing, little one. It's sad but true. The pain needs to come out. Don't worry. As much as you can, try to convince everyone to go to bed for the night because things will seem better after you get some sleep. And all is still the same. We still love you and want you."

Valeria caught Ani around the waist and hugged her hard. Ani hugged her back, kissing the top of her head.

"Thank you for putting food out for us," she said.

Then she took the two plates and let herself out, softly so as not to disturb. She could still hear the old woman's wails as she walked down the path toward Daniel's house. Her leg ached almost as much as her heart. She felt like she was a million years old.

Daniel wasn't in his house. She let herself in through the front door and called his name, softly, but he didn't answer. After a minute, she caught sight of him through the open sliding door next to the kitchen. He was lying outside on the grass, looking at the sky. Ani smiled.

"I have some food for you," she said as she walked outside. She lay it on the outside table. "Valeria wrapped it for us."

He nodded, still looking up at the sky. "Thank you," he said. His voice was raspy.

"Can I keep you company?" she asked.

He turned his head and looked at her. "I feel a little embarrassed," he said.

"What do you have to be embarrassed about?" she asked. "You handled that so well."

He let out a sigh and turned his face to the sky again. Ani could tell that he didn't believe her.

"I'm not just saying that," she said.

She left the food. They could eat it later. She went to him, easing herself onto the glass a little more than an arm's length away, turning her face to the sky to see what he saw. She drew in a breath. Out here, far away from the lights of the town and very far from the brightness of any city, she could see stars behind the stars. She didn't know many of them. But she knew the one directly above her, the three stars in a line that made up Orion's belt.

"What is the story about that constellation?" she asked, pointing.

"Orion? Hmm." She waited as Daniel gathered his thoughts, still speaking in a halting, raspy voice. "Well, he wasn't very nice, though he could walk on water. He wanted to hunt every beast on earth, so he was killed by a scorpion. But after his death, Zeus decided to set him in the stars as a constellation. His actual constellation is much more beautiful than he was supposed to be. You can see his bow there..." he pointed... "stretched upward, see it?"

"Yes," Ani said. "I see it."

"Do you ever think about how small we are?" he asked her. "These stars go out for millions of light-years, spooling farther and farther away. Each one of them is massive. And here you and I are, trying to make the lives of four people better. And I can't even do that."

"You *are* making the lives of four people better," Ani told him. "Have patience."

"I really thought I could do this, despite being autistic."

"What makes you think differently today?" she asked, turning her head to look at him lying there. His face looked so sad under the faint light of the moon.

"You saw me," he said. "I froze up. I went mute. That's not okay."

"Why is that no okay? Are you expecting perfection?" she asked.

"Well, I hurt her in the first place," he said, "by not taking the time to notice that she had planted seeds there. So I should have been able to repair it."

She watched his face, silent. He reminded her of herself, of the 'shoulds' that she held over her own head, but it was so incredibly clear to her just then that there was no such thing in this scenario. He had done nothing wrong, nothing intentional to hurt Maria. The older woman had reacted to her own story, to the things that had hurt her in the past. Ani wanted so desperately at that moment for Daniel to be free of self-recrimination. She wanted it because she needed it for herself, and she couldn't bear for him to look so sad.

"Daniel," she said. He looked at her again, catching her with those eyes of his.

She reached over and grabbed his hand. It was warm and dry, calloused. She felt a drift of sparks over her arms and legs at the feel of his skin. *This means nothing*, she told herself. *This is the action of a friend.*

He looked a little startled as she held his hand, but he didn't pull away.

"You didn't do anything wrong," she said. "You handled it well. When you melted down, you could have yelled at her or done something to hurt her further. You didn't. You did well. You are the perfect person for this job. There is nothing irreparable about this. Please believe me."

Daniel's eyes were bottomless as he watched her, listening to her words. Finally, he nodded.

"Thank you," he said.

They lay like that for a long while. Daniel didn't let go of her hand. *This means nothing*, she reminded herself. It was too bad her heart didn't believe her. Daniel told her about the different stars and the stories ancient people had shared about them. He told her about scientific discoveries in Space and the thoughts he had when he looked at the galaxy. She felt him relax, realized his voice was slowing. She grew sleepy, but she wanted to stay there forever with him, listening to all he knew.

After some time, Ani pulled away and walked to pick up the plates Valeria had set aside for them. She had no idea what time it was, but she was starving. She took the food back to the blanket, where Daniel was now sitting up. She handed him one of the plates and sat down with the other one.

"It was so nice of Valeria to set food aside for us," he said, after the first few bites. The food was cold but still delicious.

"How lucky are we that our family includes a grandmother?" Ani asked him. "Someone whose mission in life seems to be to fatten us up?" She blushed a little at her slip-up, the words "our family." This was Daniel's family. At some point, Ani would be gone, and Daniel would be with the Lorias on his own.

"God gives good gifts," Daniel said. "I'm feeling very blessed."

"She was worried that we were going to send them away," Ani said.

"Who? Maria?"

Ani shook her head. "Valeria. But she still wanted to stand up for her grandmother. She has some complicated responsibilities for a twelve-year-old."

"She's outstanding. Why would she worry about us sending them away? We would never do that."

"She doesn't understand the terms yet. This is not about their value or good behavior. They're probably all worried. We'll have to give them a lot of reassurance."

191

Daniel nodded. "I think I understand a little of how she feels. I grew up in foster care. I always worried that families would send me away. And sometimes they did, so the worry didn't exactly go away."

"You grew up in foster care?"

"Yes. I guess I didn't tell you that. I don't talk about it all that much."

Ani felt her heart give a great leap of compassion--she refused to call it love--at the look on his face. "That must have been really hard as an autistic kid."

"It was harder than anything I would ever want another human being to go through," Daniel said quietly. He put his empty plate to one side and reached for Ani's hand again. She gave it to him, wondering if this was a new thing now. What was happening? Her heart thudded like it wanted to burst out of her chest.

"But it's in the past," he said. "And look at me. I have this land, and a new family, and friends like you. A beautiful garden. And you're right. Maybe this is repairable. Thank you."

"You're welcome, friend," she said, giving his hand a squeeze.

"No, really, Ani. Thank you. It means the world to me when people stick around, even when I'm having a hard time."

"I can understand that," she said. What she didn't say was, *You are beginning to mean the world to me.*

CHAPTER THIRTY-ONE

Daniel planned to sneak away and go into town by himself for breakfast, but Ani showed up at his door and, ignoring his protests, marched him up to the Lorias' house. Inside, they found Maria and Valeria laying the table for six as usual. They put down the things they were holding and turned to look at Daniel and Ani.

"I am very sorry for shouting at you," Maria said. "You have done so much for our family."

Daniel took a deep breath, squeezing his hands into fists, trying to stay calm.

"I want you to know that you can always yell at me if I do something wrong," he said. "Although you can also tell me quietly, and I will understand. It doesn't matter what help I have given your family; you are always allowed to tell me."

"So you are not going to send us away?" Maria asked, covering her face with her apron.

"I told you, Abuelita," Valeria said.

"We are a family now," Daniel said. "Nothing will change that. And Maria..." he waited until she lowered the apron and looked at him. "I am very sorry for digging up your seeds. I did not know you had planted them. I would not have done it if I had known. We can go and buy some new ones today."

Maria looked at Valeria, at Ani, and then at Daniel. She nodded. "You are not like the men at the border," she said. "And I am sorry that I said you were."

Daniel let out a breath. He hurt all over. His skin felt raw and exposed to the elements. It had all been too similar to the accusations of the past decade. But he knew he had a responsibility to reassure the Lorias in this vulnerable moment. Leo and Gabriel came in quietly, and the six of them sat at the table eating Maria's delicious food. Daniel was thankful that they had resolved the conflict with apologies and understanding, but he felt like he had been run over by a truck on the highway. People were so hard to understand and it was impossible to plan for their volatility.

He went back to work on the garden beds, digging compost in and spreading straw over them. A few days passed in relative quiet. The kids went to school, Daniel worked at the gardens or around the house. Things were awkward in a way they hadn't been before the altercation over the garden bed.

"The honeymoon is over," Ani said, when he mentioned it to her. She was sitting cross-legged in the grass while he sifted compost with his hands. Daniel was aware that this was how they had been sitting when Maria got so angry. And that was the night when Ani had first held his hand.

"Honeymoon?" He frowned.

"You know, with any adjustment, especially a good one, there is a length of time when everything seems beautiful and amazing, like nothing could go wrong. Things are blissful and so much better than anything that came before. But that time ends as reality comes back in. And reality, in this case, is that these beautiful souls were chased from their country and mistreated along the way. That's why they're with us. And they carry trauma, pain, and so much loss from their tragedy."

Daniel nodded, feeling for more dirt clods. It was soothing to have his hands in the dirt. "I see what you mean. In a way, I feel like the honeymoon has ended for me as well. Is that normal?"

"Of course," Ani murmured. She looked down at her hands. "Is it harder to live with us, now?"

He jerked his head up to look at her. "With you? No! I'm just finding it hard to maintain this level of social activity. I didn't know how much stability I gained from quiet and my own routines. Maybe I was running on a high before, but it seems to be fizzling out."

"That sounds about right," Ani said. "You have been going at a pretty steady pace. When do you go back to work?"

Daniel made a face. "A little over a week and a half. What about you? Is your energy running out?"

Ani tilted her head and looked at him with a slight smile. She had her hair pulled up into a ponytail today, showing off the lovely lines of her neck and shoulders. She had a cup of coffee in one hand and had been taking small sips of it for ages. It must be cold by now, but it didn't seem to bother her.

"I'm feeling a bit of culture shock, mostly," she said. "The Lorias are different than the other families I've worked with. And I miss my parents."

Daniel nodded. "I would love to meet your parents one day," he said, sitting back. "We're done here. The beds are ready to plant."

Maria had some seeds, and over the next couple of days, they worked on planting those, including the ones Daniel had replaced. Then, Lewis invited the whole family to his farm to look through his seed bank and find what they needed.

They went on a glorious Saturday. Everywhere Daniel looked, the trees were blooming or in full leaf, and the sun shone warm on his head as he walked with the others to the Jeep to drive them all to the farm. He and Lewis had cut a hole in the fence between the two properties so they could get to each other's property faster. The drive was bumpy, and they laughed a lot as they were thrown around, but they got there eventually.

At Lewis's, they spread blankets on the ground for a picnic lunch. Lewis brought out food that he and Juliana had made together.

"I'm learning Venezuelan cooking," he said. "I love it. But we need to eat more salads. So much fried or heavily cooked food! My stomach has been complaining."

Ani and Daniel looked at each other. They had wondered how to bring up their need for more fresh vegetables. Maybe it was time for an intervention.

Maria and Juliana were deep in conversation, sitting a little apart on a small hill, gesturing and occasionally looking over at Daniel. He tried not to feel self-conscious, but it was difficult. He knew that Maria needed to process what had happened, and he didn't begrudge her that. But there was a hurt place in his heart from people in the town suspecting him of doing things that Cam had done. The ache had flared up again when Maria said Daniel was like the border guards. Daniel knew he was not like those men. He didn't want to take anything from Maria. He had changed his life around completely to offer a home to her and her family. But the accusation was too similar to the old allegations for there to be no pain in it.

He needed time. When would he have time to process all that was going on? Beside him, Ani nudged him.

"Doing okay?" she asked.

He nodded and tried to smile. It had always been hard for him to pretend things. He felt himself starting to withdraw to protect himself from people seeing emotions he wasn't ready to share. Without a natural way to hide, it was hard to keep some things private and be close to people at the same time. So he withdrew to a little safe place inside. It was what he had always done.

He watched the kids running through the yard beside Lewis's house, shrieking with joy. Manuel and Juliana had only one child, Layla, who was seven, just a little younger than Gabriel. The three kids played well together, and the sight was soothing to Daniel. His own childhood had been so fraught with fear and insecurity. He loved the ability of these children to be real kids, running and shrieking and pretending and climbing. Even these kids who had been

197

through so much already. Daniel prayed that from now on, only healing and goodness would flow into their lives.

After they ate, they sat for a while, soaking in the sun.

"This is something we try to do often," Lewis told them. "I had some European travelers who came to work on my farm for a while, and they taught me about a midday rest after lunch. I think it changes us, this practice of rest. When we only toil and hustle, we behave like parentless people, not acknowledging God's role in taking care of us."

Daniel hadn't thought of it that way. He felt guilty when he rested, to be honest, like if someone came along, he should jump up and start working.

Ani mirrored his thoughts with her words. "It's hard," she said. "I feel bad just sitting here, not doing anything."

"You are doing something," Lewis said. "You are resting."

After some little cups of coffee, Lewis brought them to the room where he kept his seeds, and Maria went through them, looking for what she wanted to grow. She selected peppers and tomatoes, tomatillos and lettuce, carrots, chives, and cilantro. After she was done, Daniel had a look at what was there.

"Persian cooking has a lot of eggplant in it, doesn't it?" he asked Ani. He was thinking about what she had said about missing her culture and her parents.

She was standing by the door, talking with Lewis, and it took her a minute to respond.

"Yes," she said. Daniel identified the look on her face as her surprised look.

"We should grow it, then. We can make Persian food from our own vegetables."

Daniel took the eggplant seeds and chose a few other vegetables. Lewis wouldn't take any money for the seeds, despite their protests that they wanted to pay. They walked back toward the truck in the afternoon. Daniel felt full, sun-warm, and excited to plant their new seeds.

"Are you coming to backyard night?" Daniel asked Lewis right before they left. "You've been promising forever. I can give you a ride."

Lewis smiled. "If you give me a ride, I might actually go. I've been meaning to, but I'm always so tired by that time of day. You can pull me out of my stupor."

"Okay," Daniel said. "I'll pick you up tomorrow at 5:30."

"Deal," Lewis said.

He waved at the kids in the back of the Jeep as they left.

The following day, Daniel took Maria to the little craft store on Oak Street and bought yarn and embroidery thread, needles, and fabric. Maria had confessed how much she missed working with her hands, so Daniel had offered to stock her up with supplies. She was animated in the craft store, speaking to the cashier in Spanish repeatedly, though she could not be understood.

"She says you have so much selection," Daniel said. "But your prices are too high."

The woman's eyebrows shot up. "Tell her this is just the way in this country," she said. "So much of everything you could ever want, but you pay dearly for it. Was it cheaper in her country?"

Daniel translated. Maria went into a flurry of explanation, telling the clerk how much each thing would have cost in Venezuela, while the cashier expressed her awe.

"I must go there one day," she said.

A shadow crossed Maria's face. "Yes," she said. "You should. But you must row on the surface of the waters, like a tourist, and do not dive down deep."

The clerk nodded, her face serious, then rang up all the items. Daniel paid, thinking that he had never spent so much money in such a short time in his life. He looked at Maria's shining face. He had never been happier about the way he spent his money, either.

"Let's go," he told the older woman. "I need to pick up my mail, and then we should get home."

"Yes," she said. "I need to start knitting your sweater."

CHAPTER THIRTY-TWO

Daniel got out of the car at the post office and just stood there for a moment. It felt strange to be there, as though he was meant to go in for a shift. It had been a place of comfort for him for many years, but it didn't quite feel like *him* anymore. He leaned down to the open window.

"Do you want to come in?" he asked Maria.

"No," she said. "I think I'll sit here."

"Okay. This should only take a moment."

Inside, everything was wrong. The walls, which had been covered in Daniel's posters of the galaxy, were bare. Daniel's co-worker, Jackie, wore a sour expression when she saw him.

"Hi, Jackie," Daniel said. He felt frozen, suspended in time. "What happened to my pictures?"

"Oh," she said. She had never liked him much. Daniel didn't know why. "I took them down."

He took a step forward. "You are not the postmaster," he said. "I am."

"I took photos of them and sent them to the main office in Los Angeles," she said, "and they agreed with me that it was high time those posters came off the walls. They're not protocol, you know."

"But..." Daniel started. He could feel his fists starting to clench at his sides and his jaw tightening until it seemed locked up. He forced the words out. "The regional manager said she liked the way it gave our little post office personality. She said that Aveline was such a unique town that it made sense for the post office to be different, to be interesting. And no customer had ever complained."

"Yes," Jackie said. "But the main office disagreed." She shrugged.

"Where did you put them?" Daniel asked. Jackie walked over to Daniel's desk and retrieved a box from underneath it. She straightened and shoved it across the counter toward him. He looked and saw that she had not taken the posters from the walls gently. They were all torn, ripped at the edges or even down the middle.

She stared at him, and Daniel was so confused about what to do with such malice that he started backing away. He felt a hand on his arm, a presence beside him, and he jumped, but it was only Maria, who had come and found him.

"What is it?" she asked. "And why does the woman look as though she has tasted five-day-old beans?"

Maria's presence, her lightness, helped Daniel come back into himself a bit.

"We speak English in this country," Jackie said loudly, huffing a sigh. Daniel stared. What had happened to her? She had never been his friend or particularly nice, even, but she hadn't been like this.

"We speak many languages in this country," he said. "It's one of the beautiful things about us."

He walked over to his post office box and opened it up, wanting just to get out of there and away from Jackie's poison. There was a stack of mail inside the box. Daniel frowned. As a rule, he didn't get much mail. He had canceled most junk mail, and he got his bills by email. But there more than a dozen letters in his box.

Daniel pulled them out and read his name in handwriting on the top envelope. He opened it and pulled out a sheet of paper. Just one word was scrawled on the paper: COMMUNIST.

He stared at it, mute. His heart was beginning to pound, and he felt heat in his ears, his throat. He knew hate mail. He had received it for years, in the days before, the life before.

"Someone has sent you angry mail?" Maria murmured.

"How did you know?" he asked, startled.

"I can read this word," she said. "And I know this angry writing."

"What do you mean? You know who wrote this?" Daniel's brain felt sluggish and slow. He couldn't quite process this. He felt plunged back into something he thought was only in his old life. Who would do this? Who would write communist on a piece of paper and send it to him?

"No, I don't know who wrote it, but this kind of writing. Angry writing. Angry faces. Angry voices. They are all the same. Quick angry fire, black marker scrawled on a paper."

Daniel shook himself and put the pile of mail on top of the posters in his box. He turned to look at Maria's face.

"I am sorry about the angry faces and voices," he said.

She shrugged. "If I hadn't seen them, do you think I would be here?" she asked. "It is always easier to stay home. I would have stayed home."

She sighed, and Daniel thought that it was time for both of them to get back to El Refugio, to get out from under the public gaze, to hide in the shade of their trees.

"Okay, Jackie," Daniel said. "I'm heading out. See you when I come back to work."

There was only silence from Jackie. Daniel left with Maria leaning heavily on his arm. She was tired. He opened the passenger door, shoved the box into the center of the bench seat, and then stepped back to let her inside. As he walked around the car, Daniel felt exposed, like a stadium of people was watching them. He imagined faces behind all the windows on the street. He needed to get them home. He slid into his seat and sat with his hands resting on the steering wheel for a moment before he started the ignition.

CHAPTER THIRTY-THREE

As the car tires crunched up the gravel driveway, Daniel felt a sense of great relief. He helped Maria out of the car and carried her new craft supplies up the stairs and into her kitchen. It seemed that she had already forgotten the hate mail. She showed Leo her new things, telling him all about the craft supply store.

Daniel left the house quietly, glad for her happiness. He checked his watch and saw that he only had a couple hours before he needed to pick Lewis up for backyard night. Honestly, Daniel was in no state to be social. He pulled the box of torn posters and hate mail out of the car and put it on his porch, then stood there looking at it, trying to decide what to do next. He needed clarity and could feel the beginning of a massive meltdown. His ears were ringing and his jaw was clenched.

He jumped into the Jeep and started driving, turning right at the end of the driveway to go farther around the lake.

The emotions bubbled up, and Daniel shouted a stream of words as he drove. None of this was fair. None of this was his fault. Daniel wanted something. What did he want? He wanted out. He wanted no more. Eventually, he started to calm down, and he found that he was crying.

He followed the road that curved around the lake, letting his mind empty and then start to hover over different memories, different thoughts. This worked sometimes, the random selection of thoughts keeping him from dwelling on one thing too long. Occasionally he was able to figure things out if he let himself drift.

He could see his surroundings again. The sun was like a thousand diamonds on the surface of the water. Soon Daniel was passing through his favorite section of the road, where jacaranda trees on either side formed a tunnel with the late afternoon light filtering into it, turning everything gold and purple. People drove from all over to see the long archway of purple. Daniel sighed.

For so many years, he had worked in that post office under suspicion of doing terrible things. And though many people had magnanimously tried to look past what they believed were his crimes, Daniel had always felt the malice of their mistaken beliefs. They believed lies, and lies were a thing you could taste and feel. When someone tried to overlook something about you that they actually believed, you could feel it. It didn't feel pure. It felt like oily friendship, something clinging and more about how that person wanted to be perceived.

Thinking about it made him angry all over again at the

injustice. He felt that old helpless feeling. He didn't want it anymore. He had thought he could be free of it. Would he ever be free? Would he always be an easy mark because of his neurology? And Jackie! What a betrayal. He inhaled a sharp breath at the sting of it. Jackie had taken the thing that Daniel loved, the way he had personalized that place and made it different from any other. She had so heartlessly torn his collection down.

Daniel kept driving. Soon enough, he was at the junction of the highway and the lake road, almost back where he had begun. He drove through the town and back out to his property, taking the short route through Lewis's land. He found Lewis standing at his front gate, looking up at the sky, which had begun to take on the colors of sunset.

"I was beginning to think you had forgotten," Lewis said as he climbed into the cab of the truck.

"Sorry," Daniel said. "I went for a drive, and it went longer than I thought it would."

"Everything okay?" Lewis asked.

"No, not really," Daniel said. He told Lewis what had happened, and words kept tumbling out of his mouth as he explained about the posters and the letters.

"And I feel this sickness in my stomach," he told Lewis. "That feeling I used to get when someone made a big deal about being nice to me even though I was a suspicious character. The only thing that seemed to help was getting away from everybody, staying away, so I didn't need to feel their lies, their ideas about me. But I don't want to be a hermit, either. Do you know what I mean?"

Lewis was silent. When Daniel looked back over, he saw that Lewis was smiling a little, but it did not look like Lewis's happy smile.

"I do know," Lewis said. "You've just described something that is very similar to what racism feels like. You're right. It is possible to tell when someone thinks they are a big person for being your friend. It's not a good feeling. It means that they believe the bad stuff, and they think they are amazing because they still treat you well."

Daniel felt a sensation of falling inside. He could cry. He felt pressed down to the very earth. "I thought I was beyond this," he said. "I thought that being suspected was over. It feels too hard to keep going with all the eyes on me, all the anger."

"I will never get away from it or be beyond it," Lewis said, softly. "It's hard to know what is worse, feeling the sting of people who openly hate you for what you are and their perceived ideas of you? Or the false friendship of self-congratulating people?"

"What do you do about it?" Daniel asked.

"Nothing to do. I'm finished with trying to convince people of my worth," Lewis said. "It's a waste of breath. Mostly I'm working on building a group of friends who are different. Like you and Ani, or—I hope—the men at backyard night. My volunteers. The Mendozas. Then I try to ignore everyone else. No one gets to decide my worth." Lewis was quiet for a few moments. "And I have my own business," he said. "I work for myself. I always knew I wanted to do it. At least then I can interact with people on my own terms." Lewis smiled over at Daniel. "Thanks for listening," he said. "I appreciate it."

"Thank you for pulling me out of my self-pity."

"I wouldn't call it self-pity," Lewis said. "You've had it rough. But you get to choose freedom. I try to think about freedom every single day when I wake up. I don't live for other people's ideas of me. And I know this all feels the same, but try to remember that before, people were judging you for something you didn't do. Now, they are judging you for something you did do. You sponsored the Lorias. Would you take that back if it meant people wouldn't judge you?"

"Never," Daniel said, shocked at the very idea. Lewis was right. His body and mind processed the anger in the same way, but it was completely different this time around.

They were on Francisco's street now, and Daniel parked the Jeep, his mind still processing what Lewis had said about working for himself. It was about choice, Daniel realized. Lewis could choose when and where he came under the scrutiny of people around him.

As they walked through the fence door into Francisco's back yard, Daniel had that slightly nervous, expectant feeling he often got before backyard night. He remembered how hard it had been for him to come the first time and glanced at Lewis to see how he was taking it, but Lewis seemed at ease, a smile on his face.

They were the last ones to arrive. At the sight of Daniel and Lewis, the other men broke into applause.

"What's this for?" Daniel asked when the clapping ended. "Is it because Lewis came?"

"Finally," George said, standing and clapping Lewis on the back. "Welcome, brother. But no, it's for the two of you, two single men who have taken refugee families straight into your lives. We felt that it deserved at least a round of applause. These weeks must have been intense for you."

Daniel found an empty chair and drew it closer to the fire. "I feel that Ani deserves a round of applause more than I do," he said.

Sheldon burst out laughing, and Sam handed him a ten-dollar bill. Daniel stared at them.

"I bet Sam ten dollars that you would say exactly that," Sheldon said. "You know, Danny, you can take credit for something you have done, even if you feel that someone else deserves it more. Both of you can have credit. It doesn't have to be either/or."

"It's true," Lewis said, leaning back in his chair and holding up a hand. "I'll take whatever I can get. These have been some of the most intense weeks of my life."

"Oh," Daniel said. "Then, thank you."

"And... let's welcome Lewis," Frankie said. "Welcome! We've been waiting for you to join us."

Lewis nodded in response. "I'm glad to be here. It's important to me."

He glanced at Daniel, and Daniel knew he was referring to what they had talked about in the car. Daniel almost told everyone about the conversation but remembered one of his hard-earned rules just in time. If someone says something to you in private, don't talk about it in public until they bring it up first.

He looked around at the group, listening as everyone talked about their experiences of the week. He accepted a soda with lemon and ate a burger when it was handed to him. He felt much better, warm and at ease. Lewis was right. This was important. He didn't have anything written for this life; he didn't have the rituals for what was happening, like with his old life. His things in the post office helped him deal with the difficulties his old job presented. He needed rituals and practices to support his new life. Maybe this was one of them.

CHAPTER THIRTY-FOUR

Ani sat in Mercy's comfortable home, trying to stop fretting about the Lorias by themselves at home. Women's circle and backyard night had fallen on the same night, and though Ani knew that Maria and Leo were grown people who had managed to cross several countries on their own, she was reluctant to leave them. Daniel hadn't even shown up after he took Maria shopping, so Ani couldn't tell him about her worries. Valeria hadn't allowed Ani to stay home, though, growing increasingly fierce until Ani fled the house, shaking her head, hands up in defeat.

The women had switched nights for Faith. As a therapist, she was doing so much these days, in charge of much of the counseling for the new families. Tonight was the only evening that had worked for her.

Mercy was talking. Ani sat with her glass of wine, and one foot tucked up under her on the cushy chair. She rested her other leg on the soft ottoman and massaged her thigh with one hand. She was so cozy she might fall asleep.

"It's going smoothly for the three simple cases," Mercy was saying. "At least, there are no more bumps than usual. But, Ani, despite all our research, the DHS is going to try to make an example out of the Lorias."

"What?" Ani said. Her heart began to race. "Why would they do that? Why waste time on punitive measures toward such a vulnerable family?"

"We don't know exactly, but we think it's political. They need to show that although they've opened up the doors to refugees, they're not pushovers."

Pain bloomed in Ani's chest. This, of all things, was the part of the job she hated the most--the posturing of bureaucracies and governments, as though they had something to prove about not being kinder than they should. Meanwhile, people were dying. Maybe it came from being an immigrant herself, someone who had left one country where she already had two identities-- Armenian and Iranian, but Ani could only partially understand this fierce adherence to the invisible lines of borders. Within herself, there were already bridges between three nations and multiple languages. Ani wrestled with her identities and faces every day. She felt that the country could do the same. They could be welcoming and secure, diverse and unified.

"They pose no threat," she said.

"No," Mercy said. "They don't. Nothing could be farther from it. This is where the rules make no sense. But we will fight for them with everything we have."

"Can I ask a favor?" Faith asked. She was lying on her back on the living room rug, a cloth draped over her eyes. "Can we skip the shop talk? I mean, I know we need to process. I need to process a crazy amount. But as far as actual plans and strategies go, can we leave them outside tonight? I need to just sit with other women and *be*."

"Of course," Mercy said. "Are you ever going to get off the floor?"

"Never," Faith replied.

Mercy shook her head and walked back out to the kitchen just as the front door opened. Theresa and Katie walked into the room, followed by Juanita, Dorothy, and Lucy. After a few minutes, Ingrid and Zoe came in as well, bringing the fragrance of night-flowering trees with them. Despite her what she had told her mother, Faith peeled herself off the floor and greeted the others with hugs. Ani felt stuck to her chair, unsure if she should get up and greet the others. But they didn't leave her long to wonder, coming to hug her where she sat. Once everyone was there and snacking on the wine, crackers, and cheese that Mercy put out on the table, Faith started with prayer.

"God of all, I am exhausted. There's too much in the world that is simply not right. I want to run far away, sometimes. All I can say is, please help. Help us to have what we need to do this work. We need miracles and waterfalls and joy and strength. Help us to be good to one another. Amen."

Ani found herself wiping tears away from her cheeks. Faith had somehow vocalized exactly what Ani was feeling, and into the shape of prayer, too. Ani felt that maybe she had never been quite that honest with God. Perhaps she should think about it.

"Well," Theresa said. "We're here. We've still got all our limbs. That's good."

Ani smiled, and there were laughs and smiles from around the living room. Ani took a moment simply to soak it all in. Mercy's beautiful home, cozy and colorful. The faces of the women in the soft light. The art on the walls. Ani thought of her little house, still undecorated. But what could she do with so little time? It never seemed like there was a point to decorating when she never stayed anywhere long.

Thinking this way gave Ani that feeling of despair again. Would she ever fit in anywhere? Was the depth of suffering she had seen too much to ever allow her to relax? She remembered times in the past when she had allowed herself to soften, to sink into the idea of goodness, of friendship. And then those "friends" had broken things off because of a lack of shared interests, another way to say that Ani was simply too intense.

Ani didn't know how to be restrained *and* allow herself to feel her feelings. As soon as she did, grief at the sorrow of the world hit her like a car crash.

She looked at the other women in the room. To be honest, they weren't like women Ani had met before. They had depth and honesty to them that was different. Many of them were fully committed to the refugee sponsorship project. And they seemed to know how to experience joy. Ani felt a rush of longing. She wanted that.

Juanita was talking. "I will start another, Spanish

language, women's circle next week. I thought it might be an easier way to bring our newcomers into our community. Less intimidating for them. Less learning for them to do. They are already flooded. Carlo will start something similar with the men. And of course, anyone who wants more practice with their Spanish is welcome to join."

Amanda had been right, Ani realized. Venezuelan refugees were perfect for this town.

They started going around the room, each of them sharing about life lately. Ingrid shared first. She had a minor support role for the sponsorship project, offering her coffee shop as a place to sit and look through job listings and stuff like that. The weeks had been okay for her, she told them.

"But I am lonely lately, and I wonder if there is someone out there for me." Faith and Zoe were nodding.

Ani spoke without meaning to. "Do you think there is someone for everyone?"

"I hope so," Zoe said.

"I don't even know what that means," Faith said. "I mean, I want love sometimes, but then I know how difficult I can be —don't say anything, Mom." They all laughed. "And I don't want to change. So I insist I will be single for the rest of my life. But then I get lonely."

"What do you think, Mercy?" Ani asked.

"Oh, I don't really know," Mercy said. "I think the person you are with is the person for you. But there are seasons in marriage, and the person you start with is not the person you are with twenty or thirty years later. You need to keep choosing that person."

Juanita was nodding along. "I agree," she said.

Dorothy and Lucy looked at each other. "And there is the other side," Dorothy said. "Death or the loss of a long relationship. Nothing is as simple as someone for everyone."

A long time ago, Ani had decided to close the door to relationships. No man she had ever dated had understood or wanted her to keep pursuing her work. Meeting Daniel was the first thing that had even remotely tempted her to open that door again. But it all seemed impossible. How could she know? How could she know if he was her person?

The women were looking at her. She hadn't heard what had been said.

"What?" she asked. "I asked how it's going at your place," Katie told her. "Your turn to share, if you like."

CHAPTER THIRTY-FIVE

A ni felt the heat rise to her face. "I'm sorry," she said. "I was lost in thought." After thinking about home and Daniel possibly being her person, she couldn't quite organize her thoughts. Her face continued to blaze as she tried her best to answer the question.

"It's going well," she said. "As well as can be expected. We had a few setbacks, and I think maybe Daniel and I..." she stammered over his name, "need to find what boundaries feel best for us. Maria would cook every meal for us if she could, but we're starting to realize that we need a little more space. I mean," she stumbled, "not space together. Space apart."

She looked up from where she was playing with her hands. All the women were staring at her. Theresa had a slight smile on her face and a look in her eyes that made Ani narrow her eyes.

Ingrid leaned forward. "You and Daniel currently eat all your meals with the Lorias?"

Ani nodded. "Maria is a great cook, and it seems to help her a lot to cook for us. It settles her, somehow. Makes her feel more at home."

"Is it awkward with Daniel?" Zoe asked.

"Awkward?" Ani shifted in her seat. Had she given too much away with her words or tone of voice?

"Because he doesn't talk?"

Ani stared. "What do you mean? We talk all the time."

Zoe gestured to the room. "Well, we all know Daniel from the post office, and he's notorious for never talking. We have tried over the years to draw him out, but it never worked. Theresa is friends with him, but she is the only one."

"He talks to me," Theresa said. "And to some men. But Zoe's right. He's been known as someone who never talks to women."

"I thought he was known as the postmaster—the guy you talk to."

"We talk to him," Lucy said. "He doesn't talk back."

"Does it have anything to do with the last years and the suspicion around him?" Ani asked.

Faith nodded. "Maybe. But still, he doesn't talk much to me, even though that's all over. I find it interesting that he finds talking to you so easy."

Lucy laughed. "No matchmaking, Faith."

"That's rich coming from you, Lucy," Faith retorted, grinning.

Ani's face was ablaze, like a furnace, like it was going to burst into flames.

"I don't know if it's matchmaking," Mercy said. "Looks to

me like a match in progress; we don't even have to do any making."

"I don't think that's how that phrase works, Mom," Faith said.

"Wait a minute," Ani said. "I'm not looking for a relationship. I actually can't have one. I've tried in the past, and men don't understand my work. They always think I'm putting too much attention on my clients and no enough on them. So I've gotten used to being single. I think it's my path."

All those wonderful women. All those eyes. None of them showing any sign of believing her words. Theresa's eyes were narrowed on Ani until they were nearly shut.

They went into the dining room to eat. Ani grabbed her cane as she went. She'd slipped yesterday, and it had been a bad day for her leg today. Lucy thoughtfully got her a chair with a footstool, and then the women made a big fuss about Katie being comfortable.

"I'm not even showing yet," Katie laughed.

"Let us!" Dorothy said, putting a pillow behind Katie's back. "We need to fuss."

It was Mercy's night to cook, and she had set a feast on the table, along with more wine. There was the first course of beet and feta salad, a roasted cauliflower soup, and a final course of pasta with roasted chicken and a sprinkling of parmesan and rosemary.

"Mercy, did you make all this?" Ani asked as her whole body began to feel the pleasant buzz of food satisfaction. "When did you find the time?"

"I cook for pleasure," Mercy said. "Usually, George and I

cook together in the evenings, unwinding from the day. It's such a sensory experience, and it can help me so much with letting all the mental work of the day go. And women's circle is when I really cut loose and go fancy with recipes I've been wanting to try."

"Either fancy," Faith said, "or fully southern. Mama has no in-between."

"I grew up with excellent food," Ani said, "and I can cook, but I've never *loved* to cook. I've been trying to get my mom to visit. She makes amazing Persian food."

"Yum," Katie said.

"Show of hands, who likes to cook?" Zoe asked. "My hand is down."

Around the table, the women laughed. Katie put her hand up, and Juanita asked, "Still, Katie?" after putting her own hand up.

"If I didn't still love it, I couldn't do the work I do," Katie said. "Although I can't handle any raw meat these days. I have to get the others to do it." Ani shuddered; she wouldn't be able to handle the endless cooking of running a cafe. Ingrid had her hand up. Mercy did, of course, and Theresa had her hand up. Zoe, Faith, and Ani had their hands down.

"To be honest," Faith said. "I just haven't focused on food. I'm open to it. I grew up with good food and resisted all attempts to get me into cooking. But someday, I could find my way toward making food."

"Uh, uh, not me," Zoe said, shaking her head. "My dream is to meet and marry someone who cooks."

"What about Lewis?" Faith asked. "He cooks." Then she

ducked her head, laughing, as Zoe gave her a look that could sear wood.

"You're just saying that because you know I cannot stand the man," Zoe said.

"What?" Ani said. "Really?"

"They got off on the wrong foot," Faith said, laughing.

"Oh, no, we got off on the only foot. There is no better foot. The man is a terrible human being. I wish he would move away."

She adjusted her statement when she saw the looks on Ani and Mercy's faces. "Okay, okay, I know he's good for the town, with his farm and sponsoring the Mendozas and all that. He just needs to stay far away from me."

Interesting. Almost without thinking, Ani spoke. "Daniel actually tried to set Lewis and me up," she said.

Immediately, all heads swiveled toward Ani.

"But Lewis and I set him straight. It was awkward for a while, though."

Mercy stood, shaking her head. "Y'all young folk are beyond me. All kinda strange things going on here and no one being honest with anyone."

Faith made an "O" with her mouth as her mother went to grab dessert from the kitchen.

"Y'all made Mama go back to Alabama," she said quietly, "You done drove her over the edge."

"I heard that!" Mercy called from the kitchen. Everyone erupted in peals of laughter, the tension forgotten. But Ani considered those words for the rest of the night. All kinda strange things going on here, and no one being honest with anyone. Was Ani being honest?

CHAPTER THIRTY-SIX

Ani sat at the breakfast table in the big house, holding her face over her mug, breathing in the fragrance of strong, hot coffee. This morning was a coffee morning. Her usual tea wouldn't cut it, as last night's women circle had gone on far later than Ani usually stayed out. It had been good. Very good. Over the course of the evening, Ani had stopped wondering whether she fit in. The point of the group didn't seem to be about fitting in. It was about being themselves and appreciating each other for it. When Ani looked around the table, she saw very different women. Ingrid, a coffee shop owner. Katie, a previous corporate worker who owned a cafe and loved her niece, still struggled with anxiety at times, and was pregnant with her first child. Theresa, an autistic potter who seemed to celebrate her differences fully and was dating a man who not infrequently wore suspenders and a fedora. Mercy, who had lost her son to police brutality, and Faith, who had lost her brother, two beautiful, strong, and vulnerable Black women who never held back their opinions and didn't let people tell them they were wrong for having them. Juanita, so kind and fiercely loving, Zoe an almost intimidatingly brilliant Black professor, Lucy, a Thai-American woman who could run the town if she had the chance, Dorothy, a woman experiencing a second chance at life. They were such a blend of people and backgrounds. And then there was Ani. Who was Ani?

A woman who had experienced trauma and illness as a child, survived it, and gone on to find her purpose, serving people who were displaced and had experienced trauma. She had seen many sad things. But then, so had Mercy and Faith, a civil rights lawyer and a psychologist. And so had Theresa, who had been a victim of sexual violence and had her disability taken advantage of. Ani didn't even know about the suffering of the others. At some point in the evening, she had stopped thinking of herself as other. She had relaxed, and laughed, and taken their teasing about Daniel, which only grew as the evening went on. She suspected they did it more because she was so obviously flustered by it.

Daniel seemed on edge this morning. Ani watched as he sat turning his coffee mug in circles rather than drinking from it. She heard Maria and Valeria chatting as they cooked. Light from the kitchen window streamed onto the table, illuminating the steam rising from the cup and lighting the side of his face. He was beautiful. She didn't think it was just her own bias. He had those hazel eyes, square cheekbones, dark eyelashes, defined jaw. There was something so golden about him, like he was made of gold, the darker gold of honey.

He had spoken and was now looking at her. Ani had no idea what he had said. How embarrassing.

She cleared her throat. "What?"

He smiled his gentle smile that puckered at the edges of his mouth. "Still half asleep?" he asked.

It was a good way out. "Yes," she said. "We talked for so long last night, and then someone turned some music on, and we danced. I don't normally dance, but I did last night."

"That sounds fun," he said. "We didn't dance."

"Oh right, backyard night. Was it good? How did Lewis find it? Oh, that reminds me. I met someone who hated Lewis last night."

Daniel raised his eyebrows. "Zoe?"

"Yes," Ani said. "How'd you know?"

"She ranted to me about it a few times. He insulted her somehow; neither of them will say how. It's pretty intriguing."

"Also, the other women said you don't talk," Ani said. "Which I found odd because you and I always talk."

She felt the heat rise into her face again. That had sounded way more flirtatious than she meant.

He nodded. "It's true, I didn't talk much at my old job. And I kept my after-work activities to playing in the band and going to backyard night. Maybe people haven't really heard me talk much." He looked at her. "You're easy to talk to. A lot of people make it way too hard to talk."

"In what way?" she asked, curious.

Valeria and Maria laid the plates around the table, then served the dishes, Maria shouting for Leo and Gabriel as she did so. Ani had already volunteered to help and been shooed away with a cup of coffee. Now Maria poured her a second cup. Breakfast was *arepas* and beans and vegetables.

"You don't ask too many hard-to-answer questions," Daniel said. "You just start talking, and the things you talk about are easy to answer, so I find it easy to respond. You don't ask "How are you?"" and stuff like that all the time.

Ani thought about this. She thought it was a cultural thing, actually, to just jump into a conversation. Her parents and their friends did it all the time. If it made it easier for Daniel to talk to her, she was glad for it. Other people had found it off-putting.

"Is that why it's easy for you to talk to Theresa, too?" she asked. "Because she just starts talking and doesn't do all the introductory stuff?"

Daniel cocked his head and seemed to think about it. "Probably," he said. "But the thing about Theresa is that she decided we needed to be friends when we were younger, and she just wouldn't quit."

He translated for the others, who were all seated at the table now. It was something Ani really liked about Daniel. He had a natural inclination not to leave anyone out, something that couldn't be said for everyone, she felt she could confirm after years of being left in the dust because her leg slowed her down.

She ate some of her vegetables and beans. "What were you thinking about earlier, when you were so deep in thought?"

He looked up at her from his food. "I'm supposed to go

back to work on Monday. I have to decide whether I want to."
He translated, as usual.

Ani inhaled a piece of corn and went into a coughing fit.
"I'm sorry," she said when she could breathe again. "I just
didn't realize it was even an option for you not to go back."

Maria was nodding. "Yes," she said. "This is a good
thought. Don't go back there to that woman and those letters."

Daniel translated absentmindedly, looking at Maria
thoughtfully.

"What letters?" Ani asked. He didn't answer, taking a sip
of his coffee and frowning. Ani assumed it was cold. "Daniel.
What letters?"

"Hmm? I forgot about them, actually. The last time I
went to the post office, there was a stack of mail with writing
that I can only describe as 'angry.' I haven't opened most of
them yet."

Maria snorted. "You had better not."

Ani felt her heart sinking. She had hoped that they were
past the resistance to the new families. "Never mind the
letters. You're seriously thinking about quitting?"

Daniel nodded.

"Would you have to get a new job?"

"Eventually," he said. "For now, I'm okay. I have some
investments. I'd like to really get the garden going. And be
here for all of you."

Ani couldn't exactly describe what happened in her heart
when Daniel said those words. *Be here for all of you.* What
was this feeling in her throat? She jumped up to get the
coffee pot, pouring a new cup and switching it out for

Daniel's, taking the cup right out of his hand and putting the hot coffee on the table in front of him. "Here," she said. "Yours was cold."

His face was faintly surprised. "Thank you," he said. He stared at it for a full thirty seconds, though, before taking a sip.

"You can keep helping us with our homework," Valeria said. Daniel smiled at her. "You barely need any help at all, clever girl," he said.

Valeria beamed at him.

"You seem..." Ani started. How should she say this best? "A little fuzzy around the edges."

Daniel translated, and Maria and Leo laughed. "That's a nice way to put it," Leo said. "Where are you today, Daniel?" he asked.

"I guess I don't exactly know what is supposed to happen next," Daniel answered. "I really don't want to go back to work. The thought feels like it will make me sick. Like that job is some old food that no one should be eating, least of all me. It was my life at one point, but it is not my life anymore."

"You can help me," Ani said. "With the immigration cases. We'll need some extra hands."

"Doing what?"

"I'll find something."

The sun slanted through the kitchen window onto a pitcher of orange juice at the center of the table. Light caught at the edges of Daniel's lips, at the creases of Maria's shirt, at Valeria's dark curls. Everything seemed made of light, actually.

Daniel very intentionally put his hands down on either side of his plate. "That settles it, then," he said. "If you need help, it's the last reason I need to not go back to work." He smiled, suddenly, dazzling her with his sudden joy. "I feel a dozen years younger, saying that. I feel like I could dance. Want to?"

Ani laughed. "We have no music."

"Ah, true. Well, another time, then."

"I don't really dance, remember?"

"I do," Daniel said. "I'll teach you."

CHAPTER THIRTY-SEVEN

The feeling in Daniel's heart each morning, when he stepped out of bed, seemed impossible. He made his bed and brushed his teeth, went out to sweep his porch and do his stretches, and all the while, joy! Joy! What a thing it was to have so much excitement for each day. Had he even been living before? What were all those posters about in the post office? Just a way into another universe? Now he had found his way into the universe he had always wanted: family.

He warned himself, tried to guard his wayward, happy heart. He knew about relationships. There were heartbreaks ahead. But he told himself he could handle them. With a family, he could do anything.

The garden progressed. Maria, Leo, and Daniel weeded and tended while Ani was off at work with Francisco and Mercy, and the kids were at school. They pulled every single weed out and mulched the beds with straw Daniel bought from Lewis. Tomato plants had started sprouting, along with kale and cabbage. Lewis loved the neatness of their garden.

"I don't have time to make things look like this," he said, crossing his arms as he stood next to Daniel at the end of one lovely afternoon. Daniel could hear the school bus arriving in the distance and knew that soon the kids would run down the driveway, their backpacks flopping against their backs. They would be tired and hungry and happy. School was going well for them, and they, at least, didn't get any angry notes. The other kids seemed pretty down-to-earth about having new friends to hang out with.

"You're also not autistic," Daniel said, grinning. "But it's not even all me. Maria was a gardener, you know? We still squabble over how to do things. Sometimes I want to do things I've read about or heard about, and she wants to do things she knows and has done a hundred times. And the looks she gives me!"

Lewis laughed. "I love that picture. The two of you trying to agree. Danny, she's fierce!"

Daniel couldn't help laughing himself. "But it really is tricky. Her knowledge is from a different climate, different soil. I can imagine you or I would struggle if we went to a whole different climate and had to make our gardens work."

Lewis rubbed his hands together. "I can only dream of Venezuelan soil!" he said.

"According to Maria, you would also have to deal with the bugs and fungus. Oh, wait. Don't listen to me—she'll tell you."

Maria was marching toward them with her customary

stomp, eyes on the ground, cup of coffee in one hand. Daniel
didn't know how it was even possible to drink as much coffee
as this small woman did in a day. Once he had suggested she
drink something else, and she gave him a look that would
have shriveled his stomach if he didn't know her by now.

Lewis raised a hand when she got close, and she stopped
and looked at him, then continued walking, letting herself
into the gate and plopping herself onto a stool next to the bed
one over from Daniel.

"Hola, Lewis," she said after a moment. Then in Spanish,
under her breath, "Am I going to have to listen to two men tell
me how to garden?"

Daniel felt a pang of regret when he heard her. It was
true that he was joking about squabbling with her, and that
gardening in this climate was new to her. But was that how
he made her feel? Like a man trying to tell her how to
garden?

"*Lo siento,* Maria," he told her. "I will not tell you about
gardening anymore. You teach me."

He translated for Lewis, who nodded enthusiastically.
"I've been asking Manuel a bit about his farm and wanting to
hear more about your house and garden at home."

Daniel held his breath. Maria and Leo never spoke of
home. Valeria sometimes did by accident, then stopped
herself. And Gabriel sometimes did, thoughtlessly, effortlessly. Ani and Daniel caught the jewels he threw out and
held them close.

But what would Maria do now? There was a long silence
as she pulled weeds between the tomatillos that were

233

springing out of the earth. Lewis sat on the ground beside Daniel and squished dirt between his fingers the way Daniel was doing, dispersing the clumps and tossing stones to one side.

After a long, dreamy silence, Maria began to speak.

"Our house was small, but we didn't mind. Leo and I were both farmers from when we were small. Our parents made the earth sing with flowers and food. We had one son, and he grew up to be a professor. He didn't seem to mind that we were only farmers; he always came home to visit. Later he came with the woman who would become his wife. I was worried about his wife because you don't know what a new daughter will be like, whether she will come between you and your son, but she was like another child to me from the very beginning. The very first day she came over, she planted the corn with me. I could hardly believe it. She was a teacher, too, with a lovely dress. But she came out with me and asked me what she should do. She had never worked with plants before. I showed her the way my mother had shown me. 'And your son?' she asked. 'How do I help him grow?'"

Maria paused to wipe her eyes with her apron. When she lifted the cloth from her face, there was a smear of dirt on her temple. Daniel barely dared to breathe. He wasn't translating for Lewis. He hoped Lewis was catching most of it with his beginner Spanish, but Daniel was also trying to commit it to memory, to share with the others later. He realized, suddenly, that Ani had come home and was standing with her arms draped over the fence post.

There, in the garden, four people from such different

places, all of them sharing a moment so deep and true and painful that it felt like the garden had become sacred ground, holier than a cathedral.

"I told her that she only needed to listen to him and love him," Maria continued. "Pedro, my son, was always someone who needed to be understood. She did it. She was such a good daughter. They got married, and later, they brought the kids for weekends and holidays. Valeria always loved running in the garden, barefoot. Gabriel loved holding the dirt in his hands, the way you're doing, Daniel, letting it run through his fingers, clumping it together into shapes when it was wet. They ate beans before they were ripe, and when they were around, I never got a ripe tomato—they were like birds, collecting them straight into their mouths from the vine. We were there together when we got the news that their parents had been taken and shot. I didn't know how to tell them..."

She dissolved into sobs, and Ani, who had tears streaming down her face, ran through the gate to sit beside Maria. The older woman collapsed onto Ani's shoulder, wailing into her neck. After a few minutes, Daniel heard the front door of the house open and saw Leo standing there, his hair sticking up slightly, as though he had been napping. The older man walked slowly down the steps and toward them.

Maria looked up at Daniel, her eyes wild. "And what could I do? Stay there—where the most beautiful people in the world were killed? Where the children's parents were killed? My home had become a nightmare. We heard that the police were looking for the children, so we ran. We took everything we could carry. It wasn't much. And when we heard the rumors that grandparents were not allowed to cross with their grandchildren, we lied. And here we are, and I don't understand this dirt, the color of it, or why it does not grow things the way I know. And there are letters in the mail, and people tell us they don't know if we will be allowed to stay. I do not like this place yet; I only ever wanted to stay on my farm. We built that home from nothing. But where do we go when home is not safe? We had nowhere to go."

By the time this stream of words had finished, Leo was there, walking through the open gate to take his wife into his arms. She went to him, crying and talking, and he patted her head and back, murmuring little words and humming to her. He smiled such a sad, tired smile at them that Daniel felt his eyes well up again.

"I will take her back to the room," he said. "She needs to rest. The grief goes on and on, never-ending sorrow."

"Daniel and I will make dinner," Ani said, and Daniel looked at her.

"If that's okay," she said.

"Of course," he said.

Daniel, Lewis, and Ani were silent as the couple walked slowly back up to the house, Maria leaning heavily on her husband. Several times, Daniel wanted to jump up and help them, but he sensed that they needed to be alone. He remembered other times like these, when people were lost in private grief, and he had not been welcome.

"I only caught a little of that," Ani said. "Can you tell us?"

In a low voice, Daniel told them her words to the best of

his memory. Lewis gave a long whistle. Ani sat looking straight at Daniel, but it seemed that her mind was elsewhere.

"It's good," she said. "For her to get this out. But how can anything about this really be good in a world where these things happen?"

Daniel looked from Ani to Lewis and back, surprised. She was usually pretty positive.

"Of course, things can be good," he said. "What other hope do we have?"

She bowed her head. "I've just seen this so many times before. More heartache, another relocation. I know she has to grieve, but what does it do to change things?"

Lewis gestured to the grassy space between him and Daniel. "Come sit down. Tell us what's going on."

Daniel watched as Ani swung the garden gate open and came close to them, carefully sitting and arranging her clothes and scarfs around her. She picked up a clump of dirt the way they were doing, squeezing it so that it crumbled back into the garden bed.

"Their case doesn't look good," Ani said. "They knowingly deceived the authorities, and the lawyers are going to build a case that a relationship of trust cannot be built on deception."

"Surely our lawyers can make a case that they did what they needed to do to protect these children," Lewis said.

Ani huffed a sigh and picked up another clod of dirt, this one bigger. "To tell the truth, I'm not that impressed with our lawyers. Not Mercy and George; they're doing great. But the immigration lawyers they've had to bring in. It seems as though they're willing to concede this case in order to secure the other ones. But it's all just red tape! Who cares if the grandparents lied? These are human beings who have been saddled with impossible sadness and responsibility. And to trade some people's wellbeing for others? It doesn't seem decent. And they didn't even listen to me. They talked to me as though I was a child." She squeezed the clod so hard that it showered dirt all over her. She blinked.

Daniel frowned at the idea of anyone talking to Ani as though she was a child. His mind was working quickly.

"That's the real reason I'm feeling low," she said to Daniel in a soft voice. "Sorry."

"You don't need to apologize," Daniel said. He was thinking about a lawyer friend he knew. He wanted to get a lawyer for Maria and Leo, for the kids. For Ani to have hope again. He wanted to get the best lawyer in the world.

CHAPTER THIRTY-EIGHT

Ani was still fuming. Venting to Daniel and Lewis hadn't helped. She stormed around her house, unsure of what to do with herself. In her bedroom, she picked up a brush and started to brush her hair, counting to one hundred to calm herself. At stroke number eighty, a piece of the brush broke off, and Ani held it out and stared at it, feeling slightly abashed. Her anger was spilling out everywhere.

Every time Ani thought about the meeting, she grew angrier. At the last minute, something had come up for Mercy, so it had been Ani by herself with the immigration lawyer and his assistant, men in suits who barely listened to her and acted as though she knew nothing, despite her experience.

They were so glib, so sure of themselves as they sat there and decided that the Loria family was expendable, and it broke Ani's heart. It enraged her. She blushed as she stared at herself in the mirror. She'd let them have it before she left.

"You act as though you know people, as though you know what is possible, but you have no idea what is really in the realm of possibility. You have no faith! Moses parted waters to rescue people, and you are sitting here looking at your papers and precedents like a pair of clucking birds gossiping about the world beneath you. I've had enough."

She had stood to go, and at the last minute, had turned for a parting shot. "I'm also way way way more experienced than you know. You dismissed the wrong woman."

She could die at the memory. She was sure it hadn't had any positive effect on their estimation of her, and yelling at people in a conference room wasn't exactly the way to get them to believe in possibility. She grinned at herself, suddenly, and walked out to the living room. By the time she got there, she was laughing, holding her sides. *Moses.* After a while, she realized that Daniel was standing outside her screen door, apparently waiting for her to stop laughing before he asked whatever question he had, but that only made her laugh more. She laughed until she couldn't stand and collapsed on the rugs, lying curled on her side. Daniel let himself in and sat on her sofa, looking at her with an expression she couldn't read.

When she could catch her breath, she told him the joke, but when he said, "Moses?" with a puzzled little smile on his face, Ani went off into laughter again. Eventually, she laughed herself out and realized how tired she was. She stayed there, lying on the floor, looking at the late afternoon light making patterns on her wall. It soothed her. She was close to tears. Perhaps she was going crazy, but at least she wasn't furious anymore.

She sat up and looked at Daniel.

"I'm sorry," she said. "I'm guessing you're here for a reason other than my hysteria."

He frowned. "I don't like that word. Men used it to describe women's emotions as a sickness or madness."

Ani was caught off guard again. *This man.* Of course, he knew the origins of the word hysteria. It struck her that Daniel would have listened to her today. She wished he had been there.

"I called my lawyer," Daniel said. "And he knows of an immigration lawyer that he calls a legend. He says that Mercy knows of him. So I think we should fire the lawyers who didn't listen to you and hire the legend."

"But how would we afford him?" Ani asked, throwing the question out before she would admit, even to herself, just how touched she was by Daniel's instinct to help.

"I'll pay his rates."

Hope that was almost painful flooded Ani's heart. She couldn't bear the idea that the Lorias would be deported.

"Also," Daniel went on. "I'm sure that there are many more questions to answer, but I believe we agreed to make dinner."

She nodded, grabbing a handful of her thoroughly messy hair to flip it behind her.

"We did, didn't we?" she said. "Do you have any ideas? Because I am...there is nothing in my head that seems like it could become a meal."

He was squinting at her, possibly confused by her strange wording. "Do you mean you don't know what to make? Because you were laughing so much, and you had a hard day?"

"I mean because of all of it." She gestured at the world in general.

He stood and offered her a hand. "I do have ideas. But you should rest. I can make dinner."

She waited a moment or two before taking his hand, and then felt a rush of longing at the feel of it completely enveloping hers. He didn't pull her up, just offered resistance so she could haul herself to her feet.

"No way. Don't worry about me. I think it will be restful to be in the kitchen. I find it soothing..." she looked up, and his face was very near, those hazel eyes and dark eyelashes looking at her directly. He was waiting for her to finish. She cleared her throat. "You're a restful person to be around."

He blinked, and for a moment, they just stood like that, very near, feeling the edges of each other's presence. Then he stepped back and smiled a little, crossing his arms over his chest.

"I am?"

"Well, to me, you are. Yes. Sometimes." And sometimes, he made her dizzy. But she wasn't going to tell him that.

All at once, Ani felt desperate for her mother. She wanted her mother to meet Daniel, to tell her if she felt it too —this steady beat of goodness that seemed to radiate outward from him.

She followed him out the door and paused for a moment

as he walked from her path to the common road between the three houses. The sun was steadily making its way toward the horizon; it was that gorgeous, glorious time of day that seemed like it could absorb all the world's sadness and ugliness, just take it all inside and make it disappear.

Ani was not the same after moving here. She would never be the same. The shadows on the hills made her long for things she could never have. Daniel turned to her at her little gate that did nothing useful, that only looked pretty.

The light turned his hair to gold and played with her heart.

"Coming?" he asked. She nodded and went.

The house was very quiet. Ani tried not to feel too worried about the silence. The kids were home but out of sight, and the door to the big bedroom was closed. Ani hoped they were all asleep, that they had flown away from their grief for a little while.

Is the world a place of beauty? she thought to herself. Daniel had given her tomatoes to cut, and she felt ready for deep thoughts or terrible hurt, like she could cry or laugh at any second. *Is it beautiful, or just utilitarian and full of greed and pain?*

She knew the right answer. It was both. It was neither. It was marred by wrong-doing and oppression. People took one another's lives. And yet, through the large kitchen window, she could see the sun setting, and Daniel had put an Otis Redding album on, and now he was singing along, and Ani was sick of this.

"How on earth can you sing like that?" she demanded,

turning and putting her hands on her hips, despite the tomato juices on her fingers.

He looked surprised. He was stirred onions and garlic in oil, and they were releasing their fragrance into the kitchen. This also was beautiful, as were his voice, his hands, the quirk of his mouth.

"What do you mean?" he asked. "I'm in a band, remember."

"Yes, but your voice is too good," Ani said accusingly. It was ridiculous to be angry about this. But Ani had formed her life around the need to be responsible and to right the wrongs of the world, and she didn't want her heart to be open, at least not in this way, grasping in every direction for something more than what she had come to accept for herself.

"Does it bother you?" he asked as he turned back to the stove and added chopped mushrooms to the mix he was making. Something in his voice grabbed at Ani, forced her to realize she was taking her confusion out on him, as though he should only be what he could allow her to be, no more, and this was the sum of the human error, everyone trying to rule the world and control everyone else.

He had called a new lawyer for her. He had offered to pay for it. Ani didn't think anyone had ever shown her such care. She couldn't control his goodness, the way he seemed to fit a hollow place in her life perfectly. It wasn't his fault that he made her long for good things and that the longing made her vulnerable to the abyss of pain. She couldn't be numb around him. This was either a problem or a gift.

"No, it doesn't bother me," she said, forcibly making her voice gentle. "I love it."

So he went back to singing, and she followed directions for the meal and watched the sunset, listening to his beautiful voice as he sang and cooked for a grieving family.

At one point, she did have a question for him.

"You were a foster kid, right?" she asked.

"Yes," he said.

"This is a very nosy question, but how do you have so much money?"

He laughed. "Isn't that what everyone wants to know? It's a long story, but I promise to tell you. Right now, I think we need to feed our hungry family and make sure they get some rest."

Ani nodded. He was right. "I'm going to make you live up to that," she said. "I want to hear the story. I want to hear all your stories."

He looked at her very seriously, untying the apron he had tied around his waist and washing his hands.

"Some of my stories aren't very nice to tell," he said.

"Mine too," she said, nodding. "But even those kinds of stories need to be told. They're ours, so they have value."

He nodded again. "Okay then, sometime I will tell you my stories." He waited. "And you?"

Oof. She looked at him for a long, silent moment. "Maybe sometime I will tell you mine, too."

CHAPTER THIRTY-NINE

Daniel booked an appointment for the new lawyer to come out to the house on Saturday to talk with Maria and Leo. After some thought, they decided that Ani would stay with the elder Lorias, while Daniel took Valeria and Gabe into town for an adventure. The adults needed to be able to talk freely. It was the first time they had gone anywhere in this particular constellation--just Daniel, Valeria, and Gabriel. The kids were practically out of their heads with nervousness and excitement. Gabriel bounced around in his seat, singing a tuneless song in Spanish, with Valeria singing along. She was perfectly on key, and the mix was a bit painful. Daniel winced. He was reminded again of how much his life had changed. Loud sounds and intense sensations used to be things he avoided, but he took deep breaths and steadied himself from the inside more often these days.

He had people in his life, and they had changed everything. For the first time, the difficulty felt worth it. This singing, though, had to stop.

"Let's turn music on," he suggested, handing Valeria his phone. "You choose something from the app."

"Why does she get to choose?" Gabriel whined.

"You can take turns choosing," Daniel said.

"Why does she get to choose first?"

This was another thing. Daniel had assumed that when he offered something good to kids, they would be happy. But it didn't always go that way. There was often some problem, something for them to quarrel about. Valeria and Gabriel were sweet kids who were thankful for the things in their lives and respectful to their grandparents. But they could fight about anything, and Daniel was torn between curiosity over their behavior, and the fear that it might actually drive him crazy.

"Why does it matter who chooses first?" Daniel asked.

Neither of them had an answer for that. Gabriel settled down when the song Valeria chose turned out to be one of his favorites. Daniel shook his head.

At the meeting for the sponsors a few days ago, Faith said their behavior was normal. Daniel had brought up the arguing, worried that he was doing something wrong, but she told him that kids on their absolute best behavior are sometimes worrying that they will wreck their lives and the lives of those around them if they are not perfect.

"Not that we shouldn't encourage good behavior," she said. "But every kid makes their desires known in annoying ways at times. Sibling squabbling is one of the most normal behaviors in the world. If they feel safe to do it around you, that means they're starting to trust their situation."

The words had warmed Daniel's heart, though they couldn't make him enjoy the fighting. He felt the urgency of building a good case as he gripped the steering wheel. All the safety would shatter if this little family was deported.

Mateo, the new lawyer, was the ray of hope that everyone needed. He was Mexican-American and spoke fluent Spanish, so there was no need for an interpreter, and Daniel had overheard Maria already talking to him a mile a minute as he left that morning.

As Daniel pulled the jeep onto Theresa's street, Valeria recognized the church and gave a small gasp, pointing it out to Gabe. *One day,* Daniel thought, as he parallel-parked, *this will all be familiar to them. They'll be able to run around Aveline and know exactly where they are. It will be beautiful because they'll be known and trusted. Valeria will learn to drive here, and then Gabriel.* "Let it be, God," he whispered.

The kids held back at the gate, looking shy, but then Maddie was pulling it wide open and Remus jumped up on the kids, making them shriek with laughter. Maddie ran off with Valeria and Gabriel following, heading around the house to the backyard. None of them looked back.

"Well," Daniel said. Then he shrugged and walked to the front door, letting himself in.

He could hear laughter in the kitchen and went through to find Sheldon and Theresa looking at a magazine together.

"Hey," he said, wanting them to know he was there before they said or did anything too embarrassing.

Theresa looked up first. "Daniel!" She got up and gave him a big, exuberant 'Theresa hug,' as he called them. All squeeze and then letting him go so fast he nearly fell over. Sheldon lifted a hand for a fist bump, and Daniel felt himself relax in the company of his old friends. He looked back and forth between the two of them. Sheldon wore suspenders over a T-shirt and ratty jeans, as well as a stovepipe hat. Daniel knew it was a stovepipe hat because he had made the mistake of calling it a top hat one day, and Sheldon had scorn-fully corrected him.

Theresa was her usual stunning self in a purple dress and black and red striped tights.

"My friends are circus people," Daniel said.

"Circus people looking at a bride magazine," Theresa said. "Did you ever think you'd see the day?"

"I hoped," Daniel said. "Not that you would look at the magazine, but that you'd get back together. I always liked us all together."

Theresa smiled up into his eyes.

"You're too busy for us now," she said.

"No," he protested, but Sheldon shook his head, holding up a hand. "Don't let her tease you like that. Come, tell us which dress screams Theresa. Is it this one?"

Daniel was distracted momentarily as the kids galloped by the window, riding invisible horses. Remus was wearing a cape.

"I didn't know Maddie played like that anymore," Daniel murmured, scooting a chair close to look at the picture Sheldon was holding.

"Us either, actually," Theresa said, smiling out into the yard at her daughter, who was waving one arm around her head with a glittering streamer clenched in one fist.

"Theresa, no," Daniel said, staring at the magazine, and then she and Sheldon were in peals of laughter. The dress in question was very large and poofy, a ball dress from another era. Sheldon couldn't even imagine Theresa wearing it.

"You don't have to worry about ever seeing me in that," she said when she could get her breath. "We're going to elope, just the three of us, and go on a camping adventure. This summer."

Daniel stared. "This summer. Wow, congratulations." He had just told them that he liked the three of them together; why was he now feeling a little despondent? He couldn't figure himself out. "Where will you live?" he asked.

"Here," Theresa declared.

"Well, that's good. I love this house, and it's nicer..." he stopped the sentence, almost on time.

"...than my house. Thanks, chum," Sheldon said. Theresa grinned and stood to put the kettle on.

"We're going to turn his apartment into a teahouse above the grocery store," she said. "Put all those amazing antiques and collectibles into an actual display."

"Really?" Daniel asked, looking at Sheldon. He wondered if his friend was really okay with it. Their childhoods had been similar, except that Sheldon had a parent who loved him in a way that Daniel had never had.

"Yes," Sheldon said decisively, answering Daniel's unspoken question. "I'll bring some of it over here," he said, looking around at the clean, sunny home Theresa had made. "But only some. I have found it very peaceful, spending time here. It's so airy and uncluttered."

Theresa kissed Sheldon's forehead and put a cup of tea in front of him.

"Licorice?" she asked Daniel. He nodded. It was what he always had, though oddly, he was craving some of Ani's peppermint tea.

He started telling them about how things were going at El Refugio, and in the course of telling them, told them about the dinners they had together and the vegetable garden. About the trip to see Lewis's place, and about the tea Ani made in the little glass pot and cups.

"She's had the tea set ever since they moved from Iran," he said. "It's from her grandmother."

By then, he had a mug of licorice tea, and Theresa had green tea in a little pot that she poured into a tiny cup and tossed back like a shot. The kids came roaring in, grabbed snacks, and disappeared into Maddie's bedroom.

Daniel looked up from breathing the licorice steam to find Theresa and Sheldon staring at him.

"What?" he asked.

"Talk to us," Theresa said. "What are we going to do about this?"

"What is *Daniel* going to do about this?" Sheldon corrected gently.

"Do about what?" Daniel asked, though he had a feeling he knew what they were talking about. He wanted to disappear in the steam from his mug and pretend his friends away.

"About the peppermint tea, and Ani's great way with the kids, and the way she laughs, and how she seemed to like your singing voice," Sheldon said.

Daniel stared. "Did I say all that?"

"And that was just today."

"I have never." Theresa stopped to take a breath. "Ever. Seen you like this."

"I've never been like this," Daniel said. "Not in any way. It's scary. I've never had a family, I mean, other than you guys. I've never decided to quit my job at the post office. I've never eaten dinner around a table every single evening."

"You quit your job?" Theresa's mouth was hanging open.

"Ugh, does that mean we always have to deal with Jackie?" Sheldon asked.

"Sheldon, stop, that's not the point. Look at our boy. He bought a piece of land, adopted a family, and now he's in love with a woman, though he doesn't want to admit it. And it seems like she likes him too."

"It does?" Daniel asked.

"Sheldon says her eyes follow you around the room."

"We held hands," Daniel admitted.

"What?" The word exploded out of their mouths, and Daniel had to smile at the pair of them.

"Why are you so invested in this?" he asked.

They didn't answer, just kept looking at him.

"Yes, okay, I obviously really like Ani. Maybe I love her. My heart seems to think so. It's always going to freaking bust out of my chest when I'm around her. But people like me don't get to have stuff like this."

"I do," Theresa said softly. "I'm like you."

"Me too," Sheldon said. "I'm like you too, in a different way."

Daniel wanted to protest that they weren't like him, not really. Theresa was autistic, true. And Sheldon had been homeless as a child, so he knew a little of what it was like to be a kid who was adrift. But the heartache. Daniel took a shaky breath and reminded himself that they had grief too. That Theresa had suffered because of violent things that had been done to her. That Sheldon had lost his mother.

"You really think it's possible for someone like me to have something like this?" he asked. "To have a relationship with someone as brilliant as Ani?"

Theresa smiled. Sheldon had tears in his eyes.

"I think God gives very good gifts," Sheldon said. "Sometimes he comes up with a person you couldn't have imagined you could love so much. You match each other, and it feels like it couldn't be possible, but it is."

Suddenly Daniel wasn't sure Sheldon was talking about him and Ani anymore, but he felt something like a sunrise inside his chest. Hope, that was what this feeling was called, he thought. Hope.

"Tell me more," he said.

CHAPTER FORTY

Ani watched the photographer who had come with the new lawyer. More specifically, she watched Maria watching the photographer.

The photographer was turning in circles as though she couldn't believe what she was seeing.

"This is the house for the family? Really?"

She snapped pictures of the front steps, flanked by roses and newly blooming lilacs. She took photos of the kitchen, the garden, the kids' rooms, the living room.

Maria hung back, biting her thumbnail, and Ani went close and put an arm around her. "*Que pasa?*" she asked. Maria said something in response, but Ani couldn't understand. Maria tried again, in the few English words she had been learning.

"Not good feeling," she said.

Ani nodded. It was still frustrating not to be able to communicate easily with Maria, but she at least understood this. Leo and the lawyer, a short bearded man named Mateo, came back into the house. Leo noticed Maria's wilted posture and went to her. Maria murmured something to him, and he took her arm and led her over to the sofa.

"I think all the scrutiny is making Maria nervous," Ani said. "Let's sit and talk. Talking it through and helping her understand should make her feel better."

They arranged themselves in the living room. Ani watched Maria with concern as the older woman sat with her hands folded tightly in her lap. She was such a mix of strength and vulnerability, moving back and forth between the two states easily. Today seemed like a harder day for her. Perhaps it would have been better to keep the kids close, but Ani was concerned about how much Valeria invested in the immigration burdens of the whole family. It wasn't right for a girl of twelve. She should be playing with her friends and doing schoolwork, not obsessing about deportation.

Ani's phone pinged as a text came in from Daniel. It was a photo of the kids eating ice cream with Maddie. Ani showed the picture to Maria, and the older woman smiled and straightened to sit taller.

Mateo spoke first in Spanish and then translated for Ani.

"The other lawyers were not wrong. There is very little that puts the authorities in charge of asylum on edge like lying. We will tell them your reasons and tell them the whole story. There are elements of your story that make it compelling for an asylum case."

Ani could hear his restraint because she had heard the lack of it in other cases, on the lips of other lawyers. Mateo did not say, 'It will be good for your case that members of your family have actually died.' This was the kind of statement that made sense in legal terms but could only tie asylum seekers in knots of grief and guilt. Ani was thankful he didn't say it.

"The real case we will bring to court, however, is how well-loved, wanted, and cared for you are here. To be clear," he said to Ani, "the excellent sponsorship of this town might do it. We'll focus on that, and if our judge is honest and has integrity, they should grant you asylum."

Leo leaned forward, his face earnest. "And what about work?" he asked. "Will I need to get work?"

Mateo looked startled. "Yes, they will certainly need to see that you can work."

It didn't seem at all fair to Ani that these two people who had lost their children and no longer had family to care for them should now also need to work. But the world wasn't fair.

"We'll start with job hunting next week," she said.

As he was leaving, Mateo turned to her. His photographer was already halfway down the driveway. "A couple of things, Ms. Nazaryan," he said. "One, I'm sorry, but if you are going to advocate for this community, you really need to work on your Spanish. And Maria and Leo should get some lessons started in English. It's not required in many immigration cases, but the sponsorship model is different. They want to see that you can communicate with one another."

"And the other thing?" Ani asked. She was not trying to be abrupt, but she was tired and a little overwhelmed. She was also not a sponsor who would be sticking around, but she didn't want to get into all that with the lawyer.

"Why have you not applied for jobs for them yet?"

"We were waiting...we wanted them to settle in first."

"It's been a long time."

"Yes, we'll get on it. Their sponsor here has been happy to fund what has not been covered by the amnesty grant."

Mateo looked around. "He must be made of money."

Yeah, about that. What was going on with Daniel and his money anyway? He had promised to tell Ani about it. But she wasn't discussing it with Mateo. Mateo could ask Daniel himself if he really wanted to know.

"I'm going to try to push the hearing dates forward," Mateo told her, his face softening somewhat. "I know it would be helpful to everyone if they just knew they were allowed to stay. Sometimes it can take ages, but immigration court is prioritizing the town sponsorship program."

"Thank you," Ani said softly. "I know these things take time. We're grateful for your excellent work."

After Mateo left, Ani went to see whether Maria and Leo would like to talk the meeting over, but she found them lacing up their new running shoes. Leo winked at Ani and used his translation app to tell her they were going for a walk. "If we have to get jobs, we are going to have to behave as though we are a decade or two younger. *Vamanos, mi corazón*," he said. Ani watched them leave, smiling. She missed out on so much, not being able to talk with them. Mateo was right about learning the language. She wanted more first-hand glimpses of their personalities, their senses of humor, and their resilience.

She sent Daniel a text message. "We're done here."

He sent one back immediately. "We're going to the Aveline Cafe for cake. Meet us?"

She thought about it. She could still see Leo and Maria walking down to the lower edges of the property, arm in arm. She would have to tell them so they wouldn't be afraid if they came back and found her gone. Was it worth it?

"Come," another text buzzed at her. "The cake at the cafe is so good!"

She walked down to them as quickly as she could. Maria and Leo looked a bit startled to see her. She used the translation app to tell them she was going to town to meet Daniel and the kids.

Maria said something to her husband in a shaky voice, but Leo shook his head, speaking softly to her. He nodded. "Go," he said.

She hesitated, but he nodded at her again, and she thought she understood him. It had been more than a month. Maria and Leo needed to feel more sure-footed in their new home. They were safe now, and to fully feel it, they needed to practice feelings of safety.

CHAPTER FORTY-ONE

Ani got in her car and fixed her hair in the mirror, shaking her head at herself for primping.

She was a mess. There was no other way to say it. She was confused about her feelings for Daniel, confused about her future, and unsure of whether the Lorias would be granted asylum. What did any of it mean? Did any of the events of these months fit with the life purpose Ani had been pursuing for years?

She clicked her phone into the holder and pressed the icon to video call her mother, pulling the car around and heading down the driveway. She startled a flock of quail, and they flushed from the trees, all in a panic. It made her smile. Her mother picked up on the second ring.

"Darling, are you calling me from the car? I don't like it when you talk and drive."

"It's something quick, Mama," Ani said.

"Is everything all right?"

"Yes, mostly. There are problems, but they are normal. I need..."

"What, lovely? Anything."

"I need you to come for a visit. Soon. Like, yesterday."

Silence. Ani's mother did not like to travel. She had arranged her life to suit her, like fluffing a blanket all around herself, and she had no desire to leave it. But she would never say no to a genuine need from her daughter. Ani had put Maryam in a difficult spot, and though she felt a bit guilty about it, she really, really wanted her mother to come.

"Is this about that man?"

"Partly."

Her mother heaved a giant sigh. "I will come. When do you want me?"

Ani and her mother sketched out a brief timeline and had loose plans by the time Ani reached the Aveline Cafe. She parked while her mother went back and forth about what clothes she should bring and what the weather would be like.

"I love you, Mama," Ani said. "Thank you."

"You know I love you, Ani. I will give your love to your father."

"Thank you."

Ani felt better already. She left the car, double-checking that it was locked, though it probably wasn't necessary in Aveline. She was still so used to city life. Katie's cafe was lovely and elegant, with its welcoming porches. Ani spotted her friends sitting at one of the big tables on the porch, waving at her. She waved back, ducking her face as heat rose to her cheeks, and went to meet them, reaching out to touch a sprig of orange bougainvillea on the path.

Daniel stood and pulled out a chair for her when she reached the table. Ani was flustered by the gesture but thanked him and dropped into her seat, taking a moment to settle herself, unwinding her scarf, which now felt hot, and smiling over at Valeria and Gabriel.

"Have you been behaving?" she asked.

"Not at all," Sheldon said. "They've been running around like wild horses."

"We've been good!" Valeria protested.

Ani raised her eyebrows. Valeria seemed to be growing in confidence daily, and it was beautiful to witness.

Sheldon laughed. "Yes, you've been outstanding."

Ani saw Valeria's face turn a bit red. Oops, time to distract before Valeria grew overly embarrassed.

"And you," she asked Daniel, "have you been good?" She turned to him to ask the question, regretting the words as soon as they were out of her mouth. Daniel's eyes were on hers, and, close to him like this, she sounded way more flirtatious than she had intended. She felt like disappearing right then and there.

"You'll have to ask Theresa and Sheldon," Daniel said, his deep voice making her face hotter.

"I don't even know what we're talking about anymore," Theresa said. Her eyebrows were high on her face. "What are we talking about, Shel?"

Sheldon was looking from Ani to Daniel and back, eagerly.

This conversation had gotten out of hand in record time. Ani needed to take control of it.

"My mother is coming to visit," she blurted.

"Really?" Theresa asked, successfully deflected. She leaned forward with her hand on her chin.

"Yes, I asked her to come. She'll be here next week some-time." Ani turned to Daniel again. "I hope it's okay--I invited her to stay with me."

Daniel frowned slightly. "The house is yours. You can ask anyone you want to stay with you. It'll be nice to meet her."

"What is your mother like?" Sheldon asked Ani.

And Ani remembered that Daniel and Sheldon did not have mothers and that Valeria and Gabriel had recently lost their mother. It suddenly seemed so extravagant to Ani, to be able to call her mother and ask her to come and stay. What a glorious creature a mother was.

"She will fuss over all of us," Ani said. "She doesn't leave home often, but whenever she does, she's the life of the party. She will try to give us all makeovers. She will want to cook a lot. And she is very, very smart."

"Wow," Daniel breathed. "How can we be so blessed?"

Ani looked a question at him.

"We get you in our lives," he said, "which is already good. But that means we also get to know your mother."

Daniel couldn't know how his words made Ani feel. He had no way of knowing how an immigrant daughter felt about her parents and their relationship. Other men had never seen Ani's close relationship with her mother as a gift.

Don't get too far ahead of yourself, she told herself. He hasn't met her yet.

But, in that moment, one more part of her heart melted.

CHAPTER FORTY-TWO

In the week since Ani had announced that her mother was coming, Daniel had witnessed something he had never seen before—Ani nearly out of her mind with nerves.

"Is she that scary?" he asked her one day. Ani was trying to decide whether to give her mother her own room or the guest bedroom, and had changed her mind six or seven times.

She looked at him with wild eyes. "She's not scary at all. What makes you think that?"

He chose his words carefully. "You seem... worried."

"Oh." She looked down at the bedding she was holding, apparently lost in thought, and for a moment, Daniel didn't think she was going to answer him. "I don't know if I can properly describe my mom before you meet her. She is very important to me. She is like...how can I say this? I think I can only tell you a story." She sat on the sofa with the bedding in her arms. "When I was around twelve years old, there was a writing contest at school, and I thought I might win. I had worked really hard on an essay about life in Iran compared to life in America. I didn't win. The teacher told me it was good, but they weren't looking for something quite so "ethnic." I was devastated." She smiled. "Looking back, it was just a middle school contest. But things mean a lot at that age, and my mom's response was to make me a book of poetry and essays by every incredible Persian or Armenian writer she could think of. She typed out the poems, cut them up, and collaged them with Persian art, dried flowers, and clippings of articles about prizes the writers had won."

Ani paused, looking off into the distance. She seemed far away. Then she blinked and appeared to come back to the sofa and to Daniel. She looked at him. "That's what my mom is like. That's why I want to make sure her room is perfect, and I can't decide whether she'll like the view of the lake or the jacaranda tree the best."

She turned to look at him, tears in her eyes. "I'm being ridiculous, aren't I?"

He took her hand in his own and kissed the back of it. He heard her indrawn breath and held her hand for a moment before putting it back on her lap.

"I'll go and gather jacaranda blossoms," he said, "and you prepare your room for her, since it has the view. She can have both."

Today Ani had driven to Billers to pick up her mother from the Amtrak station. Daniel and the Lorias had entered into the excitement of welcoming Maryam, planning decorations and making a special dinner for her first evening at the house. There were plans to show Maryam around Aveline, with a trip to Theresa's shop, church together on Sunday, and a fancy dinner planned at the Cafe. But tonight was just for them, for eating at home at El Refugio.

"Hurry!" Daniel heard Valeria calling. "She'll be here soon!"

Immediately he saw Gabriel tear down the stairs, running toward the flower bushes. The Gabe began collecting flowers, most likely to spread around the house for Maryam's arrival.

Now Daniel was the one with nerves. He walked down to his house to dress for dinner. He had not stopped thinking about his conversation with Sheldon and Theresa and their assertion that he could have love, even as he was. But any thought of telling Ani how he felt had been postponed in the preparations for her mother's arrival.

Instead, he was doing the very unfruitful work of fretting. Was his voice too monotone to declare love? He tried it in several different pitches in front of his mirror, but he was terrified that he would be overheard, so he stopped that. How about his clothes? Daniel had started to build up a new wardrobe after wearing the same thing for years, always choosing the most simple clothes possible. He bought some quality shirts after finding a good brand from Sheldon. He tried a different cut of jeans and found shoes he liked instead of work boots.

Now he got dressed in a midnight blue button-up shirt. He put on a pair of skinny jeans and his new black vans. After a few minutes of looking at himself in the mirror, weighing his options, he trimmed his beard closer to his face, then even closer, till he could see the shape of his jaw under his beard. He leaned back, brushed a few stray hairs from his shirt, and surveyed the results. He wet his hands and ran them through his hair. It was long-ish, but it would have to do.

Just as he was leaving the bathroom, the calm of the evening was broken by yelling from the Lorias' house. Daniel frowned. That was odd.

"Daniel! Daniel!" he heard Gabriel shouting, and he was running before he knew he had left his doorway. In the distance, he could hear tires on gravel and Maria crying. Too much was happening all at once, confusing him. He arrived at the walkway to the house, out of breath. Valeria stood there shrieking, pointing at a man in the shadows.

"What happened? Who are you?" he asked in Spanish and then in English when he got no response.

"No need to worry. I'm from DHS. Homeland Security. Just getting some pictures."

"In the evening? Without notice?"

"We put a notice in your mailbox yesterday." Daniel hadn't checked the mail today.

"You've disturbed the family," Daniel said, his voice flat and hard. "They weren't expecting you. You can't be sneaking around in the bushes."

"No one answered the door. I was knocking on the window."

"He was taking photos through the window!" Valeria contradicted, her voice angry and rough. Then Daniel remembered the sound he had heard, wheels on gravel, because headlights shone on them standing there, and an engine cut off, so they were in darkness again. Maria was shouting from the porch, and Valeria was crying while the photographer stood there stubbornly, refusing to back down.

Daniel heard Ani's voice asking, "What's going on?"

This was not how they had planned to meet Maryam. They were going to wait on the well-lit porch, ready and inviting. Valeria had planned for each of them to have a flower that they would hand to her as she walked past them. Now Valeria burst into even louder sobs and ran into the house, wailing, all her plans ruined. Daniel could feel his face freezing; he was rocking back and forth slightly, with his arms over his chest. And Leo was trying to push the photographer away.

It was Maryam who pulled it together, forming order from chaos in a moment. She walked into the fray beside Ani, her elegant silver hair pulled back in a loose twist. After Daniel gave a short explanation to Ani, Maryam moved to speak to the photographer.

"You've upset the family," she said. "Though you are perhaps only doing your job. It's not your fault, but surely another time would be better, so we can gather ourselves?"

The photographer left. Then Maryam turned and opened her arms to Maria, who fell into them. The two older women walked into the house together, letting the door drift gently closed behind them, and soon after, Daniel heard the clinking sounds of dishes and cutlery. After a moment, Leo and Gabriel followed. Daniel and Ani were left in silence. Ani sighed.

"I'm so sorry," Daniel said. He felt her gentle hand on his arm.

"It's not your fault," Ani said. She laughed. "And this is what I always do. I try to make everything good and beautiful for her, forgetting that it goes the other way. She makes everything good and beautiful for me."

Daniel was hyper-aware of Ani's small form next to him. He gazed at the steps to the big house, where a square of golden light lit the paving stone.

"Your mother--the way she immediately came *inside*, do you know what I mean?" he asked. "She immediately said 'we' without judgement or anything. Just so much love."

Ani put her arm around his waist and leaned into him. "Yes," she said. "You get it."

Daniel couldn't help it; he put his free arm around her for a real hug and kissed the top of her head, which smelled like roses.

He drew back, and she gasped, really looking at him for the first time. "Your beard!" she said, reaching up to touch his face. "Wow, it's so much shorter."

She pulled away suddenly. "Okay," she said. "Let's see what's happening. I may have to speak to Valeria."

The house was glowing with soft light, and Maryam and Maria were laying dishes on the table.

"I should be surprised that my mother speaks a bit of Spanish," Ani said, standing back to watch them. "But somehow, I'm not, and that tells you all you need to know about my mom."

Daniel helped the women finish up while Ani went to

fetch Valeria. Soon Ani was back with a tear-stained girl who came to say hello to Maryam. She held her chin up.

"It's very nice to meet you," Valeria said. "I've been looking forward to it."

"Not as much as I have, beautiful girl," Maryam said. "And I actually need to meet everyone; that wasn't a real meeting, was it?"

Maryam went from person to person, introducing herself and shaking hands or hugging, until at last she came to Daniel and stood looking at him.

"Hello, Daniel," she said, and Daniel knew instantly that he really wanted this luminous person to like him.

"It's wonderful to meet you," he said.

"You're very handsome," she said in response.

"Mom!" Ani said.

"It's true, darling. But Daniel, you and I will get to know each other more."

Introductions over, they sat in their places around the table. Maria had cooked a special Venezuelan meal, and they lingered over the food as long as they could. Daniel marveled at Ani's mother. In her presence, Ani glowed. Maryam laughed at all Ani's jokes, and her gentle words set Maria and Leo at ease. Daniel mainly watched and translated when they needed him to. He wanted to soak the night in, though it hurt as well. His mother had been gone for a long time, and even before she died, she had never been able to care for him. Daniel thought he saw what it meant to have someone like Maryam; he could see the shelter and place of belonging she made for Ani in the world, how Ani seemed to belong more in a world with her mother in it.

He helped to wash the dishes and then said goodnight to them all, walking down to the trees and farther, farther, until he could see the lake with the moon reflected on it, absorbing the feeling of this private pain.

CHAPTER FORTY-THREE

A ni never wanted her mother to leave, no matter how many squabbles they had, living in one small house together. At the end of a week, when Mateo called to tell her there was a definitive set of dates for the individual merits hearings in immigration court, Ani ran straight to her mother to tell her about it.

Her mom was in the kitchen, drying the coffee cups and putting them in the wrong place.

Ani leaned against the counter, eying her mother. "Mateo called," she said. "Each family has a date for their hearings. Also, that's not where the mugs go, Mama." She knew that her mother knew it. It was her subtle way of trying to rearrange things.

Maryam's eyes widened.

"That's wonderful. When? And I know this is not where you put them, but don't you think they should really go here?

Look how close they are to all the other coffee and tea supplies now."

"They start in two weeks, two families per week. Mateo is planning to save the Loria's for last." Ani shifted her weight off her leg, thumping her hip with her fist to loosen it up. Her body didn't seem to love the guest room bed. "I have to be there for all of them, and then the families will have their witnesses to testify for them. Frankie and the other sponsors will be there for that."

"That's a big deal! How do you feel about it?"

"I feel everything," Ani said. "If you can name it, I'm probably feeling it." She paused for a moment. "I can't reach the mugs very well up there, and I don't want to stand on a stool in my own kitchen." Her mother immediately put them back where they had been, clucking to herself. Ani waited until her mom was finished, then said, "Come and talk to me out here. I need to get my leg up."

"Let me make some tea, and I'll come."

In the living room, sipping tea and sighing as her mother massaged her calf and ankle, Ani told her about her fears. Would their word be enough? Would DHS be really tough on them because of the grandparent thing? What was the immigration judge for this area like? And, not least, would Daniel do okay with testifying.

"He tends to freeze in big moments," Ani said. "Especially if people seem to be aggressive. And DHS can be so intrusive. They make you feel like a criminal even if you're innocent as a baby."

Maryam glanced up as she continued to massage Ani's leg.

"This kind of worry has come up a few times. What do you worry about will happen? I mean, not just at the hearing, but maybe in life here? With Daniel?"

"Maybe that his disorder will cause him to fall apart, and I won't be able to hold things together by myself."

"Okay," Maryam said. "Can I ask you a question?"

"Of course," Ani answered.

"Has it happened so far? In all the stress of this family settling in, has he ever left you to manage everything on your own?"

Ani thought about the question. There was a simple answer and a complex answer.

"No," she said. "Not more than would be usual for anyone. He has needed to take time away, or steady himself, or go for a drive. But he always comes back, and it hasn't been more than I can handle."

"To be honest, darling, I think that's quite incredible for any man. For any human being! I get the feeling that he can gather his strength for this trial."

Ani looked into her mother's eyes. Maryam had always been lovely, and she seemed more beautiful with age.

"Mama," Ani said.

"Yes, love?"

"You like him."

"I really do. But it is not me that we need to worry about."

Ani did not doubt that she liked Daniel. She really, really

liked Daniel. But there was a cascade of questions in her mind whenever she thought of being with him. Where were they supposed to live? He had committed to being here at El Refugio. And Ani had committed to living out of a suitcase, traveling from place to place. She couldn't give that up for a man, could she? It seemed wrong.

"I just don't know what to do," she said. "Can't you tell me what to do?"

"We're about a decade past that, Ani-love. What is troubling you?"

"All of it. My plans for my life..." she chewed on her thumb until her mother lightly smacked her hand away. "I haven't told anyone this, okay. You can't tell anyone."

"I won't."

Ani took a deep breath. "I'm embarrassed because I thought I was beyond all this, but I'm scared that he won't like the way I look." Though it was hard to tell under skirts and pants, one of Ani's legs was way smaller than the other, her left calf withered, and her thigh twisted. She had gone through a lot of body therapy to get to a place where she could wear a swimsuit without flinching. But the looks were seared into her memory, the faces she had seen her whole life when people caught sight of her. She didn't think she could bear to see a look like that on Daniel's face.

"He hasn't seen your leg? You've never worn shorts around him?"

"I have...but I can't tell what he thinks."

"Oh, my beautiful, I see that man's face when he looks at

you. I don't think there's even one thing he doesn't like about you. You just need to decide what *you* want."

Ani made a sound of frustration, covering her face with a pillow.

"Maybe it's all too much to think about at once. You don't need to decide anything right now, love." Maryam stood and stretched. "I think I'm going to go to bed with a book, even though it's not very late. We have a big day tomorrow!"

Tomorrow was her mother's last day as well as the evening of the concert the Aveline Swing Band had been planning for weeks. Ani made a sad face at the thought of her mother leaving, and Maryam laughed. "If I don't go home, your father will be making that face," she said. "I can't win."

Maryam and Ani started the day with a long walk around the lake with Rosa, Valeria, and Gabriel, and then met Francisco for lunch at the Aveline Cafe. Frankie and Maryam got into a fiery argument over who was the best of the Persian poets, much to Ani's delight. She loved it when her mother lost her calm veneer in a debate and starting making contemptuous smacking noises with her mouth, hurling playful insults.

In the evening, they went back down to the lake for the concert. The Aveline Swing Band had added a few Latin Jazz songs to their mix, and already a few couples were dancing. Ani and her mother spread a blanket on the grass and sat to watch Daniel play bass.

"How can you resist this man?" Maryam asked, holding her palm open. "He loves God and people. He gardens, for goodness sake. And he plays music."

Just then, Daniel began to sing the harmony for El Cuarto de Tula by the Buena Vista Social Club, one of Ani's parents' favorite albums. Ani's mother put a hand over her heart as though she would swoon.

"Okay, Mama, I get it. You like him."

"You like him. That's the point I'm trying to make."

Ani did like him. She tried to keep very still so her mother wouldn't see how Daniel's beautiful tenor voice affected her, but she couldn't hide anything from her mom. She ended up with her face in her hands while Maryam laughed.

They watched as Maria and Leo stood and danced, agile and lovely in the evening light.

"Go, Mama," Ani said gently.

"And you?"

Ani shrugged. Her leg hurt already, and the evening was young. She needed to go gently if she was going to last into the night. Ani's mother looked at her with love in her eyes.

"Okay, if you're really okay," Maryam said. "I'll go show them that old Persian women can still dance."

"Mama?" Ani said, as her mother stood with a dramatic groan. Her mother looked down, her gray hair pulled up in its usual twist, her glasses on top of her head, earrings swinging. "Thank you for never making a big deal about my disability. You never made me feel as though I would break because of it. You always let me set my own pace."

Her mother looked surprised, a rare expression for a woman who seemed to know everything.

"Who else should set it? But you are very welcome. Cheer me on!"

She left and went to the dance area, swallowed immediately by the laughing crowd. Ani sat back and enjoyed the darkening sky and the music that swirled and enveloped her. It was a welcome break from the tension of the hearings. When the band finished their set, Ani went to find something to drink. She bought a glass of wine for her mother and herself, but couldn't find her mother anywhere. Finally, she returned to their blanket and sat down holding both glasses, hoping Maryam would turn up.

After a moment, she felt someone standing over her.

"There you are," she started to say, but when she looked up, she saw Daniel standing there in front of her. "Oh, I thought you were my mom," she said.

"She sent me. She said you had wine for me."

Ani shook her head. "She would." Looking around, she saw they were surrounded by people, including a few girls who seemed to be watching Daniel, maybe waiting for a chance to talk to the cute bass player. Ani also spotted Theresa, Mercy, and Lewis looking their way.

"Do you want to walk along the shore?" Ani asked. "While we drink our wine?"

"Yes, definitely," Daniel said. He took the glasses while she stood, then handed one back to her. They started walking along the lake's edge, following the line of the water.

"Is this okay for you?" Daniel asked.

Ani was limping a bit. "Here, it's fine," she said. "The bigger rocks are harder. But I'm used to it. It's okay."

Daniel seemed to accept this. After a while, the noise behind them faded. The stars grew brighter the farther they got from the center of town. Daniel stopped, tipping his head back to look at the sky. "The stars are brighter at our place," he said, "but they're beautiful anywhere." They stood there for a while in silence. Ani felt nearly perfectly content like she wouldn't want to be anywhere else.

"I told you I would teach you to dance," Daniel said.

Ani's eyes widened. "You did. But we have no music."

"I can make music."

He set both of their glasses down on a nearby rock, then held his arms out, waiting for her to step into them. She did, her heart thudding, and he held her waist and hand gently.

"The problem is that I can't rest my weight on my left leg too long," she told him. "So I will never be exactly in rhythm."

"You're more of an improvisation than a metronome," he said.

"Daniel," Ani said. He was too much.

"What?" he asked. The question was genuine. He hadn't fed Ani a line--he had offered her a thought straight from his beautiful mind. She closed her eyes and laid her face against his collarbone while he hummed and moved them both around the sand. It wasn't exactly skilled dancing on her part, but she loved it. Dancing with Daniel filled her with joy.

"Is it too damp to sit down?" Daniel asked after a while. "You asked about my story and where my money came from. Now seems like a good time."

"Sure," she said. "That sounds better than socializing. I

like listening to music, but I don't like all the shouting over a deejay that happens afterward."

He grinned, his dimple flashing in his shorter beard. "I feel the same."

"Tell me," she said.

CHAPTER FORTY-FOUR

Daniel had been so small the first time he went into foster care. Just four years old, his mother arrested on trafficking charges. Meth, of course, in the epidemic that had raged across his small Central Californian town.

Telling Ani the story, he could fill in some of the blanks: why he had been so troublesome for his foster families, why he had been returned again and again for failure to connect. Now he knew it was autism, but back then, no one had taken the time to find out what was going on with him. They'd assumed that he was just like all the other foster kids who had failed to connect.

This was the slimy underbelly of autism and all the misunderstandings about autism. For every person who turned out to be a genius, applauded by society, there were many more who could not work themselves into any kind of structure, like Daniel's mother. They got lost on the margins. Daniel's mother visited over the years when she was out of jail. She tried to get Daniel back a few times but could never hold onto sobriety long enough. By the time she was thirty-five, she had looked like she was sixty-five. She died in police custody after a violent arrest.

Daniel's mother's father sued the police department and set up a trust fund for Daniel. It was an illogical, surprising move from someone who had basically disowned his grandson. To Daniel's knowledge, he had never deigned to help his daughter or grandchild. Daniel doubted his grandfather could have gotten away with it if he hadn't been a powerful, wealthy man. But maybe by then, the old man knew it was too late. Perhaps it was an apology to the daughter he had lost to drugs and prison. An apology to the grandson who had grown up in the wilderness of the foster care system.

Daniel thought about the day that his caseworker had told him about the trust. He had trudged into her office reluctantly that afternoon. They'd had many tussles over the years, but got along better after Daniel turned sixteen. This was mainly due to Daniel's most recent foster family, a Mexican-American couple with adult children, three dogs, and a lot of peace in their home. The family was getting ready to move back to Texas, though, and Daniel was aging out of the system. He thought this was why he was being called into his case worker's office, and was unprepared for life-changing news. He was surprised when she handed him a letter.

Daniel could read his caseworker reasonably well by now, and she didn't look all that happy, so he thought the letter was bad news. He stared at the sheet of paper. The letters seemed tiny and jumbled together.

"What is this?" he asked. "I'm too nervous to read it."

"Your grandfather apparently sued the state over your mother's death."

"My what?"

Other than a few references to a terrible old man from his mom during visits, Daniel hadn't heard much about his grandfather.

"Your grandfather. Your mother's father."

Daniel nodded, still not sure where this was going.

"He set the money aside in a trust for you."

"I don't understand what that means."

"It means you get the money, but over time and with conditions."

Daniel picked up the paper again, irritated by the lights in this office, as well as the way the desk was crooked and the wallpaper peeling. It felt physically painful to be in this room.

He looked at the sum in the middle of the letter. There were a few numbers. One said one amount, one said another, and still another said even more.

He couldn't quite understand. "My grandfather has never even met me," he said.

"Well, that's why I am furious right now."

"Are you furious?"

"Can't you tell?"

"I can tell that you are not happy."

The caseworker sighed and tapped her pen on the desk. "I'm glad for you, Daniel, don't get me wrong. This will change everything for your future. But couldn't your grandfather have just stepped up when you needed a home? Does he imagine that throwing money at you right now will change the heartbreak of your childhood, of being moved from place to place like furniture?" She stopped talking and bit her lip, typing furiously.

Daniel felt like he couldn't quite catch his breath. His sternum hurt, and he rubbed at it with one hand.

"Sorry," she said after a moment. "I really should keep all this to myself. The bottom line is that you have money. The first deposit comes with the condition that you enroll in university. There is a separate tuition fund."

"University? Where?" Daniel asked.

"That's the thing, Daniel," she said, looking up. Her face had its happy look for the first time since he stepped into her office. "You get to decide that."

Daniel had enrolled in Aveline State University because he wanted to stay in California, but not too close to Fresno, where he had grown up. He barely got in and always suspected social services had done something to ensure his acceptance. He moved into the dorms, and his life changed. It didn't take long for Daniel to learn to love Aveline.

He took a job at the post office, just part-time at first, to support himself while he was in school. Something inside him didn't really trust that the trust fund would keep coming. Daniel decided to save it for something important. If he was meant to have it, it would keep coming. In the meantime, he studied and worked.

He met Sheldon and Theresa, and the three of them became good friends. He didn't have too many other friends.

It still felt odd to meet people who weren't from school or foster care. He lost touch with his social worker. He kept in touch with his last foster family for a little while, but they got busy in Texas, and they eventually drifted apart as well. Daniel graduated and moved into town.

And then the rumors started. The robberies. His suspicious newness. There was no proof, no evidence that he had committed theft, so nothing came of it. The rumors went away, but he didn't exactly make a lot of friends. When Theresa left town, Daniel lost touch with heartbroken Sheldon. Still, he liked the safety and quiet of the post office.

Daniel got the diagnosis of autism. Too late, he thought privately, remembering every teacher or professor who had been angry with him for being fixated or for interrupting, every foster parent who had accused him of being stupid or aloof. But although it was late, the diagnosis was freeing. Having Theresa move back to Aveline with her own diagnosis was a high point of life as well. They had always matched as friends, and now it felt like it was for a reason. They were part of the same tribe.

Then the rumors had started again. This time, they had nearly broken Daniel. It seemed as though he would never get to build his life on anything. He had gone into a long dark sadness. He had barely been living, he hardly lifted his head. He didn't have anything, really. He grew depressed and incredibly anxious.

But then Lydia, his therapist, had pushed him to think about what he did have. He had money that he had never used. He had a handful of friends. So when Francisco started talking about the needs of the refugee families, Daniel felt a spark ignite inside his heart. He wanted to do something, to really do something meaningful. Would he be allowed to help?

When Theresa came forward and Cam was arrested, all suspicion had once again been wiped away, though not without scars. And now. He had his new family, his new friend Ani. He didn't want to lose any of them, though he did not say it now.

The moon was up when Daniel finished the story. It was the waxing crescent of the spring moon.

"I've been investing the money all along," Daniel told Ani. "I've never spent any of it, except on university, until I bought the property. There's..." he trailed off, "...quite a lot now."

They were lying on their backs on the blanket now, having given up on sitting. Daniel felt a wash of embarrassment at the amount of time he had spent talking. Beside him, Ani shivered, and Daniel reached for her hand.

"That's the story. You got it all." He sat up, feeling a terrible vulnerability. It made him want to run. Ani sat as well, tucking her legs to one side underneath her, turning to face him. Her face was lovely in the faint moonlight. She reminded him of still water, or the peace of planets flung far out in the solar system. She was something contained, and she was drawn with lines that did not scribble or break.

"So what you're telling me," she said, "is that you inherited a fortune, and you didn't spend it until you wanted a house to host a refugee family."

"I bought a Jetta and a Jeep, too," he said. "Full disclosure."

"Is there anyone in the world like you, Daniel?" she asked softly.

He could barely think, with her so near. He could barely breathe. She smelled like roses and sunshine, like night-blooming trees.

She moved closer to him. Then closer. She put a hand on his arm, then his face. She touched his eyebrow, his temple. She cupped his face with her hand, and then he leaned all the way down to her face to breathe her in. She moved the rest of the way to meet him and touched her lips to his.

His heart exploded. He thought maybe he had died. But he hadn't, because he could still feel her, her lips so soft against his. He moved closer until she climbed up onto his lap and he put his arms around her. She was so small compared to him. He held her to warm her, and she was still kissing him.

Kissing him until he saw stars.

After a long while, he pulled away, feeling dizzy. Ani laughed softly and leaned her face against his neck.

"I supposed I should have expected how nice it would be to kiss you," she said. "We match so perfectly in so many ways."

"We do?" he asked with his raspy voice, feeling pleased.

"Yes, you ridiculously perfect man."

Ani sighed and moved away to stand up. He felt her loss like someone had splashed cold water over his head. She held out a hand to help him up, and he took it just to touch her.

He didn't put any of his weight on her as he stood. Her long black hair swung around her elbows, her dark eyebrows were like wings on her face. She looked at him very seriously.

"What are we going to do about this?" she asked. "I can't stay."

CHAPTER FORTY-FIVE

The days after Ani dropped her mother off at the train station were a blur, a collection of meetings and talks, run-throughs for the families, and shopping for suits and nice dresses. Ani thought later that if it was a film montage, Frankie would have been everywhere in it, laughing with his big smile, calming a nervous family, testifying, waiting in the audience area at the courtroom. Aveline was so incredibly blessed to have the reverend Francisco, Ani thought. She wondered if they knew it.

Slowly, the days for the merit hearings went by, and each family was interviewed. Ani and the sponsors testified to the families' need for asylum and the support the community would give them. Each family was approved. It was a dream, a hope turned reality. There were some tough spots. One family didn't have a job locked down yet. Another had unfortunate blemishes on their immigration record, from when they tried to move to Guatemala and were rejected.

But in the end, the judge approved them. Each time this happened, they celebrated until the wee hours of the morning, with the whole sponsorship committee and the families coming together to dance on the beach, or in the church, or in the Aveline Cafe. Frankie insisted they celebrate every bit of progress.

"Celebration is a spiritual practice," he said. "One we forget sometimes. Especially on this continent." Three families, three celebrations.

Ani loved how much more musical her life had become in the last weeks. There was music at El Refugio now, too, with Daniel bringing his bass up to the house to play while Leo joined him on guitar. She felt surrounded by music, and it made life better.

And then the day came. It was time for the Lorias' hearing.

Ani could feel the nervous energy as soon as she walked into the house. She knew that not one person in this brave little family knew what to expect. They had done all they could, and now they would all have to give their very best testimonies and simply hope for the best.

Poor little family, Ani thought, sitting at the breakfast table watching Maria and Leo go through their morning rituals with their whole lives in the balance. What Ani would give to have it all be over. For the hearing to be in the past for the Lorias, with nothing but school and work to look forward to.

Ani was having a hard time keeping her eyes off Daniel's

face. She kept staring at him and then glancing away when he looked at her, as though she was in the seventh grade.

Today was the first weekday since Maria and Leo found jobs that they hadn't gone in to work. Even though it still bothered Ani that they had to work, they seemed to really like their jobs. Leo worked at the Aveline cafe as a prep cook, and Maria was working part-time at the craft store, heaven, she called it. They were both signed up for weekly English lessons, and their English was improving. They were certainly better at using the translation app. Thank the heavens for technology, Ani thought several times a week.

And Valeria and Gabriel were doing well at school. Valeria and Rosa were basically joined at the hip, along with another girl named Lisa. They had nicknamed themselves the triplets, though it wasn't their looks that made them triplets, or so Maria said when Valeria told her. Maria's eyes were wide as she watched brown-skinned Valeria and Rosa running hand in hand with little blond Lisa. Valeria's trumpet-playing was still painful, but slowly getting better.

Gabriel spent a lot of time at school drawing, and lately, Ani had felt rather astounded by the sketches he showed her. She wondered if he had a future in art. He deserved all the opportunities they could give him to find out.

And Ani and Daniel had somehow gotten through the days, drawn to one another in the moments between, stealing secret kisses or just long looks, unable to resolve the big thing between them—the fact that Ani would be leaving soon.

It was nearly time for the hearing. The awareness that

this day could undo all the other days was like an electric pulse in the room. This was something they could never turn back from.

"The only way out is through," Ani said. From somewhere that seemed far away, she heard Daniel translate it.

"*Vamanos*," Maria said.

They took two vehicles, with Daniel driving the Jeep and Ani driving the Jetta. Maria and Leo sat close together in the back seat of the car Ani drove. Maria kept up a steady intonation of prayer until Ani realized she was going to go insane —it was a long way to Billers—and turned on some music. She could still see Maria's lips moving in the rearview mirror, but she could no longer hear the words. Ani's pulse calmed as she watched the trees flow by on the road, but her heart felt stretched and torn inside her. She knew, suddenly, that she would weep and weep if she were separated from this family. With a thunderbolt of understanding, she knew that she would feel the same whether they were taken from her, or she decided to walk away from them. El Refugio was the first place since Ani's parents' house that had felt like a home.

And she would be heartbroken if she walked away from Daniel.

She could see him in the jeep ahead of her, the back of his head, his hands on the steering wheel. The kids were dancing in the back seat, and Ani knew Daniel had put pop music on to distract them, even though he hated it. And then he started to dance as well, throwing his hands out at a stoplight, bopping his head. Ani could see Valeria laughing as well, but her eyes were all for Daniel. He was doing everything he could to help them feel better.

Her heart was cracked open.

What were plans without a center? What was life without love? Surely God must have seen her carefully made plans and laughed, seen all those appropriate men her mother had dangled before her and smiled knowing how Maryam would fall for this man with a heart of gold and a different way of walking in the world.

Ani couldn't pull herself away from him. It would be like taking a planet out of orbit.

She didn't want to feel this way, she had never wanted to feel this way. And yet, here she was, and what was worse, she was having this epiphany moments before arriving at court for one of the most critical merit hearings of her life. It was terrible timing.

Ani took a deep breath as she pulled into her parking space, trying to get her face and heart under control. This was not the day for confessions of love. She undid her seatbelt and opened the door, determined to be a professional, to get through the hearing without thinking about the future at all.

She offered a hand to Maria to help her out of the car, and was touched by how bravely Maria smiled up into her face, straightening and touching her hair to make sure it was in place. She wore her best Venezuelan dress, long and ruffled, carefully carried all the way from her old home to her new one. Leo came around the car from his side and took his wife's hand.

Then Daniel and the kids were there, and they went together into the courtroom, joined by Frankie, Mateo, and Mercy, everyone trying to behave as though this would be as easy as every other hearing.

Everything happened quickly after that. The judge looked through the documents, asking Mateo questions. He called Maria and Leo to the witness chair one at a time, and they did their best to answer and wait patiently for the translations. Ani heard them give the answers they had practiced —not word for word like some kind of script, but honest answers about how much they would like to live in this country, how they would like to survive and serve. They apologized for the deception. This was a point that Ani and Mateo had gone back and forth on. To Mateo, it seemed like an admission of guilt, but in the end, Leo had insisted. "I want to do my part to make it right, to start this relationship well," he said.

He apologized well, in his humble way.

Ani held her breath, and the judge didn't sneer. He merely nodded and said, "I'll take that into consideration."

The DHS lawyer asked questions as well, trying to confuse and trick the Lorias into saying something that would show they weren't eligible for asylum status. Though Mateo had warned them about this, Ani could see that Maria and Leo were rattled. Maria's hands trembled as she answered. But there was no doubt about what they knew. Their son and daughter-in-law had been executed extra-judiciously, without trial, without a chance even to say goodby to their children.

They knew they were honest in their desire to provide a better life for their grandchildren, and it showed.

The judge listened to what Valeria had to say, and then Gabriel as well. The DHS officer didn't press the children too harshly. Ani glanced at her watch. It was nearly time for Daniel to speak.

CHAPTER FORTY-SIX

Daniel was sworn in without any issue. Ani found that she was holding her breath. She tried to relax as Mateo asked Daniel a few questions about how things had been going at El Refugio with the Lorias. Daniel answered Mateo's questions with a lot of feeling, telling the judge how much meaning the Lorias had brought to his life and how much he loved sponsoring them.

"Are you confident you will go on feeling this way?" Mateo asked. "Will you be able to help them in the long run?"

Daniel leaned forward in his seat. "Yes," he said emphatically. "I am here for them as long as they need me."

Mercy grabbed Ani's hand and smiled at her. Ani could see Maria dabbing at her eyes, and felt tears prick behind her own at Daniel's sincere words.

Mateo nodded and gestured that he was done. The DHS lawyer stood.

"So tell me," the lawyer said, "why you think this family can work when it is in no way a real family. No mother, no father. No married sponsors. What will happen when the grandparents are too old to support their grandchildren? Will Valeria and Gabriel go into the foster system at a cost to the American people?"

Daniel had looked apprehensive as the lawyer approached him, Ani thought. But she could see anger building in him until he no longer looked even a little nervous.

He leaned toward the microphone in front of him and spoke softly.

"How can we say what a family is?"

"I'm sorry?"

"We've tried to force our ideal of family on people before. I thought we were starting to understand that it doesn't work."

Ani's heart started drumming in her chest. Whew, she thought. Despite his soft voice, she knew Daniel was on the attack.

"Oh, are you an expert on family systems?" the lawyer said, pretending to check his notes.

"Well, I grew up in the foster system, as I'm sure you know if you've done any background investigation on me," Daniel said.

Ani could see the lawyer deflate just the slightest bit, as though this was something he had wanted to bring out on his own. But Daniel was admitting to it readily, and he wasn't done.

"And in the group homes, there were always kids who had family. They had uncles or older cousins who would have taken them in, but those in charge thought it was better to tear all of the familiarity of their lives away rather than allow something that looked a little different from what they considered normal. It seems like the height of arrogance to break a family apart and then cobble it back together the way we want it."

The lawyer glared at Daniel. "Thank you for this answer. It highlights your...interesting background. Your Honor, I believe this is proving my point about Daniel Wright not having sufficient experience with any kind of family at all, let alone supporting one in crisis."

Ani sat forward, gripping the back of the chair in front of her. It was such a low blow that it took her breath away. She watched Daniel, worried. But Daniel kept his cool, and Ani relaxed back into her seat.

"Your Honor," he interrupted, "I have several studies here with evidence that the best thing for families is to stay together no matter whether they are nuclear or extended. Can I show you these articles?"

Mercy turned to Ani, gripping her hand again. "Brother came with research."

The judge took the papers and flipped through them, taking his time. The lawyer from DHS tried to interrupt, but the judge silently held up his hand, and the lawyer subsided.

"Continue," the judge said finally, "and please make sure we understand your point."

Ani wriggled in her seat. The point was undeniable. Was

the judge being obtuse on purpose? But Daniel still seemed calm.

"I wish my mom could see this," Ani whispered to Mercy. "She said she thought Daniel could handle the hearing. She was right."

"Maria and Leo love Valeria and Gabriel like their own children," Daniel said. "And I will do whatever is in my power, for as long as I am able, to make sure they thrive in this country that they would like to adopt as their own." He paused for a few long moments. Then came the thunderclap. "I've also attached my financials to the back of those articles," Daniel added. "In case you have any doubt about my ability to follow through with this promise."

Well then, Ani thought.

The judge looked at the papers, and his eyebrows raised just a fraction of an inch.

He nodded slowly, then looked out at the courtroom. "I'm old and hungry," he said, "so we'll adjourn for lunch. I just want to let you know, so you can be prepared, that I have some unanswered questions. It may be better to call them gaping holes. Daniel, though there is no doubt that you are sincere, your resume says you have worked at the post office your whole adult life. I'm still not sure how you are qualified for this type of work. You have Ms. Nazaryan, but as I understand it, she will be leaving soon."

"Permission to speak, Your Honor?" asked the DHS lawyer.

"Granted," said the judge.

"My file also says that Mr. Wright has autism. Perhaps

299

this should be seen as another 'gaping hole.'"

Ani gasped.

Daniel leaned toward the mic. "No," he said. "I'm autistic."

"That's what I said."

"No, you said I have autism. I am autistic. It's not something I have. It's a neurological difference that is essential to everything I do."

Oh, Daniel, Ani thought.

The lawyer looked at the judge as if to say, "This is exactly what I'm talking about."

Daniel leaned forward one more time. "Just before we break for lunch, I have one more thing. A poem to read. Can I do that?"

The judge was frowning now. "Yes, I suppose, but when we come back from the break, you all had better let me know how you are going to make this work."

Daniel took a breath. "This is a poem by an Armenian-Iranian poet named Varand."

Ani squeezed her hands together in her lap. Daniel had managed to completely shock her. He read the poem in his soft, deep voice, and no words had ever sounded more beautiful to Ani. She understood, as she listened, that Daniel had searched for this poem for her. He wanted to tell her something true. These were words of love for Maria and Leo, for the children, and for Ani.

"*I AM FORTY AND YOU, little one, are four,*

My life span is ten whole times more,
My age is ten times that of yours
Yet, I learn from you how to bloom.

YOU ARE *my small bundle of spring,*
My multiplied motive to live,
My fervent drive to go on living,
With you, I am young once more.

WE, *a devastated race and realm,*
Scattered in dozens of distant abodes,
With countless woes on our rocky road,
We've lit again the fire in our hearth.

EACH *" 1 " from you, a roof to my " 1 0 ",*
Each " 1 0" of mine, a pillar to your " 1 ",
From you till me... one small family,
From me till you... living history."

HE LOOKED up when he was finished reading. "I think it
applies to what the Lorias and other refugees need," he said.
"They are a scattered race, and they only long to go on living,
to light the fire in their hearth. We can offer this to a family
like the Lorias. I am willing to give as much as needed for the
fire in their hearth to go on burning."

CHAPTER FORTY-SEVEN

Daniel wanted to talk to Ani during the lunch break, but she held up a hand as he approached.

"Wait," she said. "Don't come to talk to me now."

Her words winded him. "I'm sorry," he said.

"No, Daniel, don't apologize; you haven't done anything wrong. I just need to hold myself together to testify, and I won't be able to do it if I talk to you. Let's wait until after, okay?"

He nodded. "Okay." It took everything inside of him to turn around without letting his face collapse. He looked for Maria and Leo; they had gotten separated from him as they headed out of the courtroom doors.

Daniel must have gotten it wrong. Had Ani been offended when he quoted the poem? Had he miscalculated everything? Daniel felt as though he had fallen from a great height. He felt as though he may never be able to get his bearings again.

There they were. The sight of the Lorias was comforting. They were sitting on two benches outside, eating the food they had brought from home. The benches were arranged so the Lorias were all facing each other, a little circle of resilience in the storm. Valeria's eyes lit up at the sight of Daniel, and she waved him over, making room for him on the bench.

"Gracias," he said as Maria passed him a container of food. He tried to speak as though his heart was not breaking. But the food was good--bean and rice and vegetables. He was hungry, and he hadn't even realized it. The food tasted like home, bringing images of their little golden kitchen, warm and brilliant against the night. "How are you feeling?"

Valeria smiled. "We were just talking about that. We don't know, actually. We can't tell how it's going. Are they going to approve us?"

He had to be honest. He always did; he always had. There were no other options available to him.

"I don't know," he said.

"Ani is next," Valeria said. "But she was crying when you read the poem."

"She cried?" he asked, startled.

Valeria nodded. "Then she said we should go eat without her because she needed to think."

Tears could mean anything. Daniel cursed his inability to intuit, to understand.

"We should pray," he said after he had taken a few more bites. He was barely holding himself together. The disinfectant smells in the courtroom, the feeling of being on trial to explain how his own differences would not ruin this family's life. This environment was unfriendly and felt like a regression. It was far from the garden, the land that had begun to heal things he didn't even know were broken inside him.

They prayed, then. They didn't have many words. But the world was broken, and Daniel knew that in God's kingdom, there were places for people who didn't have a place to be. Jesus had gestured to all of them and said, "Mine."

Let us be your people, he asked God now, there on the concrete bench in the courtyard of the ugly courthouse. *Let us live together; you say you put the lonely in families. Please help the judge to see that we can do this. And please help Ani to forgive me.*

When they filed back in, Daniel met Ani's eyes. She smiled at him, but it looked like she had been crying again, and he felt worried for her. He should never have tried something like reading that poem. His mind wanted to send him down a spiral of self-recrimination, but there was no time for it.

He sat with Gabriel and Valeria on either side of him, daring the judge to try to pull them apart. Gabriel leaned on his body like he wanted to put all his weight on someone else. He was sucking his thumb, and Daniel nudged him gently to remind him to stop.

"Let's reconvene," the judge said. "Ms. Nazaryan, are you ready?"

"Yes," Ani said. She made her way to the witness chair.

The DHS lawyer was the one to start. "Ms. Nazaryan, you have stated that your job is to help refugees become accustomed to their new homes and that you will continue that work," he said. "How is it that you think this family can continue to function? Let's take stock: Two elderly people who do not speak English, two traumatized children, and their sponsor, a man with autism? How exactly is this supposed to work?"

Ani gave the lawyer a look, and Daniel could have told him to backpedal because he was going to get more than he bargained for. Daniel held his breath, smiling a little despite the pain and fear in his heart. It would be fun to watch Ani reply to the lawyer.

"I would like to ask you," she said, her voice deceptively soft, "how many times you have climbed mountains in the dark to save your children or grandchildren? How many refugee camps have you survived? How many times have you washed the dust and bugs out of your food in order to eat it?"

"This is..."

"Because if you think that you have any idea of the strength that Leo and Maria contain in their little fingers, you are wrong. Nothing in your life has given you the opportunity for the kind of strength they have gathered and continue to exhibit. They will be fine, sir." She took a breath, clutching the sides of her chair, moving back and forth in a way that Daniel knew meant her leg was hurting.

"As for Daniel," Ani looked up at Daniel, and for a moment, everyone else in the room disappeared. He blinked.

"The Lorias have been given an actual angel to care for them. An angel who creates garden beds for them, helps them with homework, teaches them about the stars, and quotes poetry. They are one hundred percent okay with this man who has superpowers I believe none of the rest of us know about."

Daniel's eyes began to burn.

"Now that I have hopefully set your mind at ease about Maria, Leo, and Daniel," she said, "let me set your mind at ease about myself. I have decided to stay in Aveline and work in whatever capacity I can from here."

Now Daniel's whole head was burning, he nearly jumped to his feet, but Valeria held onto him.

"This is my family now," Ani said. "I think Daniel's words about family ring very true. They have become my world. And this matters enough to me to change my life. I hope it matters enough to you, your honor," she said to the judge, "for you to grant this family asylum and residency. We will light again the fire in our hearth."

She came back to sit down. Daniel did not hear a single word that Mateo said as he finished with closing arguments. His ears were ringing. He was going to have a meltdown. He rocked back and forth surreptitiously. Did Ani actually say she was going to stay? Did she quote from the poem he read? She wasn't angry? Maybe he hadn't done the wrong thing?

He couldn't turn to look at her. He was frozen. He had dreamed it. She wasn't going to stay. He couldn't bear to find out he had dreamed it.

People were moving, Valeria was talking to him, but he was frozen in place. He was alone there, sitting without comprehending, but then Ani was there beside him.

She put a small, soft hand on his neck. "Hey," she said. "Daniel?"

Like a spell breaking, Daniel found that he could move. He gulped air into his lungs.

"Did I dream that?" he asked, finally turning to look at her.

She smiled at him with tears in her eyes.

"You did not," she said. "I'm staying."

He moved very slowly toward her, giving her time to pull away in this public space, though most people seemed to have left the courtroom. He went closer, until he could feel her breath on his cheek, and then he kissed the corner of her mouth.

She turned her face to meet his lips, and then he was hugging her, and they were holding each other tight, so tight.

He pulled back, astonished to find he was crying. "Thank you," he said. "Thank you for staying."

"I meant it," she said. "I don't just mean that they are my family. Daniel, you are my family now."

It was too much; his heart would burst.

"And that poem," she said. "How? Well, my father is going to love you too. You're going to steal my parent's hearts."

He smiled then. This was real.

They were quiet for a long time. Then people began to drift back in, and Ani put her hand in Daniel's as the judge took his seat. Just as he wondered, she said it.

"Even if he says no, I would still like to stay. If that's okay with you. I will find a way that they can use my skills long-distance. I may have to travel."

He leaned close and rested his forehead on hers. "We belong together," he said.

She smiled and wiped at more tears. "What an emotional day this is. I could sleep for a month. Is he ever going to say anything?"

The judge opened his mouth. Daniel braced himself.

"The court finds this family eligible for asylum," he said. "All the best to you, Daniel, and to this very unusual family."

Then they were all hugging and crying, this very unusual family. After the congratulations and tears and squeals of joy, Maria turned to them.

"Can we go home now?" she said.

They went.

EPILOGUE

"So, what do you think?" Ani asked Mercy over the phone. "Can we start something like this from here? I think awareness is going to be the biggest hurdle if we're going increase these kinds of programs."

"I think yes, we can, and I think you're ideal for the job."

"You think it's a good way to help?" Ani said. She was aware of how her voice sounded. Plaintive, like she needed affirmation of her life choices. She sighed. "I'm sorry, I don't need to put that on you."

"You're not putting anything on me. But Ani. You are allowed to choose what is good for you. And Daniel and this family are good for you."

Ani's eyes flooded.

"And yes," Mercy went on, "I think working for Amnesty and forming a media for advertising this sponsorship method is helpful enough in this world of ours. But I understand. I always want to help everything and everyone. If you don't keep focused on what exactly God has set for you, it will never feel like enough."

"I know you understand," Ani said. "And I know you're right. Oh...Mercy, I'm getting another call. I'll see you tomorrow."

As she transferred over to the second call, Ani saw Daniel standing on her porch. Her mouth twisted upward into a smile as she went to answer the door.

"Hello?" she said.

"Ani?"

"Hi, Reesey." She beckoned for Daniel to come in, but he bent down and started pulling weeds from her flower boxes, so she went outside as well, tipping her face to the sun.

"I'm calling because I heard a rumor," Reesey said. Her voice sounded flustered and breathless, as though she was running.

Ani raised her eyebrows, glancing at the man who was pulling weeds from between flowers. "Yes, Reesey, Daniel, and I are together."

"You think that's the rumor?" Theresa laughed. "That's the worst kept secret in Aveline. No, the rumor I'm talking about is that Sheldon and I are eloping right now in Aveline Park, in case anyone felt like coming along to watch."

"Are you serious?" Ani shrieked. Daniel whirled around, looking concerned. "Right now?"

"I'd say in twenty minutes tops!" Reesey said cheerfully. "Either come or don't, no pressure!" She hung up.

Ani stared at her phone, then stared at Daniel.

"She said they're eloping right now," she said. "Like, right this second."

"Reesey and Sheldon?"

"Yes."

"Why did she tell you?"

"In case we want to come."

His face opened with joy, his smile brilliant as he grabbed her and kissed her. "I'll get the others," he said, beginning to run in the direction of the big house."

"Wait, Daniel, I don't know if she meant all of us," Ani called.

"Of course she did!" Daniel called back. "We come as a package!"

The words rippled and vibrated through the air, bringing their singing meaning right into Ani's house. The six of them, this adopted family, all of them one thing, they came as a package. Daniel was right. Theresa would know it.

Ani ran to get a shawl to throw over her T-shirt.

Something right for the occasion.

The Lost Art of Reverie, Book One in the Aveline Series, is here.

A Jar Full of Light, Book Two in the Aveline Series, is here.

What is the most important ingredient for a book's success? Besides, of course, the book itself?

It's what you, the Reader, says about it. Social proof. Reviews.

When people are out there, in the wilderness of the book jungle, looking for something to read, the main question they ask is, "Have other people read this? Did they like it?"

So if this book is your kind of book, and you think it might be someone else's kind of book, I will be over the moon if you leave a review on whatever site feeds you your books. Reviews can be the key to a book's success. Thank you!

ACKNOWLEDGMENTS

I remember the first time I read an article about community sponsorship of refugees in Canada. I felt it all through my body—the rightness of groups of people gathering together to welcome displaced people as family.

In the last number of years, this kind of sponsorship went on the back burner in the U.S. due to closures for refugees. The good news is that these programs are starting up again. One to check out is Longer Table with Amnesty USA. There are many ways to get involved!

Thank you Aveline fans, for your love for this series. I read all your comments and reviews and they warm my heart and help me to keep on with these characters who have become dear friends of mine.

In certain ways, this book reflects a lot of the stories that I have heard and witnessed. I am privileged to live in Thailand in close proximity to settlements of displaced peoples, and have heard their stories. I am always inspired by my Latinx friends, who carry their goodness around the world with them. Thanks especially to Rosa, who taught me to dance and told me about dancing as a child in Venezuela.

My friends Phiroozeh and Cypriano shared with me the strange experience of being some of the last people in the world to have gone through polio.

Thank you to my family as always, who put up with the crazed person I become in the last edits of a book. Thanks Shekina Garden Community, and all the friendships in Pai that have become like jewels over the past year.

Mom and Dad, Tj and Mark Chapman, Diane Brodeur, Rowan Keyzer, Alicia Wiggin, Annie Laurie Nichols, Bob Kohlbacher, Carrien Blue, Verena Berndt, Wenda Friesner, Julie Winslow, Stephanie Donnelly, Karen Engel, Elisha Pettit, Kathleen Andersen, Michele Lilly, and Mary Hall, you are ships carrying precious cargo, you sail through oceans with courage and love. Thank you for being my patrons.

Sign up here!

ABOUT THE AUTHOR

Newsletter

If you want to join Rae Walsh's Newsletter and learn about books and new releases, sign up here. Your address will never be shared!

~

Bio

Rae Walsh is the women's fiction/inspirational romance pen name of Rachel Devenish Ford. Rae is the wife of one Superstar Husband and the mother of five incredible children. Originally from British Columbia, Canada, she now lives in Northern Thailand with her family. She can be found eating street food or smelling flowers in many cities in Asia.

~

Works by Rae Walsh:
   The Lost Art of Reverie: Aveline Book 1
   A Jar Full of Light: Aveline Book 2

The Fire in our Hearth: Aveline Book 3

Works by Rachel Devenish Ford:

The Eve Tree

    A Traveler's Guide to Belonging

    Trees Tall As Mountains: The Journey Mama Writings-Book One

    Oceans Bright With Stars: The Journey Mama Writings-Book Two

    A Home as Wide as the Earth: The Journey Mama Writings: Book Three

    World Whisperer : World Whisperer Book 1

    Guardian of Dawn : World Whisperer Book 2

    Shaper's Daughter: World Whisperer Book 3

    Demon's Arrow: World Whisperer Book 4

    Beloved Night: World Whisperer Book 5

    Azariyah: A World Whisperer Novella

Reviews

Recommendations and reviews are such an important part of the success of a book. If you enjoyed this book, please take the time to leave a review.

Don't be afraid of leaving a short review! Even a couple lines will help and will overwhelm the author with waves of gratitude.

Contact

Email: raewalshauthor@gmail.com
Blog: http://journeymama.com
Facebook: http://www.facebook.com/rae.walsh.author
Twitter: http://www.twitter.com/journeymama
Instagram: http://instagram.com/journeymama

Printed in Great Britain
by Amazon

38227829R00189